# Against Human Nature

## Spirit Seeker Book 4

### Janna Ruth

SPIRIT SEEKER BOOK 4

# AGAINST HUMAN NATURE

## JANNA RUTH

First published in New Zealand in 2021

2nd Edition 2025



www.janna-ruth.com



ISBN 978-0-473-60399-1 (Paperback)

ISBN 978-0-473-60400-4 (Ebook)

For all Story Seekers,

young and old.

1

"Get in the car!"

The cool touch of the gun's muzzle presses into the back of my neck, pushing me forward. The getaway car is parked right in front of the bridge outside the Citadel of Spandau. It's an indistinct grey vehicle that will be impossible to pick out in a standard parking lot.

Agnes reaches around me and opens the door. As I slide in, I see Aeola swooping down at me. She looks as terrified as I am.

"Tell Wulf—" I begin.

"In!" Agnes pushes my head down, forcing me to sit down in the car.

My heart is pounding, and my breath comes out in short fits. I still haven't quite grasped what's happening here.

Aeola is still hovering, seemingly undecided. She can't help me at the moment, but Wulf can. If Agnes is really from the SSA, as she claims to be, she'll listen to him.

"I won't tell Wulf anything, sweetie," Agnes says, then snaps a pair of handcuffs around my wrists that are threaded through the door handle.

Shocked, I look up at her. "You can't do this." Surely, she can't.

But Agnes only raises an eyebrow and slams the door shut, effectively locking me into the car. She walks around the vehicle to get in the driver's seat. I glance up at Aeola, only to see her catch an updraft and fly back to the citadel. Instantly, I regret sending her away. I could use some moral support now.

As the motor starts up, I close my eyes. I tell myself Wulf will come running. He has to. But the car backs out, swivels around, and leaves the citadel behind before Aeola would even have a chance to rattle his window.

"Where are we going?"

We've reached the main road and are speeding towards the motorway circling the centre of Berlin. Instead of answering me, Agnes turns up the music, eyes fixed on the road. The tune from the radio is so upbeat it creeps me out even more than death metal would have. Her gun is hidden in the door pocket on her side, painfully out of reach from me, but close enough for her. Not that I know how to wield a gun, much less do it handcuffed to a door.

At a red light, I contemplate opening the door, but with my hands shackled as they are, I can't make a run for it. Instead, I see myself hanging from the door while Agnes pushes down the pedal. Nope, not a promising course of action. At this time of night, there wouldn't even be anyone there to see me struggle.

As if she's seen into my head, Agnes locks the doors. The vanishing nubs make me swallow. Only a few minutes later, we're on the motorway and speeding through the city.

"You know that kidnapping's against the law?" I ask, trying to sound casual, but my voice hitches with every other word. This can't be happening. When I lived on the streets I had my fair share of drama, but nothing like this. Never with a gun.

Agnes snorts but doesn't deign to give me an answer. Apparently, now that I'm in her car, there's no more need for niceties, such as answering my questions. It's not like I want to talk to her, but it leaves my mind open to all kinds of horror scenarios as we leave the lights of Berlin behind and drive south.

Agnes will throw me out at 150 km per hour.

She'll drive me to some place in the middle of nowhere and blow my brains out.

She'll kill me right in this car and throw my body in the river we're currently crossing.

Yeah, this is not going well.

Nothing of the sort happens. We drive through the night and long into the day. Whenever Agnes needs a break, she leaves the highway and parks the car on some remote country road. The cuffs around my wrists have started chafing, and my legs are screaming for a walk that'll get me further than to a bush by the road. Since Agnes has kept up the wall of silence, I've dozed in and out of sleep. When I wake again, the street signs whizzing by inform me we're still travelling South.

Soon, the scenery changes. Fields and towns give way to mountains rising in the not-so-far distance—the Alps. Under other circumstances, I would be excited. There's something about peaks of naked stone covered in snow that lifts the heart. One of my favourite memories of my mother was climbing around the mountains of Czechia when I was young. Mountains are usually teeming with spirits, whereas they keep away from cities.

Spirits.

A sudden idea gets hold of me. What if I asked the help of the spirits around here? In Dublin, the dryads were able to hide me from the world. If I could get one of the Alpine ones to do this for me, Agnes will never find me.

"I need to pee," I announce.

"You went two hours ago," Agnes tells me, keeping her eyes on the road.

"Well, I have to go again." She did give me something to drink, after all.

But we're back to ignoring me. If she's decided to heed my request, there's no sign of it. I tell myself that I just need to be patient. We're gonna stop eventually, and judging by her previous behaviour, it will be as remote as can be. Perfect for finding spirits.

As I lean my head against the windowpane, my thoughts are pre-occupied with how I've suddenly caught the SSA's attention. Back in Dublin, Wulf promised he would never tell, and even he can't be naïve enough to let it slip accidentally. Then I think of Lukas and feel the rage rising in me. He'd pull such a stunt, for sure. Or not? After what happened in Dublin, he's changed. He even wanted me to teach him more about spirits. Unless all of that was a lie or a thinly veiled attempt at reconciliation after he blew the whistle.

Maybe it wasn't anyone on the team. Spirits know not everyone is a big fan of me. Potentially Robert, the leader of the East Berlin group, could've spilt the beans, or Tallulah, the traitorous spirit seeker in Dublin, out of spite. When my mind jumps to Fez, my old friend from the streets who betrayed me before, I decide to stop this nonsense. It doesn't matter who alerted the SSA to my existence. I'm at their mercy now unless I do something about it.

In the early afternoon, we cross into Austrian territory, and still, we keep going. I wish I could enjoy the stunning sights of snow-capped mountains, rivers, and green hillsides to the left and right of us.

"Well, if you don't want me to pee on your seats, you should stop soon." I wriggle around to show her how serious it is. The urge is definitely there now, though there can't be more than a few drops in my bladder. "Please?"

Agnes lets me shift and tap my fingers for half an hour before she finally turns off the road and follows some country lane. When the pavement turns to gravel, I hope this is another break and not our destination. It's definitely remote here, in what looks like an uninhabited mountain valley. This means there should be a lot of spirits—gnomes and sylphs, and likely a few dryads.

At last, the car stops in the middle of nowhere. Agnes comes around and releases me from the handcuffs. She points to a spot right next to the car. "Pee!"

"In the middle of the road?" Not that you can call this trail a road, really. "With you watching?"

"Do you have to go or not?"

How am I supposed to converse with spirits while squatting in front of her? It doesn't seem like she's going to give me a choice. I walk as far away from her as I dare to the edge of the forest. When I hear her clear her throat, I slide behind a tree and lower myself. Instead of relieving myself, though, I observe the forest, trying to spot a spirit.

At first, it looks like the car has spooked the lot of them, but as I sit a bit longer, I hear the leaves rustle in the wind. A curious sylph is watching far above us. And there's definitely movement further in. A dryad, by the looks of it.

Quickly, I throw a peek at Agnes. Sure enough, she's keeping her gaze on me, arms crossed. "I can't with you watching!" I exclaim.

She says something in a language I can't quite grasp and turns toward the car. Alright, this is my chance. I pull my pants up again and take another quick look. She's taken out a spirit seeker staff from the back seat. Not good.

For a split second, I don't know what to do. Then the adrenaline kicks in, and I bolt.

Picking my way sensibly would have been nice. Instead, I hit my shoulder on a tree, roll an ankle in a sudden hole in the ground, and almost get myself stuck in some brambles. Behind me, I hear Agnes crashing through the woods. There's not enough distance. I won't even get fifty metres away.

Sylph. There was a sylph. "Help me, please! I need to hide," I call up to the sky. Luckily, she's still there, watching me with curiosity. "Please. Is there a dryad who could hide me?" I'm out of breath, and it's pure luck Agnes hasn't caught up to me yet.

"There are gnomes living down in the bog," the wind whispers and pushes me slightly to the left.

I take the hint and change course immediately. "Thanks," I say, just before the ground underneath me gives way. I'm on a gradient, and sure enough, I lose my footing and tumble down the hill, landing face down in the swamp at its foot.

Well, at least I finally brought some distance between Agnes and me. I push myself out of the soft ground, wiping mud off my face, and cast a glance around. Trees line the edge of the bog, which is covered with mounds of heather and other shrubs. Across from me, large boulders as tall as my room back at the citadel are strewn across the dell, some split in half, others whole.

There's no time to take in the marvellous sight. Hopping from mound to mound, I make my way over the bog until I'm between the boulders. It's darker here where the stones block out the sun. I encounter one split in half, as if struck by divine lightning. Both halves are still upright, creating a dark passage for me to hide in. Oh, yes, I can totally see why gnomes would choose to live here.

"Hello?" I ask, praying that Agnes is still making her way down the hillside. As I run my fingers across the icy surface, I continue, "My name's Rika, and I'm begging for asylum. If it's not too much to ask, could you hide me from the world? Just for a little while? There's a woman—"

"Hello," a gravelly voice interrupts from above. A mica-speckled face blocks out the rest of the sun. "You're standing in my home."

"Oh, I'm terribly sorry. I didn't know!" I can't help but check for Agnes through the gap before concentrating on the gnome. "I'm on the run from this terrible woman. She's a spirit seeker and may very well kill me. May I stay in your home, and"—I feel horrible asking this of them—"could you lock the door?"

The gnome rolls down into the gap and comes to stand in front of me, their impact shaking the walls. "Enclose you in stone?"

"If it's not too much to ask." Tears spring to my eyes. I don't know where else to run. "Please."

They roll their granite shoulders. "Why not? You look sorry enough." They put their hands on the stone and the boulder rumbles. The sides close in.

I should be relieved. Instead, panic washes over me. I hate confined spaces. I really, really hate them. Encasing myself in stone? That's the epitome of confinement. My breath hitches in my throat as I will my feet to stay put. *Don't run. Don't run. Don't run.*

When a black staff is pushed into the narrowing gap, I shudder in relief. Only problem is now I'm truly in trouble.

Agnes' staff hits the stone, and the walls shake. Gravel rains down on me and the gnome. When she bangs it against the boulder a second time, the movement comes to a standstill. My heart beats so loud it echoes in the hollow.

Agnes pushes herself inside and glares at me, then the gnome. Without hesitating, she brings the staff down on the poor fellow. Stone chips away and cracks appear on their hardened skin.

"No!" I jump over the gnome and get in Agnes' way just as she brings the staff down again. It hits my shoulder instead, and I cry out in pain, tears springing to my eyes. It feels like she's snapped my collarbone in half. Yet I hold my ground. "Run!" I tell the gnome, though I asked for protection a minute before. I meet Agnes' gaze. "Don't!"

"Are you done fleeing?" she asks with a snarl.

My shoulder is throbbing in pain and tears are streaming down my face. I want to say no, try to find another haven, but not at someone else's expense. "Promise me you won't hurt them." Behind me, the gnome is growling.

Agnes barks out a laugh. "You aren't in a position to make demands, Rika."

"Please." I couldn't bear it on top of everything else.

"Get out!" She steps back just enough to let me through. As soon as I return to the bright blue sky, Agnes grabs me roughly under my arm and pulls me away from the boulder. "You deserve a beating for that stunt."

"You already did that," I reply sullenly, trying to shift my weight so my collarbone won't hurt so much. As I glance over my shoulder, I can see that the boulder has closed, not a crack inside. Good for them.

Agnes snorts. "They'll do worse to you in Rome if you keep jumping in front of spirits to preserve their lives."

Rome.

She's bringing me to the Spirit Seeker Academy. The place where people like me who can't keep their mouth shut get brainwashed into submission or vanish in the night. In short, I'm screwed. It would've been better if that stone had shut around me forever.

2

I've never been to the Eternal City. In all our travels across Europe, my mum and I never visited Italy. It doesn't strike me as odd—we never went to Spain, either, or Portugal. But now that we're driving through the streets of Rome, I regret that we didn't. It's the very early hours of morning and the streets are mostly empty, giving me a perfect view of all the ancient buildings along the roadside. I've always been a nature girl, but there's something about the combination of overgrown ruins from ancient civilisations and modern architecture that fascinates me. Most cities would have built on top of their ruins; the Romans have embraced theirs, and not just the famous ones like the Colosseum or Forum Romanum, but little ones like the random temple ruin on the corner we're passing.

On my left, the Tiber flows in the darkness, but if there are nymphs swimming along the current, I can't see them from inside the car. After a full day of travelling, I'm exhausted. My shoulders hurt from holding them awkwardly to the side where cuffs still constrain my hands. Agnes' staff didn't break my collarbone but the spot throbs in pain, nonetheless. I'm tired, but I haven't truly slept since we left Austria, not even when Agnes holed herself up in some deserted area to snore for a couple of hours. My legs hurt for lack of movement, and my neck is strained. In some ways, I can't wait to get out of this car.

But mostly, I'm deeply afraid of it. I now wish I'd asked the others more about their training, so I'd know what to expect. I don't even know where in Rome the academy is located. Hopefully not in a ruin like Budapest's headquarters. Will it even matter, considering whatever sinister thing they've got planned for me?

To be honest, I'm at a total loss. If they wanted to get rid of me, Agnes could have shot me at any time and dumped my body in the bog, for example. It's not like the police would care if they ever found my corpse. Just another homeless person dead.

I pinch the skin between my thumb and index finger to remind myself I'm no longer homeless. Sure, I sleep under a tree, but that's by choice and as much a home as any house could be. I also have friends, and perhaps even someone who cares a little more than that about me.

As my thoughts drift to Wulf, I wonder what he's doing. By now, he's had an entire day to notice my absence, even if Aeola didn't manage to alert him last night. I know it's silly, but I keep hoping he's chasing us. That any minute, I'll see his face in the side mirror. But he doesn't even know which direction I left in, and after twenty-four hours, I could be pretty much anywhere in Europe.

At last, we veer away from the river to drive around an imposing medieval fortress surrounded by a walled-in park. On top of the castle looms the statue of an angel, wings spread in the dark, a long weapon in his hand. I shudder when I recognise it. The angel is carrying a staff to fight spirits with. Hadn't Rory told me how the spirit seekers were riding on the back of the Church?

Sure enough, we come to a stop, if only to wait for a gate to open that leads to a garage under the castle grounds. The way we drive into the black hole is an oddly fitting metaphor for my situation. As if it wasn't bad enough I was kidnapped, I'm now stuck in an underground garage below a castle guarded by a spirit-seeking angel. Claustrophobia, here I come.

Agnes parks the car in a lot, deep inside the building. As the motor dies, my stomach falls into a pit. My heartbeat, which had slowed after the long, uneventful drive down here, picks up again, making my chest hurt. Through the windscreen, I see her waiting in the darkness. It takes a thorough five minutes or longer until Agnes comes around to my door and opens it, immediately removing the handcuffs. "Get out!"

Rubbing my wrists, I comply, if only for the opportunity to stretch my legs a bit. After the long drive, they feel weak and unsupportive. They itch as blood flows back through them. I'm just about to ask Agnes what's going to happen now when I notice we're not alone. A man a good ten years younger than Agnes, and visibly more buff, is standing behind the car, waiting patiently. He has black curly hair and a short beard.

"Ready?" he asks, as if waiting to be done with the whole thing. Gee, I'm sorry to have inconvenienced him.

Agnes pushes me forward, saying, "She's yours now, Gian."

So, now I belong to this new stranger in front of me. Great. One thing's for sure. He'd win in a fistfight. "Is it time for breakfast yet?" I ask, my voice wavering.

At least, this one can smile. "Something like that." He nods to Agnes. "You'll find your own way."

"Don't worry about me," she answers, "but keep her in check. She's a flighty one."

"There's nowhere to run here," Gian says without a worry, crushing any sliver of hope I might have had. Then he offers me his arm. "Shall we?"

Yeah, I'm not going to stroll arm in arm to my certain doom. "Lead the way."

Another snort, and Gian walks away. He doesn't force me at gunpoint, nor does he order me around. I look over my shoulder, checking for a viable escape. But there's only darkness and stone, and no exit to be seen. I can already feel the walls creeping in, just like they did in the gnome's boulder. No, thanks. I'll take whatever lies outside.

With quick strides, I follow Gian up a set of stairs. Naturally, the carpark doesn't lead to the open space I saw before, but into the dark corridors of the castle. As we walk the vacant halls of naked stone, I wonder if our arrival has been timed deliberately. If this is the Spirit Seeker Academy, it should be teeming with students or recruits or whatever they call their aspiring spirit seekers. There's not a single soul awake apart from us.

Our walk is rather short. So short I can't be sure we're not still in the basement. Gian comes to a halt in front of what looks like a solid metal door. "Your room is ready for you," he says with a devious little smile, while he unlocks the door and pulls it open for me.

I don't know what I expected. Someone to explain all this, maybe. This room is smaller than a shoebox, barely wide enough to fit a single bed, a small table, and a pair of chairs. On the table, a plate with food—some thinly sliced meat or something—and a jug of water has already been set out. A door, half blocked by one chair, might lead to a closet or the world's tiniest bathroom.

"Welcome to Castel Sant'Angelo. Enjoy your stay!"

Too late, I recognise the finality of his tone. Gian doesn't set a foot inside the room. Instead, he pushes the door closed behind me. It slams into its frame, giving me a jolt. Then a barely audible click makes me break out in cold sweat.

He's locked me in. That bastard locked me into this sham of a room. This space that's hardly big enough to serve as a storage chamber.

Panicked, I look around. There must be a way to get out. My gaze flits around, but the only window I find is a fist-sized hole high up the wall, where the room narrows into a weird chimney-like hollow. I stumble towards the little door, pulling so hard on it, the stool in front falls onto the bed.

It's a bathroom, though calling it that is a gross exaggeration. There's a toilet and the tiniest washing basin in the world, no shower, just a flannel hanging from a dejected little hook. It's cold in here, drafty yet humid. I guess I should be glad they didn't just give me a bucket.

Rushing back to the main room, I try the door Gian locked. Yes, it's locked. Still. Nevertheless, I push and pull at the handle for half an eternity.

Finally, I stumble back, completely out of breath. There's no way out. I find myself wishing for the long empty darkness of the underground garage. At least there was space. In here, every step I take brings me in front of a wall.

This is not good. This is the absolute worst place I could find myself in. And this is from the girl who was ready to get herself enclosed into stone. Well, I guess I got my wish now. For all intents and purposes, I could as well be in a gnome home.

The panic attack rises in my throat. My hands are clammy, my breath shallow. I'm back at the youth home or back at a shelter, sharing my tiny space with at least three others. I can't sleep here. I can't even breathe here.

It takes me a solid hour or more to understand the room for what it is.

A cell.

Four steps. Five steps. That's how long it takes me to cross from one wall to the next, as I've found out several times now. Maybe close to a hundred times. Yes, yes, I'm pacing. A lot!

This is my own personal nightmare. A stony box with no escape. And I'm not even overreacting like those times when I stepped into an underground station or the Budapest headquarters. This is real, which is a big problem because I can't tell myself I'm just being silly. If I were, I could just open the door and walk away from it.

According to the light falling in from the tiny-ass window far above me, day has broken. People should be awake, but I can't hear a single footstep outside my door. Sound is cut off, wrapping me in cotton-padded silence. As far as I know, there's no airflow, unless you call that icy draft from the toilet fresh air. It's as if this room has become my entire world. My tiny, lifeless world.

I want to get out. I tell the door a thousand times, screaming my throat raw. I bang against the metal, shout at the window, and still no response. No one comes to see me, either, and I'm starting to think that this is it. This is how people vanish in the SSA. They get locked in a room and forgotten.

So far, I haven't been able to bring myself to touch the food. I had a few drops of water to soothe my throat but sitting down to enjoy a proper meal feels so terribly wrong. If I did that, I'd be accepting my situation. I know, eventually, I have to, but for now, the panic is stronger than the need. It's air and freedom I want, not fancy slices of meat.

Did I tell you I haven't slept yet either? That's right, I've been awake for more or less thirty hours, not counting the periods of dozing I had in the car. My body is running on adrenaline, which my claustrophobia is eager to provide.

Once again, I bang against the door to no avail. When there's no answer, I dig my nails into my palm to keep my fists from rapping on the door again.

*Step away from it,* I tell myself, and withdraw all the way to the back wall, where I stand next to the bed until I sink to the floor. Stone like everything else.

How did I get here? I've heard the horror stories, but they all came from people who more or less signed up for this. No one ever told me the SSA was recruiting at gunpoint. Yes, I told Wulf to keep his mouth shut, but only because I didn't want to deal with the potentially intense courting I thought it would provoke.

*You want to lead, Rika? Go to the academy! They'll give you a command, I'm sure of it, but it won't be over me.* I can hear his voice in my head. Which means, even if they were interested in teaching me, I won't be seeing Wulf again. They never put two people with such high NAVs into one city. Wulf will stay in Berlin, and I will... I will...

I gasp, tears stinging in my eyes. I won't go anywhere. They won't ever let me go. Shaking, I look up the chimney-style ceiling of my cell. Its dark centre is taunting me. My throat is growing tighter and tighter. The walls are moving in.

A tear runs down my cheek and neck. As soon as I wipe it away, more follow. I'm sobbing, choking on my attempts to stop it. The tears keep streaming. Snot builds in my nose, and I'm gasping for air. Terrible, guttural sounds escape my throat as I jerk my head around, trying to escape the truth of what I am. What it feels like.

An animal locked in a cage.

# 3

A creaking sound jolts me awake. I'd finally fallen asleep some time ago, still tucked into this corner between bed and wall, the stickiness of dried tears on my face.

"Are you okay?" The deep timbre of a man speaking English with a distinctive Italian accent startles me.

Hastily, I wipe the tears from my cheeks, not that it helps my appearance. Am I okay? I was kidnapped more than twenty-four hours ago and brought to a foreign city, then thrown into this horrible dump of a room. "Sure," I mumble, noticing how hollow my voice sounds.

I gaze at the new entrant. The man is in his mid-forties, his dark brown hair cut short. His moustache and beard have been trimmed so exactly I wonder if he used a ruler. It mirrors the exquisite cut of his suit. Tailored, no doubt. This is someone with money and power, the kind of person I have absolutely nothing in common with.

He still carries this look of concern, as if he genuinely cares about my well-being. "Well, I'm glad to hear that, Rika."

And he knows my name. Slowly, I get to my feet. It's bad enough he has all this power over me. I don't need to cower and fret in front of him as well.

When the silence stretching between us is just about to turn from expectant to uncomfortable, he smiles. "Let me introduce myself. My name is Dante Antonelli."

I gasp. This is Dante, Wulf's mentor and practically a father figure to him. A man he adored and who disappointed all the trust put in him. At least, I hope he did. I couldn't bear it if Wulf still believes in him after all we've learnt.

"You've heard of me?" Dante asks in the same suave, almost-caring voice. There's even a little twinkle in his eye.

*Yeah, you're the one who sent tainted spirits to Dublin—and possibly everywhere else as well.* "You're the director of the Spirit Seeker Academy."

His eyes light up. "I am." After a moment of hesitation, Dante turns towards the table where my untouched dinner or breakfast or whatever-time-it-is-right-now is sitting. "Why didn't you eat? Is it not to your liking?"

I've already forgotten what they provided me with. "I'm not hungry." My stomach convulses at the thought of putting anything into my mouth.

His smile falters and the concerned look is back. He raises an arm and waves me toward the table. "Come on. You need to eat."

"Why?" People eat to keep their strength up. For an insane second, my mind jumps to all the possibilities for why I'd need to keep my strength up. Ordeal, torture, escape. Maybe Dante has a point there.

"People usually do," he jokes, laboriously. "Come on, do me the pleasure." When I hesitate still, he winks at me. "It's not poisoned." To strengthen his words, he picks up a morsel and puts it into his mouth, chewing with delight.

With a momentous sigh, I lug myself over to the table and sit down. I only just notice that there's a second plate set out for Dante. Despite the rumbling of my stomach, I study the food with little interest. It's a plate of thinly sliced meat, rich red in colour, covered by green leaves that look a little flat now, and shaved flakes of hard cheese. If it was ever warm, it's cold now.

"It must be over twenty-four hours since you ate something," Dante says, his voice laced with concern. It has to be pretence, but my heart yearns for it to be real. Gosh, this room has truly done a number on me.

"You mean since my kidnapping?" There, I said it. I'm almost proud of how it came out. Strong, unbroken. Don't count me out just yet.

A shadow passes over Dante's face and I get the idiotic impression that I've displeased him somehow. "I apologise if your travels here have inconvenienced you."

Okay, he's definitely messing with me now. "Inconvenienced me? Yeah, I actually had plans. You don't mind if I go back to them, do you?"

My answer doesn't even get a half-smile from him. "I'm afraid to say I do mind. Eat, Rika." He nods toward the still-untouched plate of food.

But the pang of hunger has dissipated, replaced by anger. "Why don't we cut all this bullshit, and you tell me what you want from me, instead?"

My crudeness makes Dante scrunch up his nose. He sighs heavily. "Can't you guess?"

Of course I can. This is what Rebeka warned me about, what Brigid and Rory told me. "You're going to make me disappear."

Dante's eyes bulge in sudden amusement, and a laugh escapes him, which he quickly stifles with a cough behind his hand. "Excuse me." Ever so politely, he wipes the spittle from his lips with a tissue and folds it back into his chest pocket. "I don't know who told you such horror stories, but we will not make you *disappear.*" He pronounces the word as if it's a ridiculous notion. "This is an academy. We educate people. People like you, Rika." Then his lips stretch into a genuine smile. "Welcome to the Spirit Seeker Academy!"

I'm stunned. Since being abducted at gunpoint, I've replayed the horrors awaiting me over and over in my mind. And now those horrors are supposed to be nothing more than classes? "I'm in a cell." My gaze immediately searches out the little window high above.

"Ah, unfortunately, our current numbers don't leave many options. It's an old building. I'm afraid it's not entirely up to the standard of modern comforts." He rises from his chair and pats the table. "Eat up. It'll help settle your nerves."

Panic rises in my gut as I see him walk toward the door. "You've locked me in." I need to hold onto the facts.

Instead of refuting the fact, Dante puts a hand on the handle. "I'll visit you soon."

"Wait!" My heart beats furiously and sweat breaks out on my forehead. *Don't leave me alone,* an irrational voice in me wants to shout out.

Fortunately, Dante obliges. Expectantly, he waits at the door for me to speak.

My voice is trembling as I form the words, "What if I don't want to become a spirit seeker?"

Dante's shoulders sag, his hand slips from the handle, and I almost feel bad for him. I have the ridiculous notion that I just dashed his hopes.

Tentatively, he takes two steps into the room, folding his hands in front of him. "The world needs people like you. There aren't enough with your talent. God knows we're short of them." One more step in my direction brings him right up to the table. "I understand that our profession can be scary. You might think you're not cut out for this, but that's why I'm here. That's why we're here. To teach and prepare you."

"I'm not frightened," I say, though my voice betrays me. Fine. I *am* frightened, but it's not the spirits I fear.

His forehead creases. "How could you not be?" Dante shakes his head and raps the table with his knuckles, changing his tune. "Bravery will serve you well when you go up against the spirits."

"I don't want to go up against spirits," I say, much more firmly now. "Ever." There it is—the surety I've missed. Desperately, I claw at it, trying to get a proper hold of it. "Spirits deserve to live."

With a shake of his head, Dante sits back down. He clasps his hands in front of his chin and stares at me with an intensity that makes my confidence shrivel. "I wish that were a possibility."

"What?" I'd expected him to launch into this tirade about what horrible creatures spirits are and how they all need to be defeated and bottled up, not understanding.

A sad little smile appears on his lips. "Do you think you're the first person who's ever felt sorry for the spirits we capture?"

Is he suggesting he did—or *does?* "I know I'm not." There are more people out there who think like me. Rory and Brigid. Wulf, even though it took him a while.

Dante nods. "It's a common sentiment. I was the same in my youth," he admits, and I do a double take. "All full of righteous belief. Protect the spirits. Spirits have rights, too."

Okay, now he's mocking me. "What changed?" I'm not sure if I believe his claim. There's no possibility he and I were ever the same.

"I grew up." He lowers his hands, opening himself up to me. "Yes, it is unfortunate what happens to the spirits, but at the same time, humans are dying. Do you know how many people have died from natural disasters in the last decade?"

I don't. I've never been one for numbers.

Dante tells me the answer. "More than half a million. And that doesn't count those starving in Africa because of continuous desertification, or those dying of heatstroke in Europe because our summers have become so much hotter."

*Or the homeless freezing in winter,* I add silently. Those aren't spirit-related, but if we're blaming all natural weather on spirits, they might as well be. "Most of those deaths happened because we've been cutting into their habitats. What about the rainforests? We cut down their trees, poisoned their air, and polluted their seas. Of course they're angry." It all became clear to me when Aeola phrased it that way. Gosh, I miss her so much.

Dante nods, his face serious. "You're absolutely right."

Once again, he agrees with me, and I don't know how to take it. There's strength in righteous anger, but if that anger doesn't find a target, it fizzles out. "Then why don't you do something about it?"

"About deforestation and pollution?" For a moment, he looks puzzled. "We are. I mean, other people do. Those are all well-known problems for our generation to solve. But until they do, we as spirit seekers need to protect our people from the wrath of the spirits." Before I can protest, he raises a finger and continues, "There is no doubt that we are encroaching on what could be dubbed spirit territory. Though what part of the world isn't?" He shakes his head and waves the thought off. "Take Vesuvius. Three million people live on its flanks. Where would we put them? I'll be the first to admit this world has an excess of population. It's a problem, no doubt, but those people aren't just a nameless number. They aren't an indistinct mass. Every single human is a person, someone with a family, with hopes and dreams. Who am I to decide who gets to live and who doesn't?"

How did we get from fighting spirits to the ethical problem of overcrowding? I struggle to wrap my head around what he's said. And how that relates to me.

"Maybe, one day, we'll find a way to live together peacefully, but as long as spirits attack humans, it's humans we need to protect." He gives me a bitter smile and stands up again. "But you'll learn enough about that in your classes. I've imposed on you long enough."

"No..." I clamp down on the words. I have to actively remind myself Dante isn't my friend. That I don't want him to stay. "When do I start classes?" I ask instead, surprising myself that I would even look forward to them. Anything to get out of this room, I guess.

Dante takes a moment to think about it. "We'll have to see. For now, you should take care of yourself. You've had a long trip. Eat something." This time, he doesn't stop, but slips out of the door before I can think of calling him back.

As the door trembles in its frame and I hear the click of a key turning, my stomach lurches. In an instant, I'm out of my chair, knocking my knee against the table. The chair clatters to the floor as I run to the door. Frantically, I pull on the handle. When it doesn't budge, I bang my flat hand against the wall. "Open the door! Open it! Let me out! Let me out!" My voice breaks, suffocated by tears. "Come back!" I hear myself shout, then my voice is choking. "Come back. Please, come back."

I can't breathe. I can't breathe. My head swims. I don't even know who I'm calling back to me.

"Anyone!" *Just open the door!* The room is too small, the window out of reach. I need this door to open. I need to get out.

A scream, raw and frightful, tears from my lungs as I bang both my hands and my head against the door. The sudden pain makes me stumble backwards. I hit the ground. I no longer know where up or down is. The room is spinning. Am I on the floor or hanging from the ceiling?

The door. Where is the door? There's no slit of light, and I can feel myself breaking apart. Sobs tear up my throat. There has to be a slit of light. Every door has one. But not this one. This one sits firmly in its frame, sealing off the room from light and air. I grow hot and sweaty. How many minutes until all the air is gone?

It feels like I'm already dead. Encased in a tomb.

"Let me out," I sob into the cold stone my fingers dig at. "Please, let me out. Anyone. Please..."

<h1 style="text-align:center">4</h1>

Nobody visits me for several days, not even Dante. Someone replaces the food while I sleep, curled up tight in a ball. Often, I only manage to eat a few pieces before my appetite dissolves. It's good food, fresh and well-seasoned, but it tastes like ash most of the time.

I sleep when I'm tired and prowl the walls when I'm awake. Time has lost all meaning, though the window above tells me whether it's day or night. For all I know, I could've been here for two days or two weeks.

My fingernails are blackened by all the skin I've scratched from my body. They're also broken and splintered from clawing at the stone walls. Sometimes, when the panic becomes too much to hold at bay, I try digging myself out. It never ends well.

"They're going to keep you here for the rest of your life."

I'm talking to myself again, only this time, there's no spirit to listen, just me. The sound of my voice, as raspy and thin as it might be, is the only thing that tells me I'm still alive.

If only these walls were inhabited by gnomes. Or if they were playing Jenga with the entire castle, like the ones we saw in Spandau. Brick by brick, they'd dismantle it until it all came tumbling down. I find myself laughing at the image until the laughter turns to weeping.

Oh, gosh, I'm losing my mind.

"Let me out," I whimper against the stone, tapping my knuckles against its cool surface. "Gnome, gnome, wherever you are, let me out." Great, now I'm breaking into song.

With a moan, I slide to the floor and pull my legs up, closing my eyes. I try to imagine what the outside world looks like. The great outdoors with its snow-covered mountain peaks, wide, sluggish rivers, and dark, sprawling woods. I call to mind the cliffs of Croatia and the caves of Hungary, tulip fields in the Netherlands and gorgeous fjords in Norway.

But the image that comes to me from the depths of my memories is one of a similar small room. Only this one had windows, an open door, and two bunk beds for four girls who fought for limited shelf space in the cupboard. Well, all but one. I never had enough clothes to occupy much space. In fact, I only owned two pairs of jeans, a few sets of underwear, and three shirts, all the same washed-out black with nondescript logos and letters, donations from leftover marketing campaigns.

I've never been a stranger to tight spaces that fit more people than they should. The camper van I lived in with my mother our last two summers barely offered us enough space to sleep, but its darkness was comfortable and cosy.

Oh, how I missed my mum in the youth home. The social worker responsible for us had forbidden me to ask for her. She never had any answers and, if she did, I'm not sure she would've given them to me, not after I pulled out my dress from the trash can and tried to hide it. It was the second-to-last thing I owned. The last was the wooden tempest spirit I held so dearly.

I don't have that figurine now, and so I have nothing to hold onto as my mind slips back into time and space, dragging up all the memories I'd taken so much care to bury.

As cramped as the camper van was, I was always free to leave. My mum and I used to sleep as many nights under the clear sky as we did tucked in the blankets inside. At the youth home, there's a curfew. No one is allowed out of bed after ten. It's stifling and makes it even harder for me to adjust. Never in my life did I have a curfew. I can't count the times I'd stayed awake with my mum, watching the stars or sitting at a fireplace until I fell asleep in her lap, her fingers running through my hair.

But everything my mother stands for is frowned upon here. The social worker was absolutely horrified to learn I' never seen a school building from inside. And no amount of telling her that I could identify all trees, most bushes and grasses, and over eighty kinds of mushroom would appease her. Now I'm forced to complete one worksheet designed for ten-year-olds after the other. The maths ones are the worst; a bunch of abstract problems that have no relevance to the reality of my life. I can count and I can add up numbers, but finding out how many postcards some fictional person needs to buy if he wants to send all his twenty-eight classmates a postcard for each day of his week-long holiday is utter nonsense. His hand would fall off after day one, never mind the insane cost of sending them all.

Instead of doing my homework, I sit in that tiny little room by the window and stare outside. It's fully spring now. The apple trees are in white bloom, and the tulips and daffodils in the neatly manicured bed are bright spots of happiness. Only I'm locked away from all that happiness, encased in stone, wood, and glass. With a sigh, I return to the worksheet and stare at it until the numbers break my brain. I'm not allowed in the garden until I've completed the homework. A devious bit of torture, implemented just for me.

*I do my best. I solve every stupid equation on the piece of paper, or attempt to. It takes time, lots of time, and when I'm finished, the other girls are returning to the room.*

*"Are you coming down for dinner?" one of them asks. She seems nice, but then she adds, "I'm afraid it's not cooked over a firepit, though."*

*All three of them break out in laughter, and I can hear the racial slur for my people thrown around casually. I don't have the heart to correct them, though hearing it feels like needles driven into my skin. I'm dismayed because it's taken me so long to do my homework the time for outside play has passed. There will be dinner and then curfew. I'm stuck inside—yet again.*

With a shiver, I return to the current time and day, into a situation that is eerily similar and yet a hundred times worse. In the youth home, all it took to escape was a blatant disregard for the rules. One night, I walked out the door, climbed through a window on the ground floor, and vanished into the night with nothing but the clothes on my back and tempest figurine in my hand. Here, my door is locked, and the window is too high and small to climb through.

Whimpering, I dig my fingernails into the soft flesh of my elbows, rocking back and forth against the wall.

Dante returns, dressed in a similarly fine suit. Though I don't have a mirror to check, I'm sure I look absolutely feral next to his groomed appearance. I can't even remember when I last combed my hair.

Judging by the short inhale of his breath and slight twitch of his face, Dante must've had the same thought. He quickly catches himself, though. "I'm sorry it took so long to find time. As the director, I find everyone wants something from me all the time."

I stare at him. Am I expected to say something? Do I want to say something? Do I want something from Dante? Yes. Yes, I do. "I want to leave this room."

"Excuse me?" He seems mildly surprised. "Leave this room to go where?" He says it as if it puzzles him greatly that I could wish for anything like it.

For a moment, I'm equally puzzled. I wet my lips and think about it, my thoughts painfully sluggish. "Outside. I want to go outside. Take a walk."

"In the middle of the night?" Dante asks, still surprised.

My shoulders rise and fall, and my breath quickens. I feel another panic attack approaching. "That doesn't matter. I just... Please. Please let me take a walk."

Finally, he gives in. He comes closer until I can't look at him without straining my neck. Of course, he wouldn't squat in pants as expensive as these. "Tell you what, Rika. You get yourself cleaned up, maybe put on some new clothes, and when I come back in—let's say fifteen minutes—we can take a quick walk in the garden."

I want to throw something at him. Anything. But the need inside of me is too great. So what if I have to do my homework first? What if I need to make myself presentable, conforming to social standards? I get to go out.

I get to go out, and that's all that matters.

5

Fifteen minutes.

Dante has given me fifteen minutes outside, accompanied by that young, smarmy Italian, Gian. This time, I take his arm—I'm not sure it's entirely optional—and follow him up a set of stairs leading to the ground floor. The hallway is dark. Dark and abandoned. It must be the dead of night. I'm wearing the clothes provided: a simple pair of pants and a T-shirt that carries the SSA logo. I hate myself for every step I take without running, but that doesn't matter the moment fresh air fills my lungs.

As I take my first deep breath, I feel myself expand. All those muscles bunched up in my chest relax. I'm alive. Tears spring to my eyes, and I gasp. I'm outside under the clear night sky, stars above my head. The air is warm, but not too warm. And there's space. So much space.

"Is it that great?" Gian asks, amused.

Embarrassed, I wipe away the tears, then nod at him. "Yeah. Marvellous, actually."

The garden is nothing to write home about. In fact, it's more of a park than a garden. Big trees dominate a star-shaped area enclosed by high walls that block the view from the streets around the castle. Only a single motorbike cuts through the night. When I turn back to the castle, I see a bridge-like structure allowing the spirit seekers to cross the road into the neighbouring district without ever touching the ground. It's the only visible exit from my point of view.

"There are prettier parks than that in Rome," Gian says, and we begin walking.

"Really? Like which?" I hope he's right. There's nothing but trees and grass here, which is perfectly fine. It just doesn't warrant the name "garden". I mean, I'm glad the spirit seeker recruits have access to a bit of nature. In my dreams, they were all trained in grey blocks surrounded by a sea of concrete.

Gian smirks. "Well, the Botanical Garden, for one. Or the Villa Borghese. A lot of them, actually. Not that it matters. People don't come here for the view."

"No." The weight I shed earlier resettles on my shoulders. "They come to learn how to kill spirits."

"It's impossible to kill a spirit," Gian says immediately. "You can only—"

"Catch them. I know." I don't know how that distinction matters if spirits are caught, never to be freed again. Unbidden, the image of myself trapped in a spirit tube comes to the surface, and a shudder runs through me. I've never really considered the reality of spirit trapping.

Gian comes to a stop, looking at me with concern. Just as with Dante, I find myself unsure about the genuine display of emotion. "Are you okay? Should we head back inside?"

And cut my fifteen minutes short? "No, no, it's all good." I continue walking, dragging Gian along.

Light-coloured gravel crunches under our feet as we walk in the wall's shadow. A nocturnal bird is cawing at the moon, and I can almost forget that we're in the heart of a bustling city. What this park is missing is a salamander scuttling under the bushes and a sylph dancing in the breeze. I guess spirits give the grounds a wide berth, and rightfully so.

An idea comes to me, though it's more of a need than an actual plan of action. I look at Gian, watching his profile in the moonlight. He's got a prominent nose with a bump at the top. He takes a moment to notice my quiet study. "What?"

"So, how did you become a spirit seeker?" I bite my lip, stupidly nervous about his answer. What am I even hoping for?

"Who says I'm a spirit seeker?" Gian asks with a short, bark-like laugh. "I work as security for the Academy."

I frown at him. "So, you can't see spirits?" Somehow, I expected every single person around here to be a spirit seeker. But it makes sense. If he were a spirit seeker, he would be stationed somewhere fighting spirits, not taking young women for moonlit walks.

"Nope. Can't see, hear, or touch them," he admits freely. "And I've got to say, I'm glad about it."

"Why's that?" I remind myself of Leon, who thought he was going crazy because he couldn't make sense of the faint presences he noticed. I miss him and the others.

Gian shrugs. "It means I can pretend they're not really there and I never have to worry about being forced to fight wind and weather."

Hope flares up in me, sudden and strong. My heart is hammering against my ribcage. Perhaps Gian can be persuaded, like I persuaded Leon and the others. "We don't need to fight spirits."

"We don't?" he asks, mildly interested.

My breath quickens at his answer. It's like my brain is trying to overtake itself. "No. I know it's what everyone gets taught in school or wherever else they pick up their spirit knowledge. But they're wrong. Or mostly wrong. Most spirits just want to be left in peace. They're not aggressive per se. I've actually made friends with quite a few. Dryads are super nice and—"

He doesn't seem terribly convinced. "You've made friends with spirits? I've never heard of such a thing."

"That's because they suppress the knowledge. The SSA doesn't want it to get out. They even had old accounts destroyed so nobody would question them. I..." Gian holds up a hand, and my hope crashes and burns. "What?"

"Time's up. We need to get back," Gian says, not unkindly.

I deflate. With every step we get closer to the building, my shoulders drop a little further. I can't bear to leave the grounds and go back into my cell. Fifteen minutes are too short. Who even came up with the time limit? Who thinks fifteen minutes of fresh air after days locked inside is enough? How could it ever be enough?

An embarrassing whimper escapes my throat, and my feet falter. I look up, staring at the dooming complex with its spirit-fighting angel on top. "Let's go inside," I hear Gian whisper, and my eyes trail down again until they catch sight of a lit window high up. There, the face of a young man sporting a short-cropped head of ginger hair is looking down at us. If he notices anything amiss, he doesn't show any sign, but for a moment, our eyes lock.

Then Gian tugs my arm, and we duck into the doorway and back into total darkness. He might as well have covered my mouth or strangled me; it's that hard to breathe.

Dante is waiting in my room, having seemingly nothing else to do at this time of day. As Gian leads me in, he looks up and asks, "E?"

While Gian launches into a rapid stream of Italian, Dante's face sags in dismay. He dismisses Gian as soon as the young man is finished and turns to me. "I'm disappointed, Rika."

For a ridiculous moment, I'm dismayed because I disappointed the man in front of me. Shaking my head, I rid myself of the notion. "Why? What did Gian say?"

"He told me how you tried to convince him that spirits can be befriended." Dante takes a deep breath, looking sad. "It's a dangerous way of thinking, Rika. Incredibly dangerous."

The realisation hits me like a gust of wind. Gian's ratted me out the first chance he could get. No, he set me up. He let me prattle on about pro-spirit views, feigning innocence until he could stick that dagger into my back. He may claim he's hired only as security for the academy, but he's Dante's man, through and through.

I must've spaced out, because Dante turns away, ready to leave. "Think about it," he says as he closes the door and locks me in.

Think about what? I can't even recall what he said to me. He was disappointed and then? He said I was dangerous, that my way of thinking was dangerous. How is that going to help me?

*No, no, stop.* Dante is not here to help me. Why do I expect him to?

Because he's the only one that comes to visit me. There must be a reason for it. He hasn't given up on me yet. If I can convince him...

There's only one way. It'll hurt, mentally more than physically. I'll have to give in, or at least pretend I'm giving it an honest try. My chest is in pain as I imagine myself implementing my plan, and I find it hard to breathe. Still, there's no other way. Not if I ever want to get out of this room for good.

Part of me is glad Dante keeps me waiting for another two days—I've counted the periods of sunlight this time! I've kept myself tidy, just like I know he would like, eaten all my food, and even forced myself to sleep in the bed, which frankly is an insult because that mattress seems to be as old as this castle. When he comes through the door, I am as prim and proper as I can be under the circumstances.

"I'm ready," I tell him. When he raises an eyebrow, I nod sagely. "I'm ready to learn." That's the plan. Play along nicely, get through the three years or even less if I can find an opportunity to escape and walk out of here, dignity in pieces, but mind intact.

"Are you?" His eyes flit towards the table, and I quickly take a seat. Dante takes a deep breath, but sits down nonetheless. "So, you're ready to learn what it takes to be a spirit seeker. To fight spirits?"

With a rather non-committal sound, I nod. Not good. If this is going to work, I need to do better. "You said that I was naïve, full of ideas that don't reflect reality. I think you're wrong." Hey, I can't butter him up too much or he'll never believe it. "But I could also be the one in the wrong." As soon as I say it, I have the horrifying feeling that's right. Swallowing, I continue my charade. "I've never had much schooling and I've realised that, maybe, I should learn your side of the story before I make up my mind."

Dante nods with such an austere expression, my optimism wanes. He's just gonna go away again, isn't he? Instead, he says, "You do understand that we don't tolerate pro-spirit talk at the Academy?"

Nice. Censorship. "Makes sense, yes."

"And I can trust you to give this an honest try?" His eyebrows are slowly crawling upwards.

"I'll do my best," I answer, as sombrely as I can muster. "I'm ready to learn." It doesn't hurt to repeat myself.

When he says, "Very well", my heart almost does a flip. "You will start your classes tomorrow." At long last, Dante's face splits into a white-toothed smile. "I knew you would come around, my dear."

Oh, yes, I've totally come around. Whatever he wants to believe, so long as I get to leave this room regularly.

6

It's happening. After breakfast, I get picked up by Gian. "You guys don't have maps to hand out? Or is the security in here *that* compromised?" I ask him, still not over the fact he ratted me out.

"Take a guess," he says, without the slightest hint of remorse.

"I'm the security risk." Sure, I could pretend to be completely unaware and oh-so eager to have my mind changed. But if I'm in this for the long run, my evolution needs to be believable. One misstep and I'm back in that room faster than I can say, "Spirits deserve to live, too".

As we leave my room, I'm so scared of being dragged back into it, I'm shaking.

Gian pretends not to notice. He sounds bored while he explains, "You're arriving in the middle of the semester, so you'll have to play catch-up in most of the courses." Oh, that sounds just perfect for someone with my academic credentials. "Today you'll get started with a double-length lecture in SSA History." Oh, boy, whitewashed anti-spirit propaganda. Yeah. "Next, you're learning the Fundamentals of Trapping." Complex maths. I'm starting to miss my cell already. "Then lunch in the hall and on to your afternoon lecture: Spirit Species and Their Behaviour Types."

"Spirit Species and Their Behaviour Types? What does the SSA know about that?" I think of the old books in the Citadel of Spandau, depicting sylphs as cartoonish cloud women who drop out of the sky.

Gian's teeth flash for a moment, and I realise I've slipped a little too much Real Rika into my reply. "You'll find out."

"I can't wait," I say, in a weak attempt to mask my mistake. Judging by Gian's lack of interest, I guess I got away with it. Or he'll simply tell Dante about it later.

Perhaps my plan isn't as great as I thought. Sure, it got me out of my room, but quite likely into a new kind of hell. Once again, I'm not allowed to be me. I have to pay lip-service and cut away pieces of my self until I can pass for what I need to be. It's the youth home all over again.

That impression changes when Gian opens the door to the upper floor. Suddenly, my world is flooded with light and sound as dozens of recruits pass us on their way to lectures and training. The place has come alive in a way it hasn't in all the days I've spent down in the basement. I expected some sort of military discipline, the kind Wulf exhibits, but the surrounding crowd is as chatty and irregular as a horde of university freshmen. There are people from all corners of Europe and beyond here, laughing and joking on their way to class.

No one gives me or Gian a second glance. Either they're all too busy with their own day or new people—and Gian—aren't an uncommon sight. A part of me finds that blanket of disinterest comforting. Another wants to scream out at them: *Can't you see I'm not here of my own free will?* I wonder what would happen if I ran to the nearest person and told them about my abduction?

Gian would excuse my behaviour, turn me around, and lead me straight back to my comfy little room. The thought of that alone is enough to make me shudder, and I shuffle along without making any trouble.

The stone hallways have been adorned with class pictures and big glass cases displaying the latest successes in spirit seeking. The first time I see Wulf's picture on the wall, I do a double take. He's looking sternly into the camera. Behind him is the flood damage from the Elbe high water. A few steps further, he's there again, this time somewhere in the mountains. 'Avalanche avoided', the title of the mission says. Then the image of a volcanic eruption catches my attention. Wulf never posed for that one, having hurried home immediately, so instead, they've put up a portrait of him that looks like he posed for a painting. Gosh, I hope there's not a painting of him here, is there?

I knew Wulf was the poster boy of the SSA, but this is overkill. It reminds me of all the fights we'd had when he still believed the SSA could do no wrong and I was a nuisance. A dangerous nuisance. Just like I am now.

Gian mistakes my interest, noting, "This could be you in a few years."

*Never,* I want to say, but catch myself. "That seems unlikely." Let him think I wouldn't dare compare myself to the amazing Wulf Bachmann.

"True," Gian replies, with such surety in his voice, it cuts straight into my heart. He doesn't think I'm going to get there alive, either.

Well, challenge accepted. Somehow, I'll get myself out of here in one piece.

My first class isn't too far away. It takes place in a naked stone hall that doesn't even try to appear comfortable. Benches are built into it like an ancient lecture theatre, and thanks to the medieval building style, the windows are narrow and higher up, so you can't even gaze longingly at the outside. Most of the three-dozen people filing into the room are about my age or younger, but there are some who haven't been recruited straight out of school or university.

I shuffle my feet to the back row, but Gian has other plans and directs me to a seat right in the front. While I glare at him, he smiles at me. "Be a good student, won't you?" After that, he finally leaves me alone to talk to the lecturer, an older man with a straight back and frizzy grey hair.

It doesn't take long for the other students to take notice of me now. An eager-looking girl with pale, freckled arms sits down next to me, holding a ledger decorated with curly font spelling out, 'History'. "Hi, there, are you a new student? I'm Marit."

I start with a non-committal hmm-sound, not sure I actually want to get to know these people. Not that there's anything wrong with them—apart from their willingness to learn all about enslaving spirits. It's just that making friends seems too normal for my situation. All I want is to get away from this place, not build attachments. But I guess it doesn't hurt to be nice, especially if I want to convince Dante that I'm trying. "Rika, and yes. It's my first day."

"Oh. I didn't know you could start in the middle of the semester." Marit seems to be a bright cookie, latching straight onto the inconsistency. But that's the SSA's problem, not mine.

"Me neither. I thought I had to wait"—a lot longer, like forever—"but apparently, they wanted me to start straight away." I notice Gian watching me and smile reassuringly at him. I deserve an award for that performance.

At last, he leaves, and I'm able to take a deep breath. Part of me thought he'd be glued to my side for the entire day.

Turning back to Marit, I notice her confusion. "Why did they want to start you so soon? Don't tell me you're in the elite stream."

"Elite stream?" Now, it's my turn to be confused. Gian's super-short heads-up didn't cover those details.

"The one for people with an NAV higher than 400." Marit opens her ledger, showing off her neat handwriting. I bet her notes are as impeccable as they look. "Mine is only at 251."

Oh, boy, here we go. Sometimes, I think the NAV is like a pissing contest. Unless Wulf submitted my test results, no one here knows my true NAV. Not even Dante, though of course, there's no chance of concealing that I can see spirits. "Well, I haven't heard anything about an elite stream, so I don't know."

I'm glad the bell is ringing now, announcing the start of the lecture. Marit loses her interest immediately and sits up straight, pen poised on the page. The desk in front of me is empty. It only occurs to me now that Dante hasn't issued me with a schoolbag. Not that I'm a huge fan of taking notes—I can't think of a single time in my life I've ever done so—but it makes me stand out. And as if that isn't enough, I've got the lecturer's attention right from the start.

He flicks me a quick smile and announces, "We've got a new student joining us. Please welcome Rika."

There's a mostly mumbled greeting, while Marit beams at me as if I'm her favourite new thing.

The lecturer's eyes fall on my glaringly empty desk. "Could someone lend Rika a pen and some paper? As you will learn quickly, Rika, my class requires a lot of notes." Almost as an afterthought, he adds, "I'm Professor Okorie. I'll give you a reading list later."

Meanwhile, Marit has supplied me with a piece of paper and pen from her impressive collection. I try not to sigh when I set the tip on the first line. I can write, but it isn't something I've done a lot in the last eight years.

"Alright, let's continue. Last time, we started tackling the SSA's involvement during World War II," Professor Okorie begins, not sparing another glance at me. "At that point, fighting spirits wasn't particularly a priority, though it should have been. Several reports suggested a heightened spirit activity on the battlefields. Now, the SSA couldn't openly continue their recruitment drive with Europe fractured as it was. So, for a couple of years, we were forced into hiding our activities."

While Marit seems to transcribe every word, my pen hovers over the page. I feel like I've been thrown into deep water with no coast in sight. I've already missed so much, it's disorienting. What happened before World War II? Are the topics even taught chronologically? There's no framework for me to hang onto, and I'm at total loss as to what to jot down.

As the professor drones on about how the SSA recruited people in secret and smuggled staffs into countries Italy was officially at war with, I feel another panic attack rising. My hand shakes as I force it to scribble down the word 'history' just to have something on my paper. Next to me, Marit has already filled an entire page while I slip deeper and deeper into a spiral of self-hate. Why is it so damn hard for me to take notes? Why can't I simply write something down? Anything?

Lukas would have a field day with my stupidity. He, with his excellent high school diploma, would have breezed through these lectures.

I'm reminded of the teachers at the school the youth home sent us to. Of their exasperation when they learnt how far behind I was at everything, discounting all the practical knowledge I had earned instead. And the mocking of my fellow class- and roommates. It won't be long until that starts that here.

Tears are stinging in my eyes, and there's still nothing on my page. To be honest, I can't even remember what Professor Okorie talked about last.

Right now, he's putting some names on the blackboard, telling us about the feats of these extraordinary spirit seekers. "Elisha Dunning stopped a landslide that was about to crush a rescue mission in Austria. Felix Petzold brought a group of Jewish women and children to safety by leading them through a spirit-infested bog. Piotr Swalinski..."

"Are these all going to be in a test?" I whisper, vaguely asking Marit.

The look I get makes me wither inside. I assume the answer is yes. With a sigh, I resign myself to copying the names on my piece of paper.

Those two hours are the longest hours of my life. I feel like my brain has been wrung dry and left to rot. I don't even remember what we spent all that time on. Secret missions and even more secret negotiations that all blur into one thing: how awesome the SSA is.

Some of those feats sound, indeed, as grand as Professor Okorie makes them out to be, but they all leave a bitter aftertaste. The spirits they so heroically dealt with against all the odds are completely erased, and not a single person in class asks about them—including me. My jaw hurts from biting down so hard in an effort to be a good student. *I can do this*, I tell myself. I can keep quiet, keep a low profile, and get out of here. But, gosh, it's exhausting. And this is only the first lecture of many.

As soon as the break begins, people mill around me, asking me where I come from, and even more importantly, what my NAV is. Before I can decide whether honesty is the best policy or puts me even more on the spot, Gian appears, ready to lead me away.

I wave vaguely at the others and follow him. "Are you gonna be by my side the entire day?" I ask, trying not to sound too annoyed.

"I'll try to be," he says, as if it's a benefit to me. "How was your first lecture?"

I snort before I can catch myself. *No way, Gian. I'm not falling for that again.* "Interesting. I never considered how involved the SSA was in major historical events."

"The fight against spirits never rests," Gian replies.

I flick through the list of reading material Professor Okorie gave me. "It'll take ages for me to catch up."

"You'll have lots of study time in your room."

"How wonderful," I manage to say, with only a hint of sarcasm.

Gian smirks and extends an arm towards another cold room. "Your Trap Theory class."

I swallow heavily. A part of me is glad it's not a practical class. I don't think I'm ready to capture spirits for fun yet. Problem is, I'm not ready for the theory either. Just having Leon talk about it made my head spin. And he was patient and utterly understanding of my maths deficiency. Judging by my previous lecture, that won't happen here.

My mouth opens, ready to spill it all to Gian, but he's already turning away, having done his part. I quickly think about dashing down the corridor when my name is called from within the room.

"Rika?" A blond woman with a beak-like nose waves me toward her.

Bracing myself, I step inside while the others take their places. "Yes?"

She has already averted her eyes, looking at a piece of paper instead. "Do you have a surname, Rika?"

I shake my head, and then again when she looks up to me, wondering why I haven't replied. Of course I have a surname, but I haven't used it for the last eight years because my mother asked me not to before they took her away. "It's just Rika."

"Just Rika, great." She doesn't sound like that's so great. "Well, I'm Mrs Razaee. I teach trap theory and trap technology. You might find the theory daunting. A lot of my students do."

Hope flickers to life inside of me. Is she actually going to take my current level of proficiency into account?

Mrs Razaee has turned her gaze back to the piece of paper, which I assume are my enrolment details. "It doesn't say here what kind of education you've had. You're from Germany, yes?"

The hope has turned sour, and it feels like a dark pit has opened in my stomach. "Hmm." I guess having lived there for the last decade is good enough for her understanding.

"Did you study? Did you get your Abitur or... what is it called, the middle school diploma?" There are two major school systems in Germany, split by academic success. For those clever enough during elementary school, a twelve-to-thirteen-year education awaits, leading up to the Abitur that will grant you university access. Everyone else only has ten years of school and might struggle to find a well-paid job for the rest of their lives.

"I... I was home-schooled." That's not really a thing in Germany, but it sounds better than admitting I wasn't truly schooled at all.

Mrs Razaee draws in a deep breath. "Right. Then let me find out where you're at."

I've become acutely aware that everyone in the room is listening to us. Nobody even attempts to disguise their interest, least of all Marit. This will define my standing in the class. No use in pretending it will be anything other than the bottom of the barrel.

"Did you do integrals and derivatives of functions?" She looks up at me again. It feels like she's already lost her patience with me.

"No." I don't even know what she's talking about.

"Systems of equations?" Her fingers are tapping on the desk now. "Simple algebra."

I wish she would stop using these terms that make me feel even more stupid than I already do. "I can add things up and…" I stop myself because they're already snickering behind me. "Look, I don't think I'll be assigned to trapping." And if I am, I have my own way of operating the traps. "I can sit this one out if you think it's useless." Attack is the best defence, isn't it?

Mrs Razaee's eyes widen in horror. "Absolutely not. So you think your NAV is high enough you don't need to know anything about trapping?" She makes me sound like some arrogant ass. "Everybody does. Good thing is you have three years to master the necessary maths. For now, I'll be assigning you to Henny so they can work with you in private. You're absolutely right, it would be useless for you to try to follow the discussion with your current level of education."

*Hold your tongue, Rika. Hold your tongue.* So, what if I've just been humiliated in front of the entire class? That's cool. It's not like I was trying to make friends. I'm beginning to curse my decision to give this a try. Panic attacks on top of panic attacks in my confinement downstairs are better than this. A million times better.

Fortunately, I don't have to use my leaden tongue to ask who Henny might be. They're coming to the front with a big smile plastered on their face. Everything about Henny is slender, the long body, the angular face, even their nose. Their short brown hair curls behind their ears and their equally brown eyes glitter with excitement. "Hey, Rika. Let's go into the room next door so we get some quiet."

I'm eternally grateful for the little piece of grace they're offering me. At least I don't need to fail repeatedly at the simplest tasks in front of everybody else.

I follow Henny into the small office next door and breathe in relief when I notice this room actually has a proper window that allows me to see the outside. "How are you not suffocating in here?" The words slip out of my mouth.

Aghast, I stare at Henny, but they only laugh. "Well, I personally love maths. Give me a couple of equations and I'm off in my own world, not noticing whether it's night or day."

"Good for you." I take a seat at the small table, trying to keep at bay all the pain and despair that's threatening to overwhelm me now I'm in a slightly safer environment. "Well, quick warning. My maths is shockingly bad, and I don't think three years are even close to enough time to fix that."

"Don't worry about it." Henny takes their place in front of me. "Trapping isn't quite as important as Mrs Razaee is making it out to be. Sure, someone has to do it, but everyone has their strengths, and it's really only the last ring that has to be calculated. So as long as you know what kind of spirit you're fighting, you're already two-thirds on the way."

I'm slowly warming up to Henny since they're the first person in here who's trying to reassure me instead of deconstructing me further. "Can I tell you something?" Don't worry, I'm not trusting myself to the first person who's been nice. I've learned my lesson.

Henny nods. "Sure."

"I've... already got a little experience with the whole trapping system." When their eyebrows knit together, I study the table edge instead. "I guess you could call it an apprenticeship of sorts."

"Where?" There's only curiosity in their voice, no inquisition.

If I say Berlin, they'll probably connect me straight away to Wulf, and for some reason, I don't want that. There will be too many expectations if they assume I've learnt from the greatest of them all. It's bad enough they're all gonna find out about my NAV soon enough. "Ireland." Gosh, why didn't I say Hungary? After what went down in Dublin merely days ago—or perhaps weeks, considering how long I was stuck downstairs—aligning myself with a group of rebel spirit seekers might not be a smart move. I can't even speak enough Irish to save my life.

Henny doesn't seem to know about the Irish independence, or if they do, they don't show it. "You should get in touch with Eoghan then. He's Irish. Well, he's from Northern Ireland, so technically, he's from the UK, but you know what I mean." Henny is such a chatterbox, I can't help but ease into my chair a little. "He's one of us, by the way."

"One of us?"

"Of the 400-stream." Henny blushes faintly. "Sorry, I help at admissions, and I saw your name this morning."

The 400-stream, or the elite stream, as Marit called it. "I don't really know what that means," I admit.

"Well, our training differs slightly from everyone else's. Not so much in the first year, so don't worry about it. They'll probably put you into our battle class that takes place tomorrow, the day after, and Tuesdays," Henny explains, flashing me another of their encouraging smiles.

I assume that means it's Wednesday then. "And you are...?"

"A third-year, like Eoghan. Then there's his girlfriend, Wiola, who's a second-year, and Tiago and his little sister Joana, who are second-year and first-year, respectively." They stretch their neck to look into the room behind us. "You must've seen Joana already. Oh, there. She's the one with the purple streak in her hair."

I tip the chair backwards to check out my classmates, who are working in silence. The purple streak definitely helps to identify an otherwise dark-haired girl nibbling on her pencil. So, five people carry the SSA's hopes for the future at the moment.

"Right, so, trapping." Henny points both of their index fingers at the table. "Or rather maths."

Quickly, I remind myself there was a reason I told them about my supposed apprenticeship. "Uhm, so, during my time in Ireland, I already trapped a few spirits and... I don't actually need to do the calculations." Once again, Henny is looking confused. I guess it's not really that common what I do. "The rings are all about identifying the spirits, right? So, the maths is just there to help you along, but you still need to do educated guesses, and... I suppose, my guesses are a little more educated than most." Gosh, that sounds conceited. "What I mean is my intuition has served me far better than those calculations you do, so it might not really be necessary I learn them."

Henny has pushed their front teeth forward so they're sitting on their lower lip but relaxes their mouth quickly when I stop talking. "I've honestly never heard of anyone doing that. It's interesting, though. Do you think your intuition could help you with the maths?"

I groan. "I really have to learn it?"

"You're gonna be fine. You've got three years to get this down," Henny assures me, and strangely, I believe them.

At least partially. "I have to warn you though, I never received a formal education, so..."

"So?" Henny shrugs. "A formal education isn't everything. You're not stupid, Rika." How they can say that with so much certainty, I have no idea. "We just need to find a way that works for you."

I don't want to admit it, but if all the SSA's commander students are as accommodating as Henny, there might be hope for them yet. As uncomfortable as the thought is, it only makes me miss Wulf more. There must be a way to get in touch with him.

\#

The lesson passes surprisingly quickly. I don't think I've learnt anything, but Henny seems to be happy with what they've deduced of my current abilities. Even better, when Gian comes to pick me up, they lock their arm with mine and smirk at him. "I'll be taking Rika to lunch and her lecture afterwards."

I try my best not to meet Gian's eyes, fully expecting him to protest. But all he does is shrug and mutter, "Fine with me."

As he strolls off, Henny turns toward me. "What's his deal, anyway?"

I really want to confide in them, but I'm aware that would be way too premature. "I think he's supposed to help me adjust to my new situation. You know, coming in late and all that."

Henny accepts the answer easily enough and leads me down the corridor, along with the other students. "Have they given you a room yet?"

They have, but this truth is harder to mask. "Yeah." Even I'm painfully aware of how lacking that answer is.

"Great. You're mostly sorted then. So, listen. If you have a bigger break, we usually get lunch on the other side of the Tiber, though the food in here is good enough."

The other side. There might be a chance to get outside and away.

They walk through a double door into what seems to be the central room of the castle. Round tables provide space for eight to ten people each. A large canteen fills the back of the room, offering a variety of warm and cold foods. The entire place is alive with the clatter of plates and cutlery, loud conversations, and laughter. Competing melodies are playing from different corners of the room. It reminds me a little of the food banks and soup kitchens, just a lot more joyful and carefree.

"I don't have any money with me," I mumble. So far, I've gotten my food for free, but that doesn't seem to be the case here. The recruits pay for their own lunches, thus the option to leave the castle.

Once again, Henny seems surprised, but they catch themselves quickly. "I'll shout you lunch. You can pay me back another time."

That about kills any appetite I might've had. When Agnes kidnapped me, she didn't let me bring my personal stuff. I have nothing, just the clothes I wore, and even those have been replaced. "I'm not really hungry."

"Don't be silly. Don't worry about paying me back. Just pick something," Henny insists. "My parents send me enough money."

It must be nice to have supportive parents. Or parents at all. "Okay." Despite that, I grab a dry ciabatta roll and an apple.

Henny glares at me but chooses not to argue. Instead, they pay for their food and mine, and carries it towards a table on the left side.

A few people are already sitting there, among them Joana and a young man with the same bronze skin and dark hair as her. There's no bold colour statement from her brother, though. Instead, Tiago seems to go for the monochrome style, with a grey dress shirt and black trousers. Next to the siblings sits a tall, good-looking man with short red hair and equally red stubble. He's only wearing a T-shirt, its sleeves exposing several small tattoos. One of his muscular arms is looped around the shoulders of a round-faced blond woman, wearing her long blond hair in a ponytail that almost sits on top of her head. Make-up accentuates her already beautiful features. She's cuddled into his side, stealing pieces of his lunch from time to time. Meanwhile, his eyes meet mine, and I do a double take. He's the guy who'd looked down on me and Gian last night. If he recognises me, he doesn't show it, already turning his attention elsewhere.

As soon as we arrive, Henny takes a moment to introduce the group. "Alright, so this is Joana, your fellow first-year. That's her brother, Tiago. And those inseparables are Eoghan and Wiola. Guys, this is our newest club member, Rika."

Eoghan gives me another look, only this time it's one not too different from Lukas' first glance, condescending and somewhat disgusted. "How high?"

"How high?" Is he asking how tall I am?

"Your NAV," Tiago clarifies. "Currently, my sister holds the record at 454." He points to Joana, who gives a quick wave. She obviously doesn't care about such technicalities as her NAV.

Considering the way Eoghan carries himself, I would've thought he was the leader of the bunch, but he only grins. "So?"

"I... I haven't officially been tested." Wulf never sent my results to the SSA. Hopefully, Dante never actually bothers with retesting me, and I can breeze by with being vaguely talented.

"How did they know to put you into the stream, then?" Wiola asks, weirdly offended, as if I was the one that put me there. I notice her English carries a heavy East-European accent. Russian maybe, or Polish.

Helplessly, I check with Henny, who is in the process of sitting down. "Well, if she can see spirits, it's pretty clear, isn't it?"

"Not really," Wiola says, and the tone of her voice makes me think that I'm not gonna like her very much. "Every 300er can see spirits. I don't see a bunch of them being invited to our class." Class or table, it both seems to be the same.

"I can go," I say, rather lamely.

Henny tugs on my sleeve. "Nonsense. If you don't agree, Wio, you can take it up with Dante. I'm sure he knows what he's doing." For some reason, they give Eoghan a pointed stare, and he responds by pulling Wiola a little closer. Immediately, she snuggles back into him, a silly smile on her face.

"You know, Rika did some sort of apprenticeship with some Irish spirit seekers before coming here," Henny tells him.

"Oh, really?" Eoghan asks, doubt audible in his voice. "Whereabouts?"

After another tug from Henny, I sit down, though all my instincts tell me to run. "I spent some time in Dublin."

Instead of leaving it at that, his frown deepens. "When?"

"Before she came here, obviously." Henny snorts dismissively. "Seriously, Eoghan."

He spreads his arms. "I'm just asking a few questions. Last time I checked, that was still allowed." The way the two act with each other, I'm assuming they've been friends for a long time.

Wiola coos at him and pats his belly. "Cut her some slack. She only just arrived," she says in a sudden change of heart. Then she straightens herself, letting go of her boyfriend. "Welcome to our illustrious little circle." Yeah, it doesn't sound very welcoming. "How're you finding the Castel?"

"Uhm... intimidating?" I admit. "I'm used to more... airy spaces." Like the outside world. I dig my finger into the ciabatta roll, pulling out some of the white fluff, but not really putting it into my mouth.

"It can be overwhelming," Henny agrees.

"I was terribly homesick for the first month or two," Tiago admits.

"How fortunate you've got me here, then," Joana jokes, patting his leg. "Hey, Rika, if you need some notes for classes, I'm happy to give you mine. They're not as great as Marit's, but a lot more digestible. Seriously, that girl has no chill."

I've noticed that much. "Thanks. That would be great."

"And Henny is truly the best when it comes to advanced trapping. And they're an awesome tutor," Joana adds.

I've already assumed that this was why Henny was present in a first-year class. "Yeah, I'd noticed that much."

Thanks to my lacklustre participation, the talk soon strays to other topics. Apparently, there's a soccer match happening soon that needs to be examined in great detail, while I continue to murder the ciabatta in my hand. I know I should be grateful for how easily this group has admitted me into their fold, but the pressure to perform has become unbearable. I can't be myself, and thus, I'm no one, just a quiet presence at their table.

Henny bumps their elbow into mine after a while. "It's time for your afternoon class." They notice the untouched apple and the myriads of crumbs in front of me. "You weren't lying when you said you weren't hungry, were you?"

"Sorry," I say out of reflex. Feebly, my brain reaches for a workable excuse for wasting their money like that. "It's just one of those days." Hopefully, they get the hint.

Henny commiserates by pulling a face. They point to Joana, who's already got to her feet. "Jo will take you along."

"I love spirit behaviour. It's so interesting!" Joana gushes as she takes me up the stairs to another level of bleak stone. "It's the only class worth anything. The lecturer is amazing. She really knows her stuff!"

*We'll see about that*, I think to myself. To be honest, I'm not expecting much from this lecture. If it goes well, this might be a load of bullshit. If it doesn't, the upcoming class might be even more infuriating than SSA History.

Because of Gian's absence, there's no one forcing me into the first row, so I tag along with Joana, who seems more comfortable in the back as well. A little too comfortable, I notice, when she puts her feet up on the back of the seat in front of her. No one rushes to sit down near us. Instead, the others just give us a quick glance and take their seats in the front. I wonder whether my association with Joana has actually elevated my standing somehow.

"Relax," Joana whispers. "Mrs Csorba won't put you on the spot like old Razaee."

That's a good thing because I suddenly find my insides frozen solid. "Csorba?"

"Here she comes."

I slowly turn my gaze to the front, taking in the blonde woman in her early forties who's carrying a box full of class material. Her hair is shorter than it was in my memories, but her eyes are as blue as ever, and the smile she gives the people in the front row makes me whimper.

She's here. In the last place I'd ever thought to look for her, I've finally found her.

This class is being taught by my mum.

# 7

I have absolutely no idea what we've talked about during the two-hour lecture. Judging by the images on the last slide, something about gnome-salamander relationships. This class is one of the biggest I've been to so far, and I can easily see why. My mother's way of teaching is engaging and full of stories. It's effortless, breezy, and doesn't feel like a chore at all. Just as it was all my life.

If Joana has noticed anything odd about my behaviour, she doesn't show it. Neither does my mother. Either she doesn't have an attendee list, or she never bothers with it. Her focus is entirely on the students who raise their hands and ask lots of questions, Marit most of all. I'm glad because I wouldn't want any of them to witness what might pass between us.

My mother is employed by the SSA, teaching hopeful recruits all the knowledge she used to pass on to me, so they can capture spirits in their habitat. Though I've had two hours to come to terms with it, I'm at as much of a loss as I was at the start of the lecture.

"You want me to show you the recreation rooms?" Joana asks when everyone starts packing up.

I take a moment to register her question. "What? Oh, no, I need to chat with..." Mrs Csorba. I can't bring myself to say it. "My mum" weighs too heavily on my tongue.

"Suit yourself." And with that, Joana pushes past me and joins the rest of the class pouring out into the corridor.

Marit is talking to my mother, asking all the questions she couldn't fit into the class. It gives me some more time to gather my wits. I hang back until Marit notices me and smiles. "Oh, well, I'll get right to the essay."

There was an essay? I watch Marit practically skip from the room. And then I'm alone with my mother.

She has definitely aged, though she can't be more than forty-five now. In my memories, her face was smooth, apart from the little creases her smile had left on her face. Now, her much-paler skin has sagged, and though I saw her smile in class, I can't see it etched into her cheeks anymore.

"I don't think we've met," she starts, only just looking at me now. "Gosh, sorry, I probably had a notice somewh—"

"Mum?" My voice is a crippled little thing, barely audible.

Her face turns rigid as realisation kicks in. Then her hand flies up, stifling a gasp, and her eyes widen. "Rika?" Suddenly, her gaze is all over me, jumping from my blue hair to my shirt, back to my face and away again. At last, she lowers her hand, her eyes filling with tears. "I... how... what are you doing here?"

The question hurts. It sounds too close to rejection. As if I should've never attempted to find her. "I was looking for you."

My mum's face softens. She reaches out with one hand, rubbing the tips of my hair between her fingertips. "I love this colour. Makes your eyes shine." Some of the old warmth has returned to her eyes, and my heart aches for her.

"Were you here all this time?" I still don't understand how this could be. How could the woman who'd taught me all about the many wonderful spirits in the world work for the SSA? Wasn't it her who told me never to tell anyone about the spirits?

Her hand sinks back, and she sighs, leaning her backside against her desk and grabbing the edge with both hands. "Yeah, more or less."

It makes no sense. "So, you never even tried to reach out to me?"

"You don't belong here," my mum says. "You need to leave."

Her words hit me like a ton of bricks. I've spent all these years looking for her, and this is what she has to say? This isn't right. None of it is.

Someone clears their throat at the door, and both our heads turn. Gian leans against the frame, reminding me I'm still on probation. "Thanks for waiting around," he says in a razor-sharp voice.

No. He can't do this now. I need time. I need time with my mum. "They're holding me here. They—"

Two quick strides, and Gian is at my side, grabbing my wrist so painfully I gasp. "Mie scuse, Magda," he says, talking rapidly in Italian and cutting me out of the conversation. The only word I recognise is "Dante".

My mum never spoke Italian once in my life, yet she's as fluent as if she grew up here. "No worries," she finally says in English for my benefit. "I'll see you in class, Rika." There's an intensity in her gaze, but it's left unspoken.

"That's all you've got to say to me? Don't you see what's happening here?" My voice breaks, and I swallow.

The pressure around my arm intensifies until I'm sure Gian will break a bone if he continues. "We're going. Now!"

"Help me!" I cry out as he drags me to the door, but the sight of her shocks me into submission.

She takes one last look at me, then turns to sort her papers, as if nothing out of the ordinary is occurring. As if she hadn't just seen me for the first time in eight years. My heart shatters in front of her, and she doesn't even notice.

Gian brings me straight down to my room. I regret not following Joana when I had the chance. There'll be no recreation for me after a long day of lectures. Unless you count pacing my room as physical exercise. Because that's exactly what I do as soon as Gian locks the door behind me.

My thoughts are racing, while my blood rushes to my head. She's here. My mum is here. At the SSA. My mum is part of the SSA. My mum teaches spirit behaviour. Maybe I should raise my hand in class and ask why she believes all spirits should be captured and contained. Or why she never looked for me.

A scream rips itself loose from my throat, and I slam my hands against the wall, ignoring the pain that shoots up through my wrists.

How? How does any of this make sense? How did this even happen? She warned me against all the SSA stands for, taught me a different view all my life, and now I'm to believe it was all a big fat lie?

I'm done. I'm done with this place. I can't do it.

Whimpering, I slide to the floor, once again digging my nails into my palms until the pain is more intense than the one ripping my heart in two. Blood drips down onto my shoes, and I take what feels like my first breath in minutes. "I can't. I just can't."

They did it. They did the one thing I won't recover from. They took my mum from me, and she didn't even put up a fight.

\#

I guess it shouldn't come as a surprise when I get a visitor later in the day. It's not the one I want, though.

With a dinner tray in his hands, Dante enters my room. "Hello, Rika." He puts down the tray, and I notice he's brought a second plate for himself. "Come on. Won't you join me?" he asks when I still haven't moved away from the wall.

I'm too exhausted for this. My stomach informs me that I'm hungry, but I can't bring myself to rise from the floor. "Do I have to?"

"Long day, huh?" There it is again, the comforting smile that wants to convince me he's my best friend. "I've had a little feedback," Dante admits, as he helps himself to some salad. "It looks like we both under-estimated the effort your education will take."

Effort? I've got a freaking mountain to climb. My brain duly notes that he received a report on all of my lessons. Instantly, I want to know what my mum could've possibly told him. "You talked to... Mrs Csorba?" I manage to push myself up and lean against the wall.

"I did." Part of me appreciates that he doesn't beat around the bush, even though it's hell of invasive that they talked. "So, you two know each other?" he asks, with mild curiosity.

Once again, my insides feel like they've been dunked into ice water. I almost want to blurt out, "She's my mother!" but thankfully my brain remembers how to function, and I hold my breath instead.

"Léna said she was surprised to see you here." Dante studies me intensely with his dark brown eyes. "She wasn't really clear how you two know each other, though. Help me out, will you?"

I register two things. Dante's called my mother by an affectionate nickname, and my mother hasn't disclosed the nature of our relation-ship. Quickly, I rack my brain as to whether I called her mum in front of Gian. I don't think I did. He would've told his boss immediately. Part of me wants to give up the secret just to spite her, but then again what am I going to get out of that? Nothing good. So, I keep quiet. Until I've had a chance to talk to her and find out what is going on here, I want to keep my promise. It's not like I have much else to hold onto.

"How do you know her?" Slowly, I walk over to the table and sit down, pulling strength from the knowledge that something doesn't quite match up.

Dante offers me the rest of the salad. "Léna and I go way back. We were both students here."

"What?" My fork clatters on the plate, sending a piece of lettuce flying over the table. "She was a spirit seeker?"

Gracefully, Dante picks up the lettuce and heaves salad onto my plate. "Well, no. You haven't got to this part of SSA history, yet, if it's being taught at all, but during her time here, Léna... well, she staged a little rebellion." He says "rebellion" as if it was some kind of prank.

Dutifully, I pick up my fork again. My brain is racing around these fresh revelations. It's fair to say my mother never once mentioned her involvement with the SSA. "Rebellion?"

Dante waves it off. "She and a few others studied and learnt everything they could, but never entered engagement as a spirit seeker. Instead, she used all the knowledge to form her own little cult."

"It wasn't a cult!" For a moment, I'm seeing red. There's so much shit we have to take from everyone. It's a way of life, a rich culture, family. Not a cult!

"So, *that's* where you know Léna from," Dante surmises, visibly unaffected by my brief outburst. "I take it you joined her cult, then?"

Still that word. "Born into it. And it's not a cult!" I give up all pretence of being civil and cross my arms. He can eat his stupid dinner alone.

"Right, right." Dante raises a hand in apology. "That solves a lot of questions I've had about you. Like how you escaped our notice for so long." He rubs his beard while I stare daggers at him. "So, basically, you were brainwashed from birth into this pro-spirit way of thinking Léna tried to establish. But don't worry."

I snort at him. "Why would I worry?"

"We'll get there," he promises, in a soothing voice. "We'll slowly unpack all of this with patience and perseverance. It took time for Léna to come around, and you've seen how she is now. She's a valuable member of our community, teaching young minds with passion and understanding."

"So, you pressured her into joining *your* cult." Two can play this game, I guess. Slowly, the pieces fit together in my head. My mother was trained at the SSA, but she ran away because she believed, like me, that spirits don't have to be fought. She even caused what Dante called "a little rebellion". They must have not been thrilled with her. A terrible realisation hits me. "The SSA ordered the Spring Cleaning."

Dante scrunches up his nose and shakes his head quickly. "The SSA ordered no such thing." It's the most agitated I've seen him so far. "But we managed to reconnect with Léna through it. And no, there was no pressure needed. We had a few chats and ironed things out. After a while, Léna began to see where she went wrong and took up the offer to teach. She's always been good at that." A proud little smile appears on his lips, which I yearn to wipe off his face. "Léna has always belonged here. And so do you."

I want to puke. What he calls "a few chats" sounds suspiciously like what he's doing to me now. Hell, he pretty much admitted as much. "I can't wait."

The sarcasm is dripping from my voice, but Dante takes it in his stride. "Great. Well..." He gets up. "I'll be making a few changes to your schedule. There's no need for you to attend Mrs Csorba's classes. After all, your knowledge of spirit behaviour is already quite advanced. Instead, I'll see to it that more practical classes are added to your day."

"Practical classes?" Every time I think I've managed to win a bit of control over my fate, he pulls the rug out from under me. No more classes with my mum. Is it because I already know all there is about spirits, or because he doesn't want to risk the two of us scheming together? Either case, talking to her will be virtually impossible with Gian watching all my movements. And now I get more practical classes, too, whatever that means.

"You'll see, Rika," Dante says, his voice disgustingly cheerful. "One day, you too will become a valuable member of our community."

# 8

Practical classes mean physical exercising and battle training. I finally get a hold of my schedule, together with a set of stationery items Marit would be proud of. SSA History and a class called 'Disaster Case Studies' are the only lectures left. Trapping has been replaced by private tutoring with Henny, while anything related to spirits, their behaviour and markers, has been completely erased. The rest of the schedule has been literally filled up with training times and battle practise with three different streams.

"That schedule is intense!" Henny exclaims when they check it out over breakfast. Instantly, they show it to everyone else. "She's training with the first-years, the second-years, *and* our classes."

"Your physical exam must've been extremely poor," Eoghan scoffs. "They even had you running this morning."

I'm reminded of the awkward meeting we had when Gian dragged me along the paths before breakfast. At first, I'd been grateful for the chance to be outside, but the speed Gian set for me made it impossible to draw a deep breath. Even so, Eoghan and Wiola overtook us twice, barely breaking a sweat. "If you say so."

Joana shrugs. "They might just want to speed up your training. Like, put you on the fast-track." If only.

"Why would they do that?" Eoghan exclaims. I'm starting to like him less and less. "You're not special, are you? I mean, not any more than each of us." His eyes bore into me. "When are they gonna test your NAV?"

I shrug. "Does it matter?" My personal theory is that I'm getting all this training so I'll be too exhausted to think of rebelling. "You afraid it's higher than yours?" I already know it is.

Eoghan looks stunned for a moment, then he grins. "Wouldn't matter in the end. We can all see spirits, so it comes down to our other skills instead. I'm pretty good with a staff."

"Me too," Wiola says, in a deadpan voice.

It takes a moment before the entire table erupts into laughter. Henny pulls a face while Joana throws a piece of bread at Wiola. Tiago tries to keep a straight face but can't stop giggling. I'm just glad Eoghan has been brought down a peg and shut up, fighting a delightful shade of red crawling up his neck.

After that, the talk diverts to more casual topics, and I'm almost sorry when it's time to get up. Tiago knocks on the table. "Let's hope the dragon is in a good mood today. Or even better, on a mission."

"The dragon?" According to my schedule, it's time for the 400-stream battle class.

Henny rolls their eyes. "Carina Vallesco. She's the leader of the local spirit seeker group and a 400-plus seeker. If she can, she takes over our training. And, well... she's just very harsh."

"I'd be harsh, too, if my brother had been killed," Wiola says while tying up her ponytail in a tight bun. "I'll see you downstairs."

Joana pulls a face. "She was harsh before that. Now she's just mean."

Meanwhile, my heart is pounding in my chest. Carina is Wulf's ex-girlfriend and his number one contact at the SSA. I know Dante is corrupt and will probably keep my presence here from Wulf, but

Carina might be my way out. Or she's just as corrupt. Brigid once said the Vallescos were among the greatest offenders. Wulf didn't believe her, and for his sake—and mine—I hope he's right about the younger generation. After all, he knows her more intimately than anybody else.

While the others change into their workout gear, I follow Gian down to the exercise grounds, located near the back wall of the castle grounds. Just behind those walls, freedom lies, in the form of a bustling, modern city. If only I could climb them and vanish into the crowd. Unless a bunch of sylphs are looking for me, I'm pretty hard to find.

My hopes of talking to Carina beforehand are squashed when I realise she's running late. She doesn't arrive until the entire class has already assembled and Eoghan has forced us into warm-up exercise.

Can I just say, "Wow"?

Carina Vallesco is drop-dead gorgeous! I know nothing about her history with Wulf, apart from the fact he grew up with her and her brother, but I can see why he'd fall for her. I might even have a crush, myself. She's about his age, early thirties, and has the body of a swimsuit model. Her brown locks and blonde highlights are cut to shoulder length, not too different from mine, but ten times more fashionable. She's also wearing a subtle amount of make-up; it makes her face flawless. The only thing ruining her face is her scowl.

"Pick up the pace, guys," she says, in a voice that could slice through glass. "You're supposed to be examples to your teams, not slackers."

All right, I get what Tiago meant by "the dragon". Eoghan had already set a good pace before, but now he's racing through the little parkours built into this part of the grounds. Uphill monkey bars, several climbing walls, and crawling tunnels are just some of the things available to torture us. Each round comes with a new instruction: knees to the chest, heels to the bum, backwards jumping. Needless to say, I'm ready to collapse before the last round even finishes.

"Staffs!" Carina yells the instant the last of us come to a stop. That'd be me and Tiago.

I'm still trying to catch my breath when Henny passes me a weapon. I use it to prop myself up and glance at the others. Eoghan looks like he's just been through a gentle warm-up jog, while Wiola is positively glowing, sweat glistening at the roots of her hair. Tiago is utterly drenched but already going through a couple of simple attack motions with Joana. Henny's skin is glistening as well, but their eyes are sparkling.

"Second part of the warm-up is staff exercise," they inform me, demonstrating the set of motions we're supposed to be doing.

"I'm pretty warm at this stage." It doesn't help that the temperatures are already well into their twenties, despite the early hour.

"If you need water, there's the fountain, but be quick!" Henny points to the fountain at the side before throwing a nervous glance at Carina, who's already going around the other pairs, criticising their stances.

I decide to forgo the opportunity and get into position instead. "Let's go."

Thankfully, Camille and Wulf taught me some moves, so I don't make a total fool of myself. Nevertheless, when Carina comes to stand next to us, my concentration takes a dip and Henny's casual contact hits the staff out of my hands. It clatters to the ground with a painfully loud noise.

"Sorry," Henny says immediately, likely trying to draw Carina's attention to them.

"For what?" Carina's response is biting. "Are you going to apologise to the spirits, too?"

They should. The words are almost out of my mouth, but I bite my tongue and bend down to pick up the staff. If I'd thought I'd got away this time, my hopes are squashed quickly.

Carina turns her acid stare on me. "Stop cradling the staff like it's your baby. Your grip needs to be firm." When I readjust my hold, she barks, "What are you waiting for? Again!"

For the rest of the warm-up, she keeps watching us, constantly peppering me with instructions and barbs. At long last, a break is called, and Carina turns away. "Get something to drink and line up."

My fingers hurt from holding the staff so tightly, and each breath sends needles into my chest. I can't see myself going through another set of exercises. Is this what Wulf went through every day for three years or more? Is that what it takes to become so awesome?

As I bend down to drink from the fountain, I ask Tiago, "So, tell me. Is this a good day?"

"No, she hasn't had one of those since March."

Since her brother was killed in the Vesuvius mission Wulf barely escaped from. I want to feel sorry for Carina, but her harsh tone and merciless training keep me from it.

Once we line up, she walks past us like a drill instructor. If there are any instructions as to how to present myself, I never received them. It doesn't surprise me when she comes to a stop in front of me. "What's your name, newbie?"

"Rika," I mumble.

"Speak up!"

Gosh, how clichéd can this woman be? "Rika!"

Once more, Carina studies me. "You don't seem to have a lot of muscle under your skin. Or fat, for that matter. You should take better care of your body. It's your most important asset."

I'm absolutely stunned. She just managed to body shame me in front of the entire class without batting an eye. Turns out that frequent panic attacks and being locked up in a dark cell have killed my appetite. Not that there was a lot to build on. "I'll take that into account," I manage to say, already seeing protein shakes being added to my carefully monitored diet.

"Good, let's see what you've got. You're up first. Eoghan, you're her partner." Carina nods her head sharply, which is apparently the signal for us to enter the training court while the others step back.

Great, I have to hold myself up against the self-declared battle prodigy. I hope it's like fighting with Wulf. He's far superior to me, but he always matched his pace and made sure to get the best out of me when we sparred, more interested in my progress than winning.

After half a minute, it's safe to say that Eoghan is not like that. As soon as Carina gives her "Go!", he attacks with full force. I barely manage to get my staff up to block his first attack. Despite that, my elbows hurt from the impact. By then, Eoghan has already moved on, and his staff connects with my hip bone, sending a sharp jolt through my body.

After that, I'm stuck chasing his movements in a desperate effort to shield myself from his blows. More often than not, I'm too late, and his staff adds bruise after bruise to my body.

I cry out in pain when the wood hits my fingers, causing them to uncurl and drop the staff. As I bend down to pick it up, Eoghan knocks my feet out from under me, and I fall flat on my face.

"That's enough!" Carina's sharp command saves me from whatever onslaught Eoghan had planned for me while I'm on the ground. "Don't just lie there. Get up!" As I crawl back to my feet, breathing heavily and trying my best not to wince at the pain this little action causes, she adds, "Spirits won't wait for you to catch your breath. When you're down, your team goes down."

She seems to wait for some kind of acknowledgement, so I manage to squeeze out a lacklustre, "Okay."

"Watch the others!" For a tiny moment, Carina's voice sounds slightly sympathetic. "Joana and Wiola, you're next." And it's back to normal again.

Eoghan doesn't so much as glance at me as he returns to his place in the line. Meanwhile, I drag myself over, ready to plunk down back on the ground.

"Don't sit," Henny warns me from the corner of their mouth.

It's hard, but I manage to keep myself upright, using the staff as a prop. I can't even glare at Eoghan because I'm in too much pain and still catching my breath. He wouldn't notice anyway, since his eyes are fixed on Joana and Wiola, who are far better matched with each other, though they're not taking prisoners either. I guess holding back gets you a big fat minus in Carina's scorebook.

\#

I have to go up once more against Joana and once against Tiago. Both are easier to defend against than Eoghan, but if I was hoping to impress Carina, it doesn't work. Not even Eoghan gets an appreciative word out of her. Still, he beams like an idiot when, after his last bout with Henny, Carina says to him, "Don't focus all your attention on your opponent. Remember, there's a team counting on you as well."

"That's it for today. We're going to run some team simulations tomorrow, so think about a role you like to play when it's not your turn to lead. If you need inspiration, take it from your classmates." Carina turns her gaze to me. "Being yourself will suffice for now."

"She means you get the role of being the one to look out for because they're most likely to need help," Henny clarifies when they pick up the staffs to return them to the stand. "Don't worry, we all started there. You'll move out of that spot soon."

I'm not sure if I should worry more about my performance in the other team simulations or the one where I get to lead what will most likely be the most annoying bunch of recruits imaginable. Either way, tomorrow is another day, and before I follow the others to lunch, I'm keen to talk to Carina. Especially because Gian isn't here to pick me up yet.

"Uhm, hi." I'm still breathless from the exercise, and as it turns out, I don't know how to phrase my question exactly, especially when her gaze burns into me.

"What is it, Rika? I'll warn you right now, I'm not someone you can suck up to."

Stunned, I can barely keep myself from taking a step back. "Good, I wasn't planning on doing that."

Carina looks exasperated. "What is it then? I don't want excuses or anything. You'll get better with time, just continue showing up."

Is that supposed to be a pep talk? "Actually, I was wondering about something else." Now if only I could ask her straight out. "I... So..." Nice, two failed attempts. Maybe a frontal attack is exactly what I need. "I was wondering if you could get a message to Wulf?"

She certainly didn't expect that. For a moment, Carina's eyes bulge, then an angry little crease appears between her eyebrows. "Are you serious?"

Why she would be mad is beyond me. She doesn't even know me. "Yes."

"Look, little girl." Oh great, we're down to condescending terms. "I know Wulf is amazing, and you've heard a lot of stories about him, but I will not pass on your message to him. He's got far more important things to deal with than the unbecoming adoration of little girls."

"I'm not a fan! I know Wulf. He knows me."

Carina shrugs, already turning away. "Then contact him yourself."

Great idea. Why hadn't I thought of that myself? Right! "I don't have... his number." Or a phone, or any way of contacting anyone out of the safety of my cell downstairs.

Carina snorts, a lazy smile curling her lips now. "Well, then I'm pretty sure he doesn't really want to be in touch with you."

She still seems to think I'm fawning over his legend or something. Apart from the unfairness of it all, it annoys me that Carina thinks she gets to be the warden of who can or cannot contact him. "Well, I think he does," I find myself replying.

"What's this about?"

I almost jump out of my skin when Dante joins us. He looks curiously from me to Carina and back again. "Gian had to attend a meeting, so I thought I'd pick you up." Then he smiles at Carina, and her face softens ever so slightly. "Rika is our new hopeful. What do you think of her?"

"Not much," I say, before Carina can come up with some bullshit over my performance.

That actually elicits a short laugh from her. "You got that right. New hopeful, huh? Well, she's got a lot to learn. But apparently, she already fancies herself as Wulf's heir. As if he's due to retire anytime soon."

"I never said that." Gosh, she's mean. Beautiful or not, I can't see why Wulf would ever want to be around her. He's too kind for that.

"She asked me to send him a message," Carina declares, and my stomach drops to my knees. I have to remind myself she isn't part of Dante's scheme as far as I know, but it feels like Gian's betrayal all over again.

Dante studies me for a moment, then snorts benevolently. "About what?"

There's not really a point to come up with some convenient lie. "To tell him where I am."

"He knows," Dante replies promptly. "Rika, did you think I'd recruit you out from under his nose and not tell him you've started your formal training?"

Carina looks as stunned as I feel. "He actually knows her?"

My mind won't stop spinning. Wulf knows I'm here. He knows, and he hasn't come for me.

"Wulf was the one who found her. She'd been living on the streets of Berlin or so I'm told," Dante says cheerfully, as if this is a regular background of his students. Living on the streets is fun, didn't you know? "We still need to test her NAV, but she's already shown an impressive skill set in spirit awareness."

"It's 512, give or take a bit. Give more likely." I don't want to get tested by Dante, though it would be interesting to see the difference in this supposedly accurate test. "Wulf tested me the first chance he got."

Now I've definitely got their attention. Carina looks taken aback, and Dante has lost his charming demeanour. He's glowering at me. "When did he test you?" he asks at last.

"I can't remember. After he returned. Late March or early April." What does it even matter?

"Two months," Dante mumbles to himself. Then his face shows an impressive shift, and his sunny attitude returns. "I don't think I've ever heard of anyone testing above 500. All the better he found you for us."

"She could be making this up," Carina says, looking at Dante rather than me.

Leave it to her not to accept my claim. I couldn't possibly be talented in one way at least. "I can see spirits as clear as day. I can talk to them, and I know what they're feeling or if they're telling the truth. Not even Wulf can do that." He got better at it, though.

"All very remarkable," Dante says, as if to shut me up quickly. "But now we need to make sure you get up to speed with the rest of your education, as well. I believe there's a case study waiting for you. It might be that rockslide one near the Matterhorn. Very interesting stuff. Come on." He gets moving, forcing me to fall in step with him. "Carina, dear, if you could wait in my office. I'd like to have a quick chat with you."

"About me?" I mutter, severely annoyed at this point.

"No," Dante says, surprisingly firm for once. "About Wulf."

## 9

*He found you for us.*

It can't be. Wulf can't be the one who betrayed me. I know in my heart he wouldn't do that. It doesn't even make sense. We were talking under Grune's branches. I was following him inside when Agnes got to me. The details don't fit, and yet, I can't shake the suspicion.

Perhaps Dante was speaking figuratively. That Wulf reported my presence weeks ago when I hadn't yet asked him to keep quiet about it. It could all be an accident. But even that hurts.

"Are you stuck?" Henny's question pulls me out of my thought spiral and into the present. I must've been staring into space when I was supposed to be solving equations.

"No, I..." Rubbing my nose, I train my eyes back on the piece of paper. They're supposedly easy equations: one variable, simple transformations. The absolute basics for solving trap identifications. If only there were only four types of spirits and all their species were the same.

"What are you working on?" I ask Henny, who has their laptop propped up in front of them, typing away.

If it weren't for the maths, I'd come to savour these hours we have for ourselves. It's just me and Henny. No barbs, no expectations, only gentle guidance. Henny is truly invested in helping me without a single gain for them. At least, none I can conceive.

Henny turns their laptop around to show me. "Don't try to understand the maths. This is Advanced Trapping and Spirit Analysis. I've been selected to help with a research project. It's really exciting, on a theoretical basis."

"Does that mean it's theoretically exciting, but not really?" I can't see myself ever looking forward to a research project.

"No, no, I love it!" Henny clarifies. "So, this is what it's about. You know how when we catch spirits, we need to break them down?" When I nod, they continue, picking up speed as excitement takes over. "So, we identify a spirit and take energy away from them until they fit our traps. That leads to a problem because whenever spirits are being studied in the lab, they're not at their full potential."

Well, that's the SSA's fault, isn't it? It reminds me of Miriam's excitement when I'd managed to catch a spirit without harming him. Back then, I still thought he'd be released into the wild, but I'm no longer sure that's ever been true for any spirit.

"Now, in comes modelled reconstruction." Before I even have a chance to ask, Henny breaks it down for me. "We have all the data for the spirit in the trap, and using our formulas for trapping plus what we know of the initial energy measurements, we can reconstruct what the whole spirit would've looked like. And it gets even more exciting from there." Their eyes are basically glinting at this point. "We take the data from other spirits and add them up. So, basically, taking two halves of two different things and putting them together to make a whole. Like genetic recombination."

A shiver runs down my spine. I try to force a smile onto my face to match their excitement, but all I manage are weak twitches in the left corner of my mouth. "This is all theoretical?"

Henny nods energetically. "Yes, we play around with the data, not actually combining spirits. Like, can you imagine the horror? A salamander that could create its own firestorm?"

Only too well. "That sounds like it would create more problems than it solves." Each word comes out of my mouth like chewing gum.

Surprisingly, I believe Henny. It's purely theoretical for them, just some fun with numbers, but the research is anything but theoretical. It's real. There have already been multiple successful test runs. And they've been even more horrifying than Henny could imagine.

"So, how... What is it for?" I probe carefully. I need to figure out how involved they are, but not expose myself, if this is yet another of Dante's tricks. My own misery slips into the background as I get closer to the mystery behind altered spirits. "The research isn't just for fun, is it?"

"It's foundational research. Not everything has an immediate practical application, especially in maths," Henny explains. "But of course, you still need to justify it. I've got nothing to do with the grant applications, but I imagine it's the usual stuff: to understand spirit nature and find more effective ways of fighting them." They roll their eyes, as if it's annoying they have to come up with a reason at all.

I wonder if it's true. If that's really the reason the researchers gave before launching the project, or whether there's been a secret second reason—let's make spirits even stronger so we can use them as weapons against other people. "Does it work? I mean, can you combine a salamander with a sylph?"

"Yes!" Henny exclaims, and the fire is relit in them. "I mean, theoretically. It's very complicated because you have to do a lot of transformations, but it matches up."

I remember Leon and Wulf sitting together, figuring out how to adjust their equations in order to catch these combined spirits. Would it have been easier for them if they'd known what combinations they were dealing with from the start?

I take a few moments to form a proper question that masks what I already know and tells me what I want to know. "Sorry, but this all sounds like you make up some data and add whatever you need, and behold, it works. How applicable is it to real spirits?"

Henny pulls up the image of a trap and the data from the three rings, plus the initial energy reading. "We don't make up a data set at all but work with what we got. Spirit seekers catch spirits every day, so there's a lot to choose from when you look for a partner. It doesn't always match up perfectly. Sometimes, you need three or four, but that's what I'm working on."

The ring position in front of me drives it all home. "I know that snow sprite," I say, before realising I spoke aloud.

"What do you mean, you "know that snow sprite"? How do you even know it's a snow sprite?" Henny pulls up some additional data, a mission log as it looks. "It *is* a snow sprite. Caught in Berlin on the 23rd of February."

She'd been dancing on the footpath, turning the surface into slippery ice. It was more of a nuisance than a threat, with people slipping and potentially hurting themselves, but no more than they would on any icy surface. One of the first spirits I'd caught on my own. I can't say that, though, without giving away my lie about Ireland. "I can just sense it. What they are." Hopefully, Henny doesn't remember I claimed to know this spirit.

"From one look at the trap?"

How do I get out of this? "Trapping has always been intuitive to me. I think it's the rings themselves. They're made of spirits, aren't they?" Everything in the SSA is, so let's call this an educated guess.

Henny nods. "Just a smidgeon. You'll learn more about that in year two when they add Spirit Technology to the schedule. I'm not really an expert, so I can't explain to you how it all works in detail. It doesn't really matter either because they've been built in a way so everyone can read and adjust them."

"With maths." A sigh escapes me. How exactly is this more advanced? Just because it makes it look more complicated than it is and gives me a headache?

Henny doesn't reply immediately, but studies me instead. "You said that before."

"What? With maths? Sorry, I'm really struggling with it." Lukas would be delighted. Or maybe not. He seemed changed after our time in Dublin.

"No." Henny shakes their head, letting their short curls fly. "I meant that you'd been trapping spirits with intuition."

Oh, that. I told them that hoping to get out of maths tutoring. It hadn't worked, and it looks like I've set myself up for something worse.

"How do you do that?" Henny asks, their brows knitting together. I can't see the usual excitement in their eyes, probably because this is something unheard of.

For a moment, I entertain the idea of feigning ignorance. There's still the chance they'll report me. I mean, they're nice and all, but so was Gian. And Henny is involved in a special research project that directly relates to the horrible alterations the SSA is doing to spirits. If that's not a sign the SSA places a lot of trust in them, I have no idea what is.

And yet, I feel a connection with Henny. Or perhaps less of a connection, but more their absolute genuineness. Like a spirit. Only, humans don't work that way, and I've been the worst at reading human intentions lately.

I pick up my pen, twisting it between my fingers while I search for the right words. Truth or lie? "One ring for the nature of the spirit, one for its strength, the third to adjust." My eyes are fixed on the small silver ring in the pen's cap. "The nature is obvious when you see them"—if they haven't been altered, that is—"and their strength becomes apparent when you fight them. As for adjusting... I sense the spirits. I recognise them. There's only one possible combination."

The soft clearing of their throat pulls me out of my fixation. Henny looks at me with awe in their eyes. "I know they haven't tested you yet, but when they do, I'm sure you'll break all the records."

Breaking all the records doesn't get me a seat at the dinner table, though. I have no idea what Henny and the others think about me skipping so many meals. I'm torn between whether I like the reprieve from keeping up the act or fear the extra hour I am locked up in my room. The fact that I'm getting frequent breaks from it makes my situation a lot more bearable, but I still find myself waking up in terror or clawing at my arms when the walls seem to close in.

Tonight, the feeling of purpose keeps me alert. I can do this. It will be hard, but I can bide my time. I can learn what I can and then take my shot. This might even be a good thing. If I can get into the research program, I can find out how they do it, and potentially gather enough evidence to expose the SSA.

Focusing on something bigger than myself helps a lot. I can bear the torture of being in this room, of having to listen to all the SSA glorification in my lessons, or the ridicule I experience from teachers and students alike. I can get through all of this if it means I'll stop that awful program.

But first, I need to find more, and who better to ask than Dante himself when he comes to join me for dinner.

For the first time since my arrival, I have an appetite, and it's a good thing because the steaming hot cannelloni is amazing; all cheesy gooeyness with spinach and ricotta and pasta. It doesn't get much better than that.

"I'm happy to see you enjoying the food," Dante comments, potentially because he didn't have to coerce me into sitting down for once. "You need to build up your strength for training."

"Yes. Carina might've mentioned protein shakes if I don't eat, and that warned me off pretty good." It would be yet another level of horror if all my meals were replaced by thickshakes.

Dante laughs. "That's one way to get you into shape quickly."

"Fortunately, I have three years to get there, don't I?" It doesn't hurt to challenge him a little.

"That's true, though we might fast-track you later down the line if things outside keep developing as they are." For once, he sounds uncharacteristically sombre. I almost buy his worried face.

I help myself to another piece of cannelloni, thoughtfully poking my fork into it. "How are things outside?" Come on, give me the whole sob story, so I can pretend to lap it up.

Dante has finished his meal after only eating a little. I guess he gets this kind of rich food every day, so doesn't need to savour it like I do. The smell alone is to die for. Unfortunately, that makes me think of Aeola and how she would mingle with the flavour. One day—when I'm free again—I'll have to take her to Italy so she can enjoy all the good things it has to offer.

"Spirit attacks are on the rise," Dante says, sipping a glass of water. "First, we had Vesuvius, then the Erlking, then incredibly powerful nymphs in Budapest. The spirits are getting stronger, more organised. We need all the support we can get."

It's incredibly hard to keep a straight face throughout. I think if he'd added the dryads of Dublin to the list, I might've screamed. But I manage to keep a straight, even pained face by filling my mouth with burning-hot cannelloni. "And so, you're forced to extreme measures, such as... well, recruiting people like me, for example." Or, you know, kidnapping me.

Dante smiles gently and nods. "That's true. I'm glad you see that now. If times were better, we wouldn't need to, but with things being as they are... I'm sorry, Rika, but someone with your potential had to be drafted." Yeah, it's still kidnapping.

"I understand." I also understand I need to be delicate with my next foray. "Today, Henny told me about a project they're involved in." I watch him lean back and squint in anticipation. Part of me wants to believe that means Henny is not on his personal payroll. "We were talking about trapping and how my high NAV makes it possible for me to guess the trap settings. It's something Wulf noted, as well. My intuition is more accurate than the equations you use. I thought that would get me out of maths, but now I think I might be able to help instead." Look at me, campaigning for more academics to be inserted into my life. As if it weren't bad enough.

"I'm not sure I follow. Help with what?" Dante leans forward again, still confused.

"The project Henny is working on," I say, as innocently as I can. "You're trying to combine spirits to study them, and I might be able to match them naturally. It could speed up the whole trial-and-error process."

"Intriguing," Dante admits, finally lighting up.

My heart is pounding as I wait for his verdict. *Please let me join the project. Show me the lab. Let me learn all there is about spirit alteration, so I can shut the program down.*

Dante looks inward for a moment, then shakes his head softly. "We should keep that in mind for year three. Right now, I want you to focus on laying the foundations for your education. I appreciate your enthusiasm, though." He smiles openly. "I like it. Looks like you're finally finding your stride here."

I smile back, knowing that if I push now, I'll lose whatever progress I've made. "I'm trying my best."

"And you're succeeding. Well..." He gets up, ready to leave. "It has been a pleasure, as always. I'll see you again soon. Make sure you eat the tiramisu as well. It's delicious."

"Okay." *Don't question me. Eat dessert.*

Dante leaves the room, and I breathe a sigh of relief. That went well, didn't it? Semi-well, considering I didn't get what I want, but I feel like I earned his trust tonight. Not that I'm kidding myself. He's still nothing more than a glorified jailer, but if I keep this up, he might drop his vigilance soon.

And it needs to be soon. As the darkness creeps into my room and the walls begin closing in, my breathing flattens. *Just a little longer,* I tell myself. *Don't think about the closed door or the little window. Don't think about the massive stone walls.*

*I can do this.*

*I can do this.*

*I can...*

# 10

Everything about the academy is brutal; the training, the teachers and students, and most of all, my lodgings. I grit my teeth through all of it. I sleep in my bed, pretending the uncomfortable slats I feel through the mattress are Grune's roots instead. My training is demanding as hell, but I've decided to embrace it and get better for my own purposes. I even keep up with my homework, giving everything an honest try while keeping my mouth shut when I have to and repeating what they tell me instead.

Interestingly, not everyone has succumbed to the SSA propaganda yet. There's a boy in my class—Yvann—who loves getting into discussions with Professor Okorie, constantly questioning why we never learn the spirits' side of things. Honestly, I just want to kiss him on that dark fluff he calls a beard every time he raises his hand, but instead of supporting him, I keep my head down and my distance outside the classroom. And for all his eagerness for debate, he never questions his place here. In two years' time, he'll be just as brainwashed as the others, eager to wreak havoc on the spirit world.

Of all the classes, Carina's is the worst. I don't know if it's my mention of Wulf or the death of her brother, but her class can't even be called training. It's pure maltreatment. I'm pretty sure Eoghan is the only one who is enjoying himself, but when she's unavailable and he takes over as the most senior student, he's not even half as bad. I'm glad it's not just me who sighs a breath of relief every time Carina has to leave for a mission.

Today, however, she's waiting for us when we come down after lunch. One glare from her and all of us break into a run. I'm pleased that I'm starting to keep up with the others, or at least Tiago and I are now battling it out for the last spot.

"You gonna get beaten by the newbie?" Carina calls out after the first three circuits. "Whoever's last needs to do two extra rounds."

Tiago and I share a quick look, neither willing nor capable of adding even more "warm-ups" to our plate. Then we both scramble over the climbing wall as fast as we can. Perhaps sprinting through the rest of the course and using up all my energy isn't the best idea, but I've at least got to try.

We're neck-and-neck as we crawl under the net, but I gain the edge when I get up again. The three wall obstacles that are the end of the course are my favourite ones. Thanks to my expertise at climbing fences, they pose no problem whatsoever, and I almost manage to overtake Wiola.

"Not bad," Carina comments in such an offhand way, I can't even pretend that it was a compliment. Poor Tiago looks at me as if I told him his cat died. He has to go another two rounds as promised, but he's running out of steam before he's even halfway around.

Meanwhile, Carina tells us to grab our staffs and meet her in the fenced-off corral near the outer wall. Looking up, I notice even the sky is covered by an intricate mesh. I've never been in here, but the third-years seem on edge. Eoghan grabs his staff tighter, and Henny shifts her weight from one foot to the other. It doesn't take long for me to understand why when my gaze falls onto a cart with an array of metal tubes—traps.

I guess not all spirits are used for research.

"The other streams use the virtual arena," Carina explains as she walks up and down in front of the cart. "But you don't need those auxiliary devices. So, pick a tube from the top. That will be your adversary for today."

The traps have been fitted with a kind of velvet band that covers up the rings, so there's no guessing what kind of spirit is in it or how strong they'll be. I watch the others approach the cart and pick their traps at random, but I can't bring myself to move. We're going to fight spirits. Spirits that have already been beaten once are subjected to further aggression, just so these elite students can have something real to practise on.

Tiago enters the facility, soaked with sweat. He checks with me first. "You not gonna pick?"

I'm unable to form words, let alone shake my head. Tiago waits a few seconds, then he shrugs and makes his choice.

Only one tube is left in the top row.

"Today, Rika," Carina calls, and there's some snickering from Eoghan's and Wiola's corner. "It's not gonna bite you in the tube."

I need to fall in line in order to survive. And yet, dragging my feet to the cart leaves me even more breathless than the warm-up we just did. My hand hovers over the trap, eliciting another giggle from Wiola. I grab the trap, not thinking about the icy touch of it as I return to my place in the line-up.

Carina rolls her eyes and turns to Eoghan. "Come on, show them how it's done. What do you have?"

Eoghan slips the velvet from the tube and studies his trap for close to twenty seconds. "A spring nymph, on the weak side."

"Let it free. I will readjust your trap. You've got five minutes to break her down before attempting to recapture her," Carina explains, stepping towards him.

Eoghan nods. He opens the trap, and it fizzes like shaken soda water. Fresh spring water sprays everywhere as the nymph rushes to freedom. Little does she know, there's only pain to be found.

As Eoghan hands the trap over to Carina, I wish I could walk away. If I do, Dante will lock me up again. I need to join in to keep up my cover. But how? I can't even stand watching the others do it.

The nymph is an elegant spirit, all wavy shapes and glistening eyes. But there are scars all over her body. Dark pools of standing water where nothing flows. And the fear in her eyes when she realises she's facing yet another spirit seeker tears my heart in two. I know then I won't be able to do it. Let them do with me what they want. I won't hurt a spirit just to satisfy Carina's blood thirst.

Eoghan doesn't share my reservations. He rearranges his staff almost lazily before he attacks with a burst of sudden speed.

"Leave me alone!" the nymph screams, but he doesn't hear her.

Water splashes everywhere, soaking Eoghan's shirt and hair, and yet he never slows, raining down blows on the nymph left and right until there's nothing left of her except a weeping puddle. Carina hands him the trap, and he sucks the spirit back into it without a sliver of compassion.

One by one, I watch the other students go up against their chosen spirits. Henny is the fastest to identify their spirit, taking only ten seconds to do so while Joana struggles the longest, trying to make sense of the ring placements. Wiola's spirit is by far the strongest, a hot-tempered ifrit who is not much more than a dark face in a ball of fire. He gives up a good fight, snarling and hissing insults at her. At the five-minute mark, Wiola isn't even close to her set target, instead nursing a large second-degree burn. Carina sighs, resets the trap once again, and does the trapping for her.

"You can't be afraid of the flames." Her cold eyes turn to me. "It's your turn, Rika. Henny may help you with identifying your spirits since you just started…"

"She's a greenschist gnome," I tell them, barely even looking at my rings. "Rather strong before she was captured, but beaten down in the process."

"Very well…" This time, even Carina can't quite keep the surprise out of her voice.

Meanwhile, Tiago frowns. "How do you know it's a she? It's just a bunch of stones."

"Same way I know you're a boy." My nerves are already frayed enough without having to explain gnome anatomy to the others or how I just recognise their gender.

Carina claps her hands twice, then stretches her left out toward me. "Come on, set it—or her or whatever—free and show me what you've got. You have five minutes. Try not to die."

Five minutes. That's how long I need to endure whatever the poor gnome throws at me. It doesn't sound terribly long.

I open the trap, but nothing happens. Good. That's even better, then.

"Give that to me!" Annoyed, Carina rips the trap out of my hands and shakes it violently, making it sound like a bunch of marbles set loose. One by one, the rocky parts of the gnome materialise in front of our feet.

She's a green-greyish colour with a clear schistosity that layers her body in near-horizontal lines. Quartz veins cover most of her knobbly abdomen, but more prevalent are the brittle planes where the rock has been reduced to fine grains that have eroded into her body. Her deep green eyes look at me in near terror.

"This is not a staring contest," Carina reminds me sharply, then shoves me forward. "Attack, Rika!"

"I won't." My voice is merely a whisper, and yet I feel it scraping over the courtyard. No one has ever refused to spar with a spirit. "I can't."

Carina sighs. "You don't need to be afraid. As you noted, it's been broken down before. Look! It's not even attacking you. So go!"

"I'm not going to fight her." This time I'm much louder and more agitated. How can Carina expect me to fight a harmless spirit, one that's been hurt beyond repair already?

"You've got three minutes left, but I don't mind keeping you here longer if you don't move. So stop wasting everyone's time!"

The others are starting to mumble. When I still don't move, Eoghan weighs in, "It's really not that hard. She can probably only take one or two hits."

But I keep my ground. Stubbornly, I set my jaw, staring at the gnome instead of engaging her. Suddenly, Carina grabs my staff and tries to force it in the direction she wants it to go. I can barely keep my hold on it. "Fight!" she commands, and something snaps in me.

I whirl around, putting myself between her and the spirit, then scream at her stupid face, "Can't you see how scared she is? What's next, beat up a dryad sprout? Extinguish the flicker of a salamander? What the hell is wrong with you people?"

For a moment, there's utter silence. Only my blood rushes loudly through my ears. Then Carina tugs at my staff again, and this time, she manages to pull it from my fingers. A second later, she slams it into my shoulder. "Go! I want you to run the circuit until I tell you to stop. Now!"

Her eyes are blazing, but I don't care. I don't mind running myself to exhaustion if that means I'm exempt from hurting spirits.

Actually, I do mind, or at least, my body's screaming for a rest when, forty minutes later, Carina still hasn't told me to stop. On the contrary, every time I try to sneak in a break, she notices immediately, pelting me with insults until I pick up speed again. I swear, that woman has eyes at the back of her head. Meanwhile, my muscles are hurting so much I want to cry. My mouth is completely dry while my clothes are soaked in sweat. And to top it all off, my head's been hurting for the last ten minutes, making me really nauseous. So nauseous that when I pull myself over the climbing wall, I spill my entire breakfast down the back of it.

Is my defiance worth all this? Absolutely.

"Have a drink." Henny's come over, their brown eyes full of compassion.

With their help, I manage to drag myself to the fountain. Never has water tasted sweeter. I splash some of it over my face and hair for good measure, enjoying these few breaths more than I ever thought I would. "Is it over?" I manage to say after a minute or so. Please don't let that be a temporary reprieve before I have to get back onto the circuit again. I might collapse this time.

Unfortunately, Henny shakes their head. "No, you're supposed to come back with me. Carina wants you to have another go."

"I'm not gonna do it." If she thinks a little physical exhaustion will break me, she's in for a surprise.

"You might not have a choice this time," is all Henny has to say.

The others give me wary looks when we return to what I've now dubbed 'the Cage'. I understand the walls and ceiling are to keep spirits from fleeing. There's probably mesh under the ground as well, stopping gnomes from burying into the earth. The only non-metal part is the back wall, hiding us from the city behind it.

Carina throws the staff at me, but I let it clatter to the ground. I hope I'm not the only one who looks stupid. She snorts. "You'll pick it up soon enough. Everyone else, out! You can tell me what mistakes Rika made when we're done."

The others file out of the Cage and watch from outside. Great. This way, they can't be tempted to help me. And now Carina will whoop my ass. It's not like it's going to be a challenge for her, as aching and tired as I feel.

But instead of attacking me with her staff, she pulls out another tube. I only have the opportunity to notice the spirit inside is on the stronger side when they explode into a dusty whirlwind. A dust devil.

"It's all yours," Carina says, retreating towards the door and leaving me alone with the spirit.

To my chagrin, I'm tempted to pick up the staff just to defend myself. The dust devil swirls around at high speed, picking up more dirt from the ground and flinging it at me. The sand hits me with hate similar to that of altered spirits, and yet much more natural.

"I'm not gonna hurt you." I tell the dust devil, though my mind jumps ahead, telling me that, with a vicious vein like that, they're not worried. "I know you're here against your wi—"

Okay, talking only leads to a mouthful of dust. I spit out as much as I can, which is pitifully little, and raise my hands in a pacifying gesture instead. I've barely lifted them when the wind picks me up from the ground. For a moment, I can't see anything but yellow murkiness. Then I land hard on my bum, gasping for air.

"Pick up the staff!" I hear my fellow students shouting. It's one of many tips they're trying to pass on, if they're not outright jeering like

Eoghan and Wiola. The only one who's quiet is Carina, her eyes burning into mine with unspoken command, and I understand it's live or die for me.

"Stop," I plead quietly with the dust devil, who's turning around, gathering more strength for another attack. "We don't have to fight each other. It won't matter. It's just—"

Once again, my body's lifted into the air. My head's whipped around. Grains of sand pelt my cheek, giving me road rash. Then I'm flung against the walls of the Cage. The mesh is almost like another spirit, digging its metal into my face, elbow, and thigh, its wires grabbing hold of my hair.

"Come on, Rika! You can do this!" Henny's voice rings out above the others.

My eyes flit towards the staff, now a good five metres away from me. "I will destroy you," the wind howls, but the words don't sink in like they did with the Erlking. They're flung at me, superficial injuries like the dust. Their heart isn't truly in the fight despite all the hate. Maybe the dust devil has realised that they're still in just as much of a cage as before. "Show me what you've got, little seeker."

Though my legs are far from steady, I cross my arms, hoping to exude confidence and calm. "No. I won't." It would work much better if my heart wasn't racing at the same time.

The dust devil howls and attacks once more. This time, there's no reprieve. I'm sucked into their vortex and spit out again, only to be flung against one of the walls. Even if I wanted to attack the spirit, it's become impossible. I don't know up from down or left from right. My entire world consists of dust in my ears, nose, mouth, and every fold of my skin. And pain. So much pain from all the impact I've endured. I'm exhausted, and I haven't even lifted a finger to defend myself.

My forehead smashes into the stone wall at the back of the training court, and my world explodes into searing pain. Something wet and sticky runs down my temple. My vision doubles while my breath is like a thousand needles stuck in my chest. This is bad. This is really bad.

I brace myself for the next attack, but it never comes. I blink, my eyes sticky with sand. Someone else has engaged the spirit, wielding their staff with frightening proficiency. It almost looks like a dance. A dance the spirit is quickly losing.

Carina is impressive, but I can't help but wince at the pained howls of the dust devil. It takes her less than a minute before the spirit is broken down enough to be trapped again. As the dust settles, my heart aches. Now the spirit who fought so valiantly for their freedom is back in tight confinement.

There's applause from the sidelines, but Carina glares at the others, and they shut up instantly. She blows a windswept strand of her hair out of her face as she regards me. A fine layer of dust covers her skin. "Can you stand?"

Dragging myself to my knees and then my feet while clinging to the wall seems to confirm it. Should the blood running from my forehead really have softened her?

"Very good." Then Carina's face evolves into a sneer. "Now get out of my sight. And don't dare come back to my training."

Though it's everything I ever wanted, I shiver at her icy tone. As I drag my sorry ass out of the Cage, I hear her address the others. "Don't bother listing her mistakes. We all know that refusing to fight is what would've killed her in the field."

Only, in the field, I wouldn't have been stuck with a dust devil in a confined space. If they'd been free like they were supposed to be, there wouldn't have been that much hatred, making it impossible to reason. I'm positive we would've found an understanding away from the ruthless practice of the SSA.

For once, I'm in luck, and Gian isn't yet here to pick me up. If I can evade him, I might be able to sneak out of the fortress and flee. My pulse races once again, filling me with the sort of energy you only tap into with adrenaline. Carina doesn't want me here. Dante will learn of this. It's absolutely paramount that I take this chance to leave this horrid place behind.

I hobble down the corridor as fast as I can. The students are still in class, which plays to my advantage. I don't encounter anybody on my way.

"Rika?" Well, almost anybody.

My blood freezes as do my feet. This isn't a male voice, ready to drag me back to my cell, but the voice that haunts me in my dreams. My mother steps out of what looks like a small office. Her eyes run over my bedraggled figure and are drawn to the wound on my forehead.

"What happened? Come here. Let me have a look at that." She ushers me into her office and closes the door.

It's tiny. There's only space for a desk and two chairs, plus a corner shelf behind the desk. But there's a carpet shielding us from the cold stone, and pictures of spectacular landscapes on the wall. And what really draws my gaze is the row of potted plants near the window. There's life in here.

My mother tries to push me into the chair in front of her desk. Instead, I find myself hugging her as tightly as my aching muscles allow. Gosh, I've missed her so much. The other day we didn't have a chance to get close to each other, and after Dante's change of my schedule, I doubted I'd ever see her again. Before long, tears are streaming down my face.

"Why didn't you come for me?" An incredibly whiny voice inside of me wants to know.

"Oh, darling." Carefully, my mother untangles herself from my embrace and ushers me into the chair. She produces a tissue and starts dabbing at my forehead. "What happened to you?"

Everything. But I guess she wants to know about the visible wound. "They had me go up against a dust devil. A real one, no simulation. I refused to hurt the spirit."

The gentle smile that graces her lips is not like the one I remember. There's too much sadness inside of it. "So, you let the spirit hurt you?"

"There was no other choice. Carina... Signora Vallesco forced us into the Cage. The dust devil had nowhere to go and so much hate pent up inside. It's not their fault they have to fight for survival." Surely my mum can understand this. She was the one who taught me how to listen to the wind.

Instead, a little sigh escapes her. "Their fight for survival endangers us. If there were a chance to deal with the spirits without fighting them, we'd do that. But it's not possible. It's in their nature to cause disasters. And as much as you sympathise with them, they'll always be a danger to us."

Her lips are moving, but her words make no sense. Or rather, they make all sense, the same sense Dante's words made. Spirits aren't bad per se, but humanity will suffer if we don't fight and capture them. The spirit seekers are heroes; I'm an idealistic fool. Pretty much everyone I've ever met in the SSA has said so. Now my mother's singing the same song. What if they're right and I'm wrong?

"Rika, darling." Her hand on my hair feels so good, so comforting. "You need to be open-minded. The people here have been doing this for centuries."

I want to. At this moment, I really want to give up the fight. Open myself to the process. Be with my mum. After all, if my mother believes this after a lifetime spent in the wilderness, it must be true. Who am I to say differently?

The person with the highest NAV on record, the most inherent understanding. Untrained and uneducated, but insightful and intuitive beyond their wildest dreams.

Or I might just be conceited, thinking I know better than anyone else just because my natural attunement is slightly higher than everybody else's. But then I remember Grune's vision, his memories of the true spirit seekers, and I wonder if there's a reason they're called seekers and not fighters. There's Aeola and everything she said about human-spirit relations, and the Liffey who took Rory as her literal husband in order to blaze a trail for constructive interaction. It's possible, and it was my mother who taught me that. The same woman who's now feigning ignorance. The woman who's become a valuable member of the SSA community—after Dante brought her back into the fold.

"You never looked for me." What mother does that? "It wasn't hard. I was in Berlin all these years. Living on the streets."

Her hand falls into her lap as tears fill her eyes. "I'm so sorry."

"How could you not look for me?" A wave of emotion breaks inside me. I spent so many years searching her. I checked every police record, wandered through every homeless camp. I even travelled to Budapest to find word of her. And all this time, she was here, betraying everything she once stood for, while I barely scraped by, lonely and frightened, with enough nightmares to last a lifetime.

"Rika..." Her voice falters, and suddenly I can't bear this anymore. This isn't my mother. This is some well-conforming nightmare of her.

I jump out of the chair and rush from the room, ignoring her pleas for me to come back. Tears are blinding me, while my throat feels tighter and tighter. And promptly, I run into someone.

Quickly, I wipe my cheeks. Of course, it has to be Eoghan, the perfect student; everything the SSA hopes for. "What?"

"What?" He sounds amused. "I've been looking for you."

Great, there goes my chance of slipping out of this prison. "Why?" I ask a lot more aggressively than he deserves. Well, maybe only a little more. Eoghan has been pretty aggravating so far.

"Because you're just as stupid as my brother says."

What a weird thing to say. What do I care about his brother? And why does his brother think he can pass judgement on me? "And who's he?"

"Well, who do you think it is, Miss Apprenticed-in-Dublin?" Eoghan looks over his shoulder, almost as if he's checking we're alone. "Half-brother, so we have different names, thank god."

I'm starting to see it in the line of his jaw, in the dimples he so rarely shows, the dark amber of his eyes. "Rory?"

Instantly, Eoghan clicks his tongue and rolls his eyes. "Could you be any more obvious?" For a quick second, he lowers his voice. "No one knows. Doesn't mean I'm not on their watch list."

"They're—"

"Oh, shut up!" Once again, he checks the corridor. When there's no one to see, he hisses, "I almost made it. Just a few more months and I'm out of here, so could you please stop ruffling feathers? What you pulled off in Dublin was bad enough."

Slowly, his words fall into place. Eoghan has only been playing the part of the star student. I mean, he's good, but he's biding his time, just as Rory did, in order to survive training unscathed. It's what I was trying to do, but failed miserably at. "I'm sorry." I could never pull it off, not if it means hurting spirits.

"Well, I'm gonna tell him just how annoying you really are." He grabs my arm and pulls me down the corridor.

"You're—" Quickly, I shut my mouth. It's much harder to fight the smile creeping onto my lips. Eoghan gives a great show, but the meaning isn't lost on me. He's going to let Rory know where I am. I don't know what Rory can do, seeing as his "antics" already got him into trouble, but at least someone will know where I am. "If you have to."

Now it's him that can't fight off the smirk. It's quickly wiped off his face, though, when we run into Dante. "I found her."

"Thank you so much, Eoghan." While he's pleased with Eoghan, the glance Dante gives me is one of disappointment. "Rika, I heard what happened during training. I'd better show you to the infirmary. I'll take it from here, Eoghan."

Part of me wants to hang onto Eoghan's arm for dear life, but the thought I might blow his cover sobers me. I let go and take Dante's proffered arm instead. I doubt we're really going to the infirmary, but even though I'm back in his hands, it doesn't seem so bad anymore. Rory will know, and help will come. I'm sure of it.

11

I'm out of commission. I assume everyone's been told I have a cold or was hurt worse than I was, or perhaps it doesn't matter. I appeared out of nowhere. I can vanish back into nowhere. But I know the truth: my so-called sickness is punishment.

While it gives me time to nurse my wounds—and there are a lot of colourful bruises all over my body—the extended time back in my cell is doing my head in. What if I've failed? What if I've blown my only chance of getting out of here? Nobody's told me how long this punishment will be, so what if it goes on forever? Just the thought of it speeds up my heart rate and my breathing. I feel like a spirit trapped in a tube. Only my tube is made of stone.

From that train of thought, I arrive at the spirits who are here for amusement. Well, not amusement directly, but it's hard to see the necessity. I know from my training with the second-years that there are state-of-the-art virtual reality facilities in the castle. I don't mind batting spirits in a game the same way I wouldn't mind going up against humans. But beating up a spirit that's already been diminished by active spirit seekers? That just seems cruel. And you can't tell me it prepares these people for reality in any meaningful way.

It seems like a lifetime ago Camille told me the spirits would be released into the wilderness. I've mulled over her words for far too long, trying to discern whether they were an outright lie to reassure me. It didn't seem that way, but Camille could've genuinely believed it was a possibility. Her NAV is below 300. I've already learnt that the first-years only train in staff-handling, and the second-years make use of the virtual reality room. Maybe the third-years are split at the 300-mark, and so Camille never encountered a trapped spirit and had to wonder where it came from. Wulf, on the other hand, definitely knew.

I wonder where they keep the traps they receive from all over Europe. There must be thousands and thousands of them. My fingers itch at the idea of freeing them all. It's a wish that only grows over the length of my punishment. If I can't be free, they should be. If only I'd figured out where they stored them. Oh, and that minor matter about getting out of my room.

Worrying about somebody else helps keep the panic at bay. At least for the short while my mind can focus on it. In the room's timelessness, my thoughts are scattered all over the place, and one of the biggest problems is the constant silence. The room is insulated so well, I can't even hear water rushing through the pipes. There's no wind, no rustle, just me and my racing heartbeat. I miss the stars most of all. That endless sea of darkness is better than any blanket could ever be.

In my worst moments, all thoughts follow the path to my mother. It physically hurts that she's so close and yet so far away. And not just because I'm locked in this room. Something's happened to her and trying to figure it out is like scratching at a scabbed wound. Does she wonder where I am? Why would she? She didn't care for eight years. I know there must be an explanation. My heart's all too ready to accept the horrors of the SSA brainwashing her into this mindless follower. But doubt keeps creeping in, questioning all I ever knew, and it breaks my brain.

When the door finally opens, it almost frightens me out of my skin. If it's Gian, my classes will continue. But, of course, it isn't. Instead, Dante enters carrying a pile of papers, several of them stapled together. Quickly, I avert my eyes and study my splintered fingernails instead. Turns out clawing walls is not a good manicure.

"How are you feeling?" he asks in that unnervingly soothing voice that always trips me into thinking he actually cares.

Well, let him care. If Eoghan can keep his head down for three years, I can manage a simple conversation. "Everything hurts."

"That dust devil got you good, huh?" Dante commiserates. He sets down the pile of papers on my table. "I'll be the first to admit that Carina's training was a little too intense for someone who's just started out. Unfortunately, we have to train our students that hard. As you are undoubtedly aware, reality is much harsher."

"Harsher than Carina?" I doubt that's possible.

Dante chuckles. "Hard to believe, isn't it? But don't worry. I've talked to her, and once you've recuperated, you're welcome to go back."

Fantastic! More spirit bashing with a vengeful harpy hard on my heels. "Thanks, I guess." I really don't get how Eoghan does this. How can I shut out everything I believe in and not lose myself in the process?

"You will have to apply yourself, though." Dante switches to a sterner tone, and I can't help but feel sorry I displeased him. "This wouldn't have happened if you'd listened to Carina's instructions."

Instead of outright refusing them? He doesn't say it, and it bothers me that he never directly blames me, as if they're all unfortunate mistakes, not wilful acts of rebellion. As my mind jumps to correct him, it's me that puts the blame on myself.

"What happens if I can't do it?" Even if I wholeheartedly commit myself to nodding and going along with everything my teachers say, I know I can't raise my weapon against a spirit. No matter how carefully I listen to Carina's instructions.

"This." Dante pats the pile of leaflets. "While you're recovering from your injuries, you'll have to keep up with your studies. This is a collection of case studies. They're spirit attacks from the last twenty-five years. I want you to read them carefully and fill out this worksheet I've prepared." He lifts a thin booklet from the top of the pile. The thing has at least eight pages. "You'll hand it to me when you return to class."

In other words, I won't be able to leave this room until I've completed his assignment.

Slowly, Dante walks over and sits on the edge of my bed, mere centimetres away from where I'm perched against the wall. "Listen, Rika. I know you think I'm mean or a horrible person."

"I don't," I hurry to say, but it's far from convincing. Fact is, that's exactly what I think of him. If only Dante weren't so compassionate and kind while being so.

"You have your reservations based on your experience, and I get it," he continues, leaning forward ever so slightly. "I understand how foreign all this is to you, and I'm not expecting you to trust me after only two weeks. You've been raised in a cult that reveres spirits. That's a lifetime of lies and deception."

My breath quickens, and my head feels uncomfortably light. My mother led the supposed cult he's talking about. If he's right, they're her lies and deception. The problem is she must've lied to someone because the person I grew up with and the person who lives and teaches here are not the same. They stand for fundamentally different things. What if she was just as misguided as me, spewing all her delusions into my trusting mind? Children always believe their parents. At least until they're taught differently. And even then it's a struggle to dissociate from what you learned growing up and what is real. What if she... *I* was wrong?

Dante puts a hand on my knee. I hold my breath. "It's a long road, but I'm willing to put in the effort."

"Because I'm valuable to you?" I hold onto it like a drowning child. *Love me. Care for me. Accept me. Tell me what's right or wrong.*

Realising how much I long for Dante's approval, anyone's approval at the moment, makes me want to bash my head into the wall behind me. Instead, I dig my fingernails deep into my palms, close my eyes, and groan.

"I value you a lot, Rika. I want to help you."

"Why?" Despite wanting it to be true, I can't accept anyone would care enough.

And in a dark corner of my mind, I'm sure Dante doesn't care, either. He's just pretending to.

For a moment, he looks at the floor instead of me, as if he can't quite bring himself to say it. "Because I was the same as you. You're not the first student to come through here who thinks we're all just monsters." He chuckles, almost sadly. "It's hard to change your ways, even more so when you've been spoon-fed these ideas from early childhood. But trust me, Rika, it's worth it. The world will thank you for it." With a last pat to my knee, he rises again. "Do the assignment. It'll help you understand the true nature of your spirit friends."

I find myself drinking in every word he says. I want more, but Dante is finished for today. He looks around the room for a moment, then nods and leaves. Once I hear the familiar click, I'm stuck again. My head hurts from all the conflicting feelings: the things I thought I knew, and the things I have to learn. Irrationally, I want Dante to be proud of me. I want him to feel his investment is worth it, but then I'm reminded of Eoghan, who's played his part so well, but who, after three years of learning differently, still believes in a peaceful relationship with spirits.

Has Dante ever talked to him? Was he locked in a cell like me? Or did he manage to slip by, allowing him to keep his belief intact? Aeola, Grune, Szirom. I need to remember them, their truth. The spirits are actually talking to me. I sense their nature with a sure-fire intuition that has never been wrong. I wonder what Dante would tell me if I asked him about the altered spirits. Or will my knowledge of them condemn me even further?

Grunting in frustration, I run my hands over my face. I need to get out of my head, but I'm stuck in there the same way I'm trapped in this room.

The assignment. Surely, that'll help me keep my thoughts at bay. And if I complete it, I might be let out. It's worth a shot for nothing more than that.

Tentatively, I sit at the table, side-eyeing the pile of leaflets and booklet on top. Disaster study. Great. If my life is one thing right now, it's a disaster. I can't bring myself to touch the pile, which is ridiculous. It's just paper, probably full of SSA propaganda. I can handle this. Eoghan could. And Rory did, in his time.

I take a deep breath and snatch the booklet from the pile.

*Question 1: How many people died in the Izmit Earthquake 1999?*

What the hell? My heart races as I scan the rest of the questions. Tally death numbers here; describe the damage wrought there. Which spirits brought on this disaster? Which spirits joined in?

My hands are shaking as I pull the pile to me in order to find a stupid earthquake I've never even heard of. All these leaflets are marked as European spirit disasters. Some reports are only half a page long, some are half a novel. They contain the details of each natural disaster or weather extreme over the last twenty-five years, which spirits were involved, how the catastrophe evolved, and what grief it caused. What they don't do is detail the SSA's involvement. I can't blame any of them for mishandling the situation. They can't be everywhere at once, after all.

Flicking through the leaflets, the headings all blur into one. Nine dead in a storm in Spain. Zagreb hit by earthquake. Awakening volcanoes in Iceland. French flood leaves five dead. Ireland braces itself for powerful storm. Gran Canaria wildfire. Siberian forest fire. Record heat wave in Central Europe. Teenagers killed in Austrian avalanche. Tonnes of rock falling from cliff in Greece.

*Total: 17,127 deaths.*

My eyes water as I stare at the leaflet that provides the answer to the first question. Over 17,000 people died in the Izmit earthquake more than 20 years ago. Seventeen thousand. And that's not all: 250,000 further people lost their homes in the widespread damage. That's a quarter of a million people displaced or dead. Gnomes, of course, caused the earthquake, but hundreds if not thousands of spirits joined in, including salamanders who set a petroleum plant on fire, and sea water sprites that caused a tsunami, killing a further 155 people.

I can't comprehend how anyone, spirit or human, could do such a thing. How can anyone cause such destruction and suffering?

Because we poison the seas, pollute the air, chop down the forests. Aeola's words still ring deep in me. Thousands of spirits have lost their lives because of our careless destruction of nature. A stretch of dying land, of yellow grass and corroded trees, may not shock us as much as human tragedy, but it's there, invisible to most. There's grief enough for both sides.

Tears fall onto the image of a collapsed building, burying who-knows-how-many people. A shout tears free from my throat as I grab the entire pile and throw it against the door. Paper rains down, reminding me of the fallen spirits and humans alike, and I start sobbing uncontrollably.

# 12

My confinement lasts three days. Filling out the assignment well and truly broke me. Tallying all those numbers was like inscribing them into my flesh. To a certain extent, I assume each of these deaths to be my fault. It's my attitude that causes deaths like that. Each year, the spirit seekers risk their lives to prevent even more disasters, and here I am, thinking it could all be solved by listening to a few select spirits.

And yet, I hold on to this ever-thinning thread of my self. I realise I'll fall if I ever let go, and there'll be no climbing up after that. Just like my mother.

I see her again when I'm finally allowed outside to have dinner in the dining hall as a treat. She sits alone, away from students and teachers alike. Despite spending eight years here, she's made no friends as far as I can see, and it breaks my heart that she's given up so much to gain so little. I'm tempted to walk up and sit with her. I still miss her badly, especially with all these doubts in my heart, but I remind myself that this isn't the same woman I knew, and getting close to her will only tear up wounds I'm unable to face in my weakened state. Besides, even here at dinner, I'm being watched.

Instead, I join the group of people I'm studying with, and they meet my return with delight. "Are you feeling better?" Henny asks, making room for me.

"I guess so." I'm exhausted, but not for physical reasons.

"Well, that spirit got you good," Eoghan exclaims, stuffing his face with risotto. "You looked like a rag doll."

Wiola sputters her drink as she bursts out giggling. Her cheeks almost burst trying to hold in the rest of her laughter. I realise that though she may be like Eoghan and it could all be a front, it doesn't change how grating her behaviour is.

"Yeah, I certainly felt that way." Being caught in a whirlwind is not an experience I intend to repeat anytime soon. "I guess fighting spirits is harder than it looks." So much harder if you can't bring yourself to do it.

On that note, Tiago slams his cup on the table. "That's for sure. I almost shit myself the first time the traps came out."

"You almost shit yourself at anything," his sister teases.

"Fighting spirits is scary!" Tiago shrugs, giving up the argument before it's even started. "I'm glad I still have one-and-a-half years before I have to go out there and do it for real. And hopefully not mess it up for my team." He shudders.

Now that I consider it, he always seems so uncomfortable, forlorn, or resigned. "Did you not want to become a spirit seeker?" I hope I'm not putting him on the spot. The last thing I want is to get anyone else into trouble.

"Had little choice once the test results were there. They were basically begging me to join, and... the promise of all that money is pretty good. I could buy a house for mae e pai. Gosh, an entire street of houses. And they deserve it. They gave up everything for us." Next to him, Joana's nodding emphatically.

He talks about it in the way someone who's never had much money would. I can get behind that. When Camille offered me half a spirit seeker's salary, I didn't even know what to do with it. "Won't they be scared, though, with both of you taking on such dangerous jobs?"

"No, my pai is the proudest man in Cerdeira. He thinks we're like Superman and Superwoman," Tiago declares, brightening for the first time.

"Far out!" Eoghan cries out. "I never saw Superman dragging his ass over a wall."

And just like that, Tiago deflates again, staring glumly at the leftovers of his risotto. "I'm trying."

"Not enough." I wonder if Eoghan gets so lost in playing the role of boisterous, eager, star student he doesn't notice how much he hurts people or whether he does it anyway to save his own hide. He might do well with his act, but I believe there should always be room for kindness.

Henny seems to think the same because they hit him on the shoulder. "You're insufferable. It's like you're getting worse every day."

I leave them and Wiola to their spat and give Tiago my sole attention. "Well, now we can drag our asses over the wall together," I say, trying my best to smile.

He snorts. "No way! You look like you're hopping over them."

"I might have had to jump a couple of fences in my life," I admit. Letting the others know a little of myself helps me hold on to who I am.

As I look around, my gaze falls on Henny. "Why did you want to become a spirit seeker?"

Confused, Henny looks at me. "I've wanted to be one since I was little. My older brothers used to tell me scary stories. I'm the youngest of five—horrible! Anyway, they were telling me all those creepy stories about how the spirits will get me, and for a time, I was terrified because, obviously, I could totally see spirits. My parents thought I was just making them up at first, you know, like childhood monsters under the bed, but when my nightmares became really bad, they showed me documentaries about the spirit seekers. I believe I was six when they took me to the Rotterdam headquarters, and I remember the woman there showing me around and explaining to me how they fought the spirits. And then she said I could become a spirit seeker when I was big. And I've never been afraid again. The monster you can see is something you can beat."

"Easy for you to say," Tiago complains. "You're able to move on to the research program once you're done."

Henny shrugs and smirks. "Impress your teachers with your amazing academia and you can, too."

Apparently, Tiago isn't so strong in that either, because he pulls a face as if the risotto was filled with kumquats instead of mushrooms. "Great."

"Well, for me, it was a near miss," Wiola says, for once keen to join in the conversation. "I was on a class trip in my final year, and we were somewhere in the Carpathians. One day, we were doing one of those annoyingly long and boring hikes all over the mountains when I noticed some gnome activity above us. I managed to warn my classmates and got us out of there safely before a landslide completely obliterated the track. We would've been so dead, but we weren't. I knew then that I was special." She smiles smugly, probably replaying her heroic moment in her mind.

It almost makes me want to puke. Then her eyes settle on me, and I start getting major mean girl vibes.

"So, what about you, Rika? In which hole did they find you?"

Maybe sharing my story with them isn't such a good idea. I've already been through this with Lukas. I'm not interested in hearing all the insults about Travellers or the homeless again, so I decide to ignore the question and go with a different answer. "I want there to be peace,"

I announce. "I want to make sure high school students don't have to worry about being hit by a rockslide on their class trip or that stories about spirits don't frighten little kids. That's why I'm here." All true, if not necessarily in that order.

For a brief moment, Eoghan looks right at me, forgetting he's supposed to be arrogant and put off by my presence. There's something in his green-grey eyes that hungers for more. *Only a few more months,* I want to tell him. When he gets back to Ireland, Rory will show him how it's done.

Then the moment is over. He shakes his head and scratches the short hair on his neck. "All right, enough of all these sob stories. It doesn't matter what we've been through, just where we're going. And I say we're going on a trip this weekend. Let's take the train up to Florence. We leave Friday after classes."

Excitement bubbles up around the table while my heart races. Leave the castle. Take a train to Florence. I could get away there. They won't even notice when I hang back and slip away. I could hide in the city or travel north on country lanes the SSA will never be able to check.

My blood's rushing to my head. This could be my chance. But I have to be careful and not appear too excited. To hide my true emotions, I look around the room. Inadvertently, it lands on my mother, and I do a double take. She's no longer alone. Dante has joined her, and they're laughing. My mother's enjoying herself with the man who's taking my re-education into his hands.

Just as I'm staring at them, Dante's sweeping gaze falls on me. His face already bears a laugh and it doesn't falter when he sees me. Instead, he acknowledges me with a quick nod, as if I'm some dear friend, and focuses back on my mum.

He doesn't know we're related I tell myself as my joy sours. He thinks we're just two women from the same family group—or cult, as he calls it—and he's keeping tabs on both of us. Either that, or he's actually managed to worm his way into my mother's heart, forcing her to shed all that was between the two of us. I don't know which is worse. I only know that I can't allow myself to fall for his charms like she did.

I *will* get out of here. And I'll leave them both behind.

# 13

"So, my friends are planning to go to Florence at the weekend," I tell Gian as he accompanies me to yet another battle class.

"No."

"You don't even know what I'm asking!" I complain.

Gian stares at me, as if he can't believe I'm serious. "No, Rika, you will not be leaving the castle anytime soon. You haven't earned that kind of trust yet."

I expected as much. And at least Gian doesn't pretend I'm anything other than a prisoner in these halls. Compared to Dante's sickening kindness, he's like a breath of fresh air. "Will I ever?"

"I don't see it happening soon," Gian replies, entirely unaffected by my accusatory stare.

"So, how do I explain this to my friends? I'm a grown woman who should have agency over her own time." And body and mind. But that went out the window the moment I stepped into Agnes' car.

Gian leads me outside and down the path to the training circuit. "Well, then I expect a grown woman can come up with something inconspicuous, like not wanting to go."

"Oh, yeah, I hate sightseeing." I roll my eyes and step away from him. I guess I could explain how much work I've got to do. It wouldn't even be a lie as far behind as I am. In any case, there goes my shot at escape. It would've been too easy, I suppose.

I join the others. Despite wanting nothing more than to leave this place, I'm also sad I can't go with them. They aren't bad people, and I'm beginning to like some of them. Definitely Henny, who helps me out so much without ever nagging me about my deficiencies. But I also have a soft spot for Tiago, who's like my partner in crime for being on Carina's chopping list. I hate that he feels obliged to do something he hates just to get food on the table. I wouldn't be surprised at all to find out the SSA has his and Joana's family under some soul-crushing debt.

Dante may have said that Carina had agreed to let me back into training—damn her!—but she certainly hasn't forgiven me for blatantly questioning her authority. We're now in breaking-down-Rika mode. Despite Tiago lagging behind, Carina's on my case, her tongue constantly lashing out to whip me along the circuit. Overtaking Wiola in the crawl? Not good enough. Practically jumping over the mid-size walls? Not fast enough.

In the end, she makes me run a bonus round because I didn't give it my all, and I'm consumed by hate for her. She's horrible all around, and it speaks volumes that even the others aren't really keen on her. I can't wrap my head around the fact that she and Wulf were ever a thing, or that he'd hold her in high regard despite their break-up. Wulf is thoughtful and compassionate, capable, but always aware of his team's needs.

And Aeola and Grune both said he was in love with me. For a moment, back in Berlin, I believed them. I had been ready to confront him and see where those feelings might take us, but now I'm not so sure. How could anyone be in love with me *and* Carina? We're polar opposites. She's tall and beautiful; I'm as regular as they come, plain if it weren't for my blue hair. She's born and bred in the SSA, breathing in and exhaling anti-spirit propaganda every single minute of the day, and I can't even bring myself to face captured spirits during practice.

That last one is a real problem, since Carina continues her training program with the trapped spirits. This time, we're all set up with a spirit at the same time. Carina's brought a whole wagonload of traps and distributes them whenever a student finishes off their current spirit.

I try to escape her notice by picking a spot near the back wall where the spirit—a nymph—and I just stand around and stare at each other, neither moving to attack. His glossy black eyes remind me of the deep sea, and I wonder in which event he got trapped. Did he drag a submarine into the depths of the ocean? Or did he launch himself at hundreds of thousands in the Boxing Day tsunami in Indonesia? Or perhaps he got picked up on a deep-sea mission just because a spirit seeker could. He looks so sad. Homesick, probably. I can't ask him, though, or Carina will come rushing over here.

Instead, I avert my eyes to study the wall. There's still a smudge of dried blood from where I crashed into it. Did no one notice or did they leave it there to remind me about the danger of spirits? The wall is old, probably as old as the castle itself. If it's been proofed against spirits, I can't see how. In fact, cracks are visible not too far from my impact site.

A crazy plan hatches in my head. A plan that will get me in so much trouble I'll never see the light of day again.

I look around the Cage. The nymph is still standing there, watching me. He's probably unsure what to make of this weird inaction. All around us, students are busy fighting. Tiago is put under pressure by a willow dryad who uses their hair like a hundred-tailed whip. Eoghan takes a heavy hit from a basalt gnome, who rams his head into his stomach. I wince as the Irish student goes down with a grunt. Joana and Henny are teaming up against a sylph and salamander pair, who've combined to a firestorm. On the other side, Wiola is handily disposing a sylph who makes me think of Aeola. My heart aches for her. That might've been one of her sisters.

"Stop staring. Fight!"

Shit. Carina's noticed me. After giving Wiola a new opponent, she approaches me, crossing her arms. "Come on. Unless you want to be sick again."

So, she knows. Of course she does. She's one of them, after all. I remember how Brigid warned us about the Vallescos and Antonellis. They're in the thick of it. And though Wulf won't see it, I can. There's no help in this direction.

But the warning gets my crazy plan turning again. If I can be sly about it, it might just work. I just need the right spirit. I strengthen the grip around my staff and face the nymph. He can sense my determination, his body rippling now like waves lapping on a shore. "Where do I hit him?"

"It doesn't matter," Carina answers, already annoyed. "Let's see if you can hit a spirit at all."

Yeah. Let's see about that. I swing wildly and miss the nymph by the breadth of a hair. Oops.

Now that I've broken the stalemate, the nymph rushes towards me. A wave builds higher and higher, and despite all this going according to plan, my heart skips a beat in terror. I move backwards in awe, not daring to take my eyes off the crest. The moment the wave breaks, I jump aside, swinging my staff through the water that isn't part of the nymph. The rest of it crashes into the wall, filling the cracks in the stone just as I'd hoped it would.

"It's a start, I suppose," is all Carina has to say about that. "Have another one."

The nymph hasn't even taken damage yet, but Carina releases a second spirit before continuing her rounds. It's a tempest, and she's vicious. One moment, I'm checking what the nymph's doing. The next, a horse made of storm and lightning is charging at me. Thunder booms as I throw myself to the side, straight into the pooling water at the nymph's feet.

The cold shocks me wide awake. It really is deep sea water of only four degrees Celsius. But when I gasp, my mouth fills with water. The nymph has put his arms around me, keeping my head underwater. Meanwhile, I can feel the floor vibrating under the tempest's hooves.

"Wall," I try to say, but it turns into a gurgle. So much for my awesome plan. I guess dying is another way to get out of here.

I owe my life to the sand that covers the ground. This close to summer, the weather has been dry for weeks, and the ground is thirsty, soaking up the water quicker than the nymph can call it to himself. My reflexes take over as soon as I take that first breath of hot air. I thrust my staff backwards into the nymph and roll myself to the wall.

It's like I've poked a hole into a rubber boat. The nymph screams in pain while his water flows out of him. I've reopened a wound that's barely healed. "I'm so sorry."

Quickly, I clasp my hand over my mouth, but it's too late. Carina heard me. "Sorry?" she says. "I didn't have to save your ass. There's nothing to be sorry about. You get a new one, congratulations."

"A new one?" I look around. The tempest is definitely still there, charging her energy for a new attack.

It's an odd sight. Normally, lightning rolls effortlessly under their storm grey, cloud-like fur, but this one looks like a motor with starting issues, all sparks and no charge. Just like the others, this spirit has already been beaten once. Nevertheless, she has enough hate in her to fuel herself.

Just as Carina releases not one, but two spirits, the tempest charges again. I raise my staff in defence, but duck at the last minute as if I've lost my bravado. The beautiful horse slams into the wall behind me, releasing another thundering boom.

For all her volume, the damage is pitiful. Some dust trickles down, but if there are new cracks, I can't see them. Before I can investigate further, my attention is drawn to the two new spirits that have been added to my light training exercise. One of them is a sandstone gnome. Once their sand was compacted to hard rock. Now it's trickling all over their body. The other is a spirit I've never seen before, all white and jagged edges, with a long, gaunt face that's as beautiful as it is terrible. His mono-lidded eyes are glassy, devoid of any colour. And he's cold, terribly cold. Behind me, the tempest is chomping at the bit, her breath raising the hairs at the nape of my neck.

Screw Carina. I won't die here pretending I'm something I'm not.

"Hush," I tell the tempest, putting a hand on the side of her head. I get zapped immediately, but it's no worse than any of the fences they use to keep cows in their paddocks. "Calm down. I'm not going to hurt you."

She doesn't believe me. The hurt she's already endured at the hand of spirit seekers has made her deaf to my words. Trust has to be earned; it's not freely given, and right now, I don't have time to convince her of my intentions.

A chill of cold air hits me, practically freezing the wet clothes on my body. Then something hard hits my hip. The sandstone gnome is pelting me with blows. It hurts, but worse than that, the gnome is crumbling, their fists dissolving into sand. I don't care about getting hurt as much as I care about the gnome practically killing themselves to take their vengeance on me.

Anger fills me, wrestling for control with the fear and pain I feel. I have to stop this madness. With a rage-fuelled scream, I force my stiff body to whirl around and thrust the staff into the wall, barely missing the tempest. I'll break this thing down myself if I have to.

The tempest rears, slamming her hooves into my back, sending me down on the ground. Once again, an icy chill engulfs me. My cheek is cut and a tear of blood rolls down my skin. The ice spirit, or whatever he is, is as ruthless as he's cold, his eyes not giving away any kind of emotion.

"Hit. The. Wall." I don't dare speak the words aloud in front of Carina, instead forming them with my lips and all my intentions.

If he's understood me, he doesn't show any sign. A second shard of ice slices down my chin. When I try to stand up, the tempest is stomping all over me, sending small jolts all over my body. They're nothing against the lightning strikes I endured from the Erlking that scarred my arms. She's losing steam fast.

A glint of ice flashes before my eyes, ready to strike me. Quickly, I bury my face in the ground, expecting the shard to slice open my scalp. I feel the gust of air rushing through my hair, but the ice never strikes.

Confused, I raise my head. The snow spirit has followed my lead. He's attacking the wall with everything he has.

Just then, a sucking noise rings through the Cage, and my beautiful ally is sucked back into his trap. Moments later, the tempest is withdrawn as well. Carina is calling them all back. The last to go is the gnome, who's not much more than a pile of sand now. I can only hope they won't have to go up against prospective spirit seekers any time soon.

I'm afraid to get up. Carina has foiled my plan, but I don't know whether it's on purpose. If it was, I'm screwed.

Instead, Henny runs to my side. "Are you okay?" They help me to my knees, fussing over the minuscule cuts on my cheek and the slightly bigger one on my chin.

I must look a mess; my clothes soaked and half-frozen, my face bloodied and dirty, sand all over my body and in my hair. "I'm alright."

"You wouldn't have been," Carina informs me, ever one to rain on my parade. "Do you have any sense of self-preservation?" She doesn't wait for me to answer. "Tell Dante to retest you. I don't believe you belong here, much less have an NAV over 500." She scoffs once more before turning around to the others gaping at her. "Clean this mess up. I've got some proper spirits to attend to."

She's barely left the Cage when the others group around me. "Wow, 500," Tiago exclaims. "Far out!"

"There hasn't been a spirit seeker with an NAV that high for eighty-two years or so," Joana nods to herself, probably recalling some SSA History lesson I didn't attend.

"Wulf came close, but that's about it," Tiago says.

Meanwhile, Eoghan covers his mouth as if he's bursting with laughter. Sure enough, his condescending act comes out in top form. "It's such a joke! I mean, who honestly believes that? Have you seen her fight? She missed those spirits by a mile."

"Yeah, Carina's right." Leave it to Wiola to join her boyfriend. "I don't believe you can actually see them."

"I can't wait to tell my brother about you again," Eoghan says, still snickering. "He'll piss himself when he hears that."

*Keep your face straight! Don't give yourself away! Don't give him away!*

It might be the hardest thing I've had to do today. Hope is rushing through me faster than the nymph's wave, but I'm supposed to be horrified, hurt even. Eoghan's made fun of me. He hasn't let me know he's told Rory about my whereabouts. Just plain bullying, no secret message at all.

It must have worked, because Henny puts themselves between me and the rest. "Don't listen to him. Eoghan's just jealous there's yet another girl that's better than him this year." Behind them, Eoghan snorts. He should really consider a career in acting if this spirit seeker thing doesn't work out. "I, for one, believe you. With everything you told me about the traps and how you intuitively know how to set them, I pretty much expected your NAV to be that high."

"Well, she can become the trapper on her team," Wiola says. "I don't see anyone following her command."

"Oh, shut your mouth, Wio!" Joana barks. "She's just started out. In three years, Rika will be awesome, and you'll wish you'd been nice to her."

In three years, I won't even be here. Not now that Rory knows where I am. And not with the plan I intend to carry out.

"Let's go and leave these losers to clean up this mess." Eoghan puts an arm around Wiola's shoulder before she can say anything else, and strolls off with her.

Tiago snorts and rolls his eyes. "Sometimes, I can't with those guys."

Henny scrunches up their nose. "Eoghan didn't used to be that bad. I don't know what's got into him, but he's been shocking this last month."

I know what's got into Eoghan. Dublin. Somehow, he must've learnt about the rebellion. Maybe Dante paid him a special visit and reminded him of the SSA's expectations of him. With only a few months left, they must be anxious about him. I doubt a return to Ireland is on his cards, no matter his performance.

Tiago squats down next to me, sighing. "Man, Rika. Carina truly has it in for you. I bet she's jealous, too."

To my surprise, Henny nods, their face uncharacteristically sombre. "What she did was totally out of bounds. She's pushing you much harder than anyone else. We need to report her."

"Report Carina Vallesco?" Tiago asks. He knows how useless that is.

"Perhaps she wants to challenge Rika, accelerate her process, or something," Joana says, then quickly remembers the state I'm in. "It sucks, though."

"Majorly," Tiago echoes.

And for the first time since arriving here, I find myself truly smiling. Once I get out of here, I think I might just miss these folks.

# 14

"While the SSA was officially founded at the end of the eighteenth century, the history of the spirit seekers is much longer."

Now that we've had a rough overview of the organisation's history, we're covering the advent of spirit seeking. For a few minutes, Professor Okorie has my full attention. In Dublin with Wulf and the others, we'd been trying to unearth the true origins of spirit seeking, which had been a lot harder than we'd thought because the SSA had destroyed a lot of those records. For once, it might not be the current leaders at fault, though it was some ancestor of Carina's who'd struck a deal with the Irish. Either way, the SSA has a long-standing tradition with writing their own history, so I'm interested to see if there's any acknowledgement of that.

Professor Okorie keeps walking up and down in front of the whiteboard, using his hands to gesticulate, but in a thoughtful, restrained manner, not like Carina's passionate hand movements. He's a talented storyteller, I'll give him that. But it seems like stories are all he's got. "Spirits, of course, have haunted us since the Earth was young. And while we didn't learn how to defend ourselves against them for a long time, there were always those who could sense, hear, and see them. Who can tell me when humanity started to fight back?"

Naturally, Marit's hand shoots up. She's likely inhaled every textbook. "About 2,500 years ago, when the first spirit seeker staff was made."

The professor displays an image of a staff I'm so familiar with my throat tightens. It's Wulf's.

"Very good, Marit." After a quick nod, Professor Okorie addresses the rest of the class. "Now, you'll notice how different those first spirit seeker staffs look to the ones you're used to. But don't let that trick you. These ancient staffs, as we call them, are more powerful than the ones we have today. However, we've yet to figure out why."

I know why. But then again, I'm the only person who owns a similar staff that is far from ancient.

"Unfortunately, only a few of them have survived the test of time, and we'll get to that in a minute. We had three in our vaults but lost one a few months back on the Vesuvius mission. So now there's only two left." He sighs as only a History professor can when faced with the loss of valuable artefacts. I'm almost tempted to tell him there's a third now, or even four, counting Rory's. And if only the spirit seekers would change their ways, they'd have access to even more.

Professor Okorie claps his hands once. "So, what happened? How come we don't have any records about those early spirit seekers or how they forged these weapons? Yes, Marit?"

"The Dark Ages," she announces, proudly.

Next to me, Joana rolls her eyes, but I like Marit. There's nothing wrong with a passion for learning. I wanted to learn everything about spirits when I was a kid. I still do. I just don't do well with the whole read-a-book-and-study approach.

"That's right—like so many other advances in the ancient world, they were lost in the Dark Ages. For people with a high natural attunement value, those centuries were even harder," Professor Okorie continues.

"Remember that most people can't hear or see spirits, so our kind were essentially hearing voices and having visions. And that's never a good thing when it happens right before a natural disaster. For a long time, spirits were confused with the Devil. So people like us were rounded up for talking to the Devil."

And now, we still see spirits as devils and seek to destroy them. I roll my eyes almost as hard as Joana did. Am I supposed to be proud of how far we've come because, at least, we're not prosecuting people like me any longer? We're still treating spirits as a malicious force that needs to be banished. Something else strikes me, and for the first time, my hand rises.

Even Professor Okorie seems surprised. "Do you have a question, Rika?"

"Yes." And all eyes are on me. Great. "Does that mean people were able to actually talk to spirits, like, have a conversation?" I really want to know. If so, the SSA can tick off something else they've lost over time. As far as I know, none of them have ever bothered to talk to spirits.

"No." Professor Okorie chuckles. "As far as I'm aware, it's impossible to hold a proper conversation with a spirit. However, they have been known to pick up words from our language. Spirit seekers with a high NAV have reported several occurrences of words flung at them over the years. I don't think any of them held a sensible conversation, though, however short." I'd better not tell him how Aeola and I have talked for hours, then. "Anyway, that mattered little to those who sought to persecute these early spirit seekers."

For a while, he talks about various people from old texts who may have been highly attuned to nature. It quickly descends into another incredibly boring list of brave martyrs who chose to expose themselves to save other lives, the only ones defending humanity against the evil spirits.

"You talked to a spirit," Joana whispers. "In the courtyard. I heard you talking to them or trying to."

I'm not sure how to react to this, so I give a non-committal shrug. Hopefully, she didn't pick up on how I asked the spirits to hit the wall.

Joana doesn't give up easily. "Maybe it's a 500 thing."

"Just because I said something doesn't mean they answered."

"Is there something you want to share, Rika and Joana?" Professor Okorie's voice rings through the room, and sure enough, everyone turns towards us.

Joana shows off another of her magnificent eye-rolls, crosses her arms, and shakes her head. "No."

I shake my head as well, and the professor continues, "Over time, our perception of the world changed. We had Copernicus questioning geocentrism, explorers sailing around the world, people rebelling against the established structure. The Italian Renaissance can be seen as one of the starting points for modern spirit seekers. In fact, it was at that time that secret cabals gathered: groups of like-minded people who all believed in the reality of natural spirits. Not all of them could see the spirits, just like most of you can't, but those who could led groups, gathered information, and conducted experiments on how to fight them. One of the most famous figures of that time was Paracelsus, who was born around 1494. Not only was he a gifted physician and alchemist, but he defined and studied the first four spirits in his element theory. Who can tell me which four those are?"

This time, a boy with curly hair answers, "The earth spirit gnome, the fire spirit salamander, the water spirit undine, and the air spirit sylph."

Professor Okorie nods. "About thirty years later, dryads were added to the base groups. Of course, nowadays, we know not all water spirits are undines, and there are also spirits of mixed elements. It's not quite as simple as Paracelsus thought back then. But back to our Italian cabals.

Italy has always been a country heavily under attack from the spirits. There have been too many tragedies due to earth and fire spirits in many earthquakes and volcanic eruptions. It's not known how they found out a wooden staff was the most effective weapon against these spirits, but they did. At first, these groups fought in secret, building up an impressive underground network. But since many had been organised by well-standing noblemen, they sought approval early. After several years of discourse, the Church agreed to validate this fight against the Devil. Giordano Ficino, Francesco Antonelli, Giuliano Vallesco, and Luca Masaccio were the first four men blessed by the Pope to undertake this noble crusade."

Of course, the Vallescos and Antonellis have managed to keep their coveted spot at the top, poisoning countless generations to come with their extremist views. I know most spirit seekers believe they're absolutely needed, and that protecting human lives is a heroic cause. It's just that not long after this advent of spirit seekers, spirit attacks began rising, and even more lost their lives. So I don't see how fighting spirits has done us any good.

As we dive deep into the biographies of these pioneers of spirit seeking, an overwhelming sickness builds in my stomach. "Where are the women?" I want to ask. Did they only start seeing spirits today? If spirit seekers were always this progressive and altruistic, then why are we solely focusing on the same white men who seem to be the only people who ever did something worthwhile? And of course, they all come from prestigious, well-off families who could afford this exciting adventure. The worst part is, not much has changed since then. Despite more than half the class being female, it's still a male Antonelli who oversees the education of future generations, and a Vallesco who leads the largest spirit seeker team, right here in front of the Vatican. I bet the council or whoever leads the SSA are full of descendants of these supposedly distinguished men. Their views are the non-plus ultra, while people like me or my mother need to be re-educated.

"This is bullshit," I whisper ferociously, causing Joana to look at me. Annoyed, I wave her off and pack up my things. Then I raise my hand.

"Another question, Rika?" Professor Okorie smiles encouragingly, as if he appreciates my newfound enthusiasm.

"I'm afraid not. I'm not feeling very well. May I be excused?" This whole topic is giving me cramps.

The smile falters and the sigh returns. "Yes, of course. I hope you feel better soon."

Joana hisses my name, and for a moment, I'm afraid she'll follow me, but then I'm out the door and breathing in fresh air. Compared to this corridor, the classroom was suffocating. There's no sign of Gian yet, which I count as a blessing. Why didn't I try this earlier? He only accompanies me from class to class. He doesn't actually wait in front of the door and twiddle his thumbs all day.

As I come across the door to my mother's office, I'm tempted to knock just to see her face once more before I leave. It's a useless sentiment. She never looked for me; she won't miss me now.

Instead, I step out into the garden. The sensation of the wind on my skin, the air heavy with citrus and the sweet aroma of flowers, makes me almost giddy with hope. Technically, I'm still in the castle, but I'm on my own, outside, under the blue sky. While the training also takes place outside, most of it's in a fenced are and under the scrutiny of Carina and the others; it truly isn't the same.

"Enjoying yourself?"

How does he do that? I haven't even been outside for a full minute when Gian steps into my way, arms crossed. So much for secretly taking off. "I wasn't feeling well."

"Is that so?" He raises an eyebrow.

"Period cramps. The first few days are always the worst." I actually had my period last week, but unless he's been going through my garbage, he doesn't know that.

Sure enough, the stalwart man pulls a face, as if I'd asked him to do just that. "I don't want to hear about that."

"You asked."

Gian manages to get over himself, though he still keeps an awkward distance. "Well, then, off to your room, so you can lie down or whatever it is you need to do."

"Actually, fresh air helps a lot." It's worth a try at least.

"You'll have to do without." Gian gives me a sharp nod. "Room or get back to class."

Room it is. I don't want to explain why I suddenly feel well enough to listen to more whitewashed history. To be honest, I'm not even particularly mad at Gian for foiling my spontaneous flight plan. I can't leave with a good conscience, anyway. There's a foolish plan I still have to see through.

# 15

"Rika, you're up."

Today, Carina has announced we're doing midterm tests or something like that. Each one of us will get a spirit carefully selected to match their skill level. For Eoghan, that means a sylph who must've been caught pretty early in the fight, because she's barely been damaged. Though he usually excels in training, this battle leaves him bruised. I assume because sylphs are the hardest spirits to see, and his NAV isn't quite high enough.

Now it's my turn, and I hope Carina doesn't pass up the chance to humiliate me and gives me a nice, powerful spirit who's happy to go along with my plan.

"Ready?" she asks. "This one has been captured whole." Told you. This woman just can't help herself.

I grip my staff tight. "Ready." It might not happen today, but it will happen.

Carina opens the trap and evicts the spirit. A devilish smile curls her lips. "This one's tiny. You should be able to manage it."

Her vitriol is completely lost on me as I stare at the spirit in front of me. The spirit seekers trap thousands and thousands of spirits. How could this be one of the few I captured?

Black eyes look at me, and recognition strikes as fast as it does me. The last time I saw the little salamander, he had been frightened. Now, he's angry. "You promised."

"I'm sorry." I almost choke on the words, not realising how much this is hurting me. It was my fault. I coaxed the spirit into the trap with promises of fields of lava, a gloriously free life in Iceland's volcanoes. Instead, they brought him here to be studied in a lab and thrown against wannabe spirit seekers. "I'm so sorry. I didn't know any better. I really thought they'd set you free."

Carina lets out a mighty groan. "What is it now, Rika? Can't you just attack a spirit like a normal person?"

"I'm not a normal person," I reply, glaring at her. *Focus, Rika. She's not important, the salamander who you involuntarily betrayed is.* I drop down to a crouch, putting my staff to the side and stretching my hand out instead. "I know I messed up. I promised you a warm place and condemned you instead."

"You promised," the salamander hisses, as if he hasn't picked up a single word of what I said. The disappointment hits me like a wave even before he spits fire, singing the hairs on my hand. My fingers curl in reflex, but I force them straight again. I deserve so much more than that.

My lack of knowledge might excuse my misguided promise and capture of the salamander. But I have learnt better. Even back then, Miriam mused that she'd love to study a perfect spirit like this, and Camille admitted that it was up to the SSA to decide his fate. Did I do something, though? Did I snatch the trap out of the delivery box? Did I follow up on what happened to him? Did I even think of him? Turns out, I'm just as bad as my mother. Too busy with my own life to look out for the ones relying on me.

"I failed you, and there's nothing that can excuse that," I admit. "I can only vow to do better, and I will. You won't be captured again."

"Oh meu deus, she really can talk to spirits." That one's from Joana, and I'm pleased to note she doesn't sound aghast, but awed.

Eoghan clicks his tongue. "Don't be silly. Just because she's talking at a spirit doesn't mean it understands her." Satisfied, I note his delivery isn't quite as smooth as usual.

The salamander hisses again, his entire back on fire. I try to tune out the others and get closer, still keeping my hand outstretched. It's an offer, not a demand. He gets to choose whether he wants to forgive me.

His tongue lashes out, and this time, I don't shrink back. It hits me right on the palm, leaving behind a searing row of blisters. The salamander glares as if I've denied him the response he needed. Now, all that pent-up anger dissipates. The flames on his back flicker before they extinguish.

"Feeling better now?" He's still as adorable as he was in Berlin.

"I didn't realise you could do that," Tiago mumbles. "Calm them down like that."

Something moves in the corner of my eye, and panic shoots through me. "Come here!" I shout just moments before the sweeping sound of a staff arises. It hits the ground a split second after the salamander has scurried onto my arm, hiding his face between my shoulder and neck. "Why did you do that?" I shout at Carina while getting to my feet.

She points the end of her staff at the salamander. "Because that's what you were supposed to do. You've failed."

"No, I haven't." I know she means her stupid test, but if anything, the test is a sign of a much grander failure. "This spirit's never hurt anyone. We need to stop treating them like they're mindless beasts, hell-bent on destruction."

Carina gasps. "So, now you're an expert on spirits? A newbie?"

"I'm only a newbie to the SSA. I've been around spirits my entire life. If it weren't for salamanders like this one or friendly dryads, I wouldn't even be alive." Not with eight years on the streets.

A dam has broken, and all the words I've been biting back come spilling out. Bit by bit, I rediscover myself. "Spirits aren't evil. Some are, but so are humans." I know a bunch of them living in this castle. "And yes, they can talk. If you've never heard a nymph gurgling on about all the rubbish thrown into their river, that's on you. Because despite all your natural attunement, you decided to close yourself off to them."

Carina's nostrils flare, her eyes blazing. The others are too stunned to say anything or have decided not to get involved. The latter is definitely the case for Eoghan as he lowers his head, studying the sand at his feet.

"Are we going someplace warm now?" The salamander asks, not quite grasping the tension in the Cage.

I gently stroke his back and tail. "Soon."

That brief exchange sends Carina over the edge. She marches down to the cart and starts opening all the traps. "They're friendly, yes? Let's see about that, shall we? Everyone else step back! Rika is going to show us how it's really done."

"Signora Vallesco, please," Henny pleads, but Carina is too lost in her rage to care.

I'm not sure if I should keep quiet or egg her on. My heart beats faster as the first spirits materialise. Convincing the salamander was one thing, but a whole lot of spirits that might have spent years in confinement, damaged and stewing in their anger? Some of them might be too far gone to be reasoned with. But I need them. I need all of them.

Picking up on my anxiety, the salamander's back has reignited. "We're gonna get out of here," I whisper to him.

The last spirit to be released is the ice spirit from the previous training, and his beautiful face gives me hope. He listened before. Maybe he'll do it again.

Carina throws the last trap on the ground, and I'm impressed she hasn't thrown it at me. She's certainly furious enough to do it. "There you go. Show us how far talking will get you." She joins the others at the exit. A bunch of them are gripping their staffs tightly, whether to help me out or just from fear, I have no idea.

The spirits are confused by each other's presence, giving me a small window to act.

"Listen!" I call out to them. A dozen sets of glowering eyes focus on me. "I know you're all angry and want nothing more than to take out your frustration on me, but if you follow my lead, I can get us out of here."

I no longer care if Carina can hear me. She released the spirits, and now they're in her way.

An old, weathered gnome looks up at me. "Why should we listen to you?"

"Because I want to get out of here as much as you do." I could've told them how I'm a true spirit seeker, but honestly, who would believe that? They've been tricked before, maimed and captured.

"She's nice," the little salamander pipes up.

"She doesn't attack," a voice as brittle as a thin layer of ice says. The snow spirit gives me a nod. "I won't attack, either."

I can't even describe the rush of relief flushing through my veins. "Thank you," I say sincerely. I realise they can feel my honesty. "But I do want you to attack something." A sharp gasp can be heard from the side, and I almost roll my eyes. Sure, here comes Rika, the Spirit Queen, sending her forces into battle.

Instead, I point to the side where the weak spot on the wall is. "Do you see the cracks? Break through there and you're free."

It's mayhem from here on out. A storm builds, much more terrifying than any I've ever seen, picking up sand, fire, lightning, and ice shards. I almost get sucked into it as it passes me, finding myself stumbling in its direction. But then, something digs into my thighs, and I fall flat on my side, unable to protect the little salamander before we impact. A dryad, all brambles, has decided I'd be a much better target. "Woodchopper," she calls. "Weedpuller!"

"Leave her alone!" the salamander hisses. Fire licks along the brambles, causing the dryad to shriek in agony.

She lashes out, but I bring myself between her and the salamander, scooping him up once more. Thorns that couldn't truly penetrate my jeans are biting into my arm. Then they're sliced off by clear, shimmering ice. "Move, dryad!" the ice spirit snarls.

The bramble dryad drags her cut-off brambles through the dirt and decides the spirit seekers at the door are an easier target. She's not the only one to think so. Several spirits have chosen to attack the humans with black staffs rather than the one with a salamander on her arm. And, of course, the prospective spirit seekers and Carina are rising to the occasion.

"Are you okay?" the salamander asks, licking my arm where the thorns have ripped away the skin. His heat sears the skin just enough to cut off the bleeding.

I nod, unable to speak in the chaos. "Thank you," I tell the ice spirit, whose colourless eyes refuse to give anything away.

I'm just about to stand up again when a loud explosion throws me back to the ground. Boulders are rolling over the courtyard, and I can see the mesh of the ceiling bending inward. A vast pile of rocks is lying where the wall once stood, dust rising in the air. Already, some spirits are fleeing.

"Get up," the ice spirit tells me. "It's time to go."

I glance back at the other spirit seekers. Eoghan is lying on the ground, not moving. Henny and Tiago have left the Cage and are staring wide-eyed at the chaos. Joana and Wiola are defending themselves against two spirits, a cackling thunderina and a water devil.

Carina is handily knocking a sylph against the mesh and turns to glare at me, her hair pasted to her cheeks. "Don't you dare!" Behind her, I see people running into the garden to check out the noise, Gian among them.

That settles it. Without another look, I run over to the pile of boulders, scrambling up high to reach the footpath above. The rocks are still moving, and once, my foot gets painfully stuck between two, but the ice spirit cracks the rocks open, and a gust of chilly air sends me upwards again.

Outside the compound, onlookers have gathered, oblivious to the spirits who have just stampeded through them. I ignore their bewildered looks and run down the first alley that presents itself. I need to get as far away from here as I can. If they catch me again, I won't be leaving here alive.

# 16

I feel like I've been thrown eight years back in time. Once again, I'm the little girl with nothing but the clothes on her back, in a city she hardly knows. Only this time, I can't even speak the language of the people here, and there will be spirit seekers on the lookout rather than the police—or perhaps both. But eight years did happen, and I know things about survival now I didn't know when I was fifteen. And I'm not alone.

The salamander is still sitting on my shoulder, dozing lightly while the ice spirit strides alongside me with his long legs. He doesn't look too good, losing water with every step.

"We should go into a supermarket," I tell him. "They've got AC." It might not be officially summer here in Rome, but the heat is already sweltering.

"A supermarket?" His voice is dripping, as if it's melting as well.

I realise he's probably never been in a city. "You're from the tundra, right?"

He nods then raises his hand, mirror-glazed palm facing me. It's a strangely peaceful gesture. "Demyan." A greeting.

"My name's Rika." With a smile, I raise my hand in the same way, even though mine's dirty and blistered. Then I nudge the little salamander on my shoulder. "What's your name?"

Lazily, he opens one eye. The heat is comforting to him. "Glut."

"Hello, Glut." Just then, I notice people staring at me. Normally, I wouldn't mind—I couldn't care less if people think I'm crazy—but I don't want anyone to be able to pass on information about my whereabouts to the SSA. I take Demyan's hand, hoping I'm not offending him with my body warmth, and say from the corner of my mouth, "Let's go."

It takes us a couple of blocks to find a proper supermarket with a large chilled-food section. My grumbling stomach tells me it's had no food for lunch, and I don't have the heart to tell it that we probably won't have food for dinner, either. I'm sure there must be food banks in Rome, but I don't know them yet, much less how they work. I'll have to find some other homeless folks and hope they lead me to one later.

Demyan is slowly getting back into shape. He leans into one of the ice cupboards while I pretend to browse the chilly bins in front of it. It feels wrong to stand still after my spontaneous flight from the castle, and looking at food I can't buy doesn't help. The danger is far from over. For all I know, I've doubled back to the Castel Sant'Angelo. Wouldn't that be glorious?

I need to leave the city, or even better, the country. Return to Berlin or perhaps go to a new place altogether. Sure, the SSA has people everywhere, especially in the cities, but it's summer now and there'll be plenty of food in the countryside and forests. I could accompany Demyan to Russia. Surely Siberia is remote enough to hide.

And then?

When I ran away from the youth home eight years ago, I had a goal. I wanted to find my mother. I know where my mother is now: sitting and laughing with Dante. So that's out of the picture. But I also found something else in between: a family, a purpose, a home. And surprisingly, I find it difficult to let go of it. My soft smile is reflected from the glass doors. Berlin it is, then.

"Demyan, I'd like to go now." There are cameras in the supermarket, and I'm nearing conspicuous behaviour with the amount of time I've spent here. I don't know how far the SSA network extends, but I have to assume they've got eyes and friends everywhere.

The tundra spirit looks at me with his colourless eyes. "Then I wish you swift winds."

I try not to be disappointed he won't accompany me. Somehow, our brief communication in the Cage and subsequent prison break had given me a sense of communality. But apparently that's a far too human response. The spirit is happy here in the cold box, not in the warmth outside. "I wish you cold days and even colder nights." I hope he returns to Siberia, or he might extend his newfound love for supermarkets and become one of those weird spirits shunning nature for the comfort of human inventions. Either way, I'm sorry to leave him.

On the way out, I snatch a packet of biscuits from the trolley behind the checkouts that's collecting surplus food for the shelter. I figure it's not technically stealing if I'm one of the eventual recipients. The heat hits me like a wall after all the time spent in the cold, and it wakes up Glut, who's been still in the supermarket. "Where are we going?" he asks, stretching out around my neck.

"I don't know yet," I whisper, trying to decide where to go. One of my issues is the standard T-shirt I'm wearing, showcasing the SSA logo. People are probably wondering why one of the SSA students looks like they've had a rough day, with dried blood and dirt caked into my skin. Then again, they might be used to the sight. Nevertheless, the T-shirt is one thing that stands out, so I duck into one of the many small alleyways and turn it inside out. Chucking it would be better but wandering around in a bra will make me even more noticeable.

Fortunately, the city is teeming with tourists, which gives me more than enough cover. I follow the crowds around as they make their way down cobbled streets with charming little eateries. From time to time, the throng makes way for a moped cruising through, eliciting shouts from the Italian restaurant owners, some angry, some welcoming. It's really hard to tell which it is. The city itself is beautiful and peculiar in the best way. Each house has its own charm, often with plants hanging from the windows or black iron signs dangling over the street. One street has countless strings of fairy lights strung from one side to the other, and I almost want to stay until night falls so I can admire the myriads of lights.

And in between all modern Rome, millennia-old ruins are standing. Some of them are completely ignored, though I can't fathom why, while others are the target for my fellow tourists. Among them, I find my sleeping place. Surrounded by busy streets lies a city-block wide complex of ruins in a lowered lot. There doesn't seem to be any way to enter the ruins, so the tourists stay out of it. That doesn't mean they're empty, though. Quite the opposite. The place is overrun by cats. They laze in the sun in the nooks and crannies of shattered walls, slink around the shadows at the bottom, or nestle into the grass overgrowing the ruins. It's like they've established their own little colony out here. That works for me. Cats are like spirits. They've got their own mind, but they don't mind some company from time to time if you don't bother them.

It's too early now to settle in. Far too many eyes are watching but, judging by the restaurants filling up along the streets, it's close to dinnertime. I decide to continue my stroll, feeling more at ease when I'm moving around.

The tourist streams around the monuments lessen, which gives me the opportunity to use one of the many fountains to wash my face and arms. It doesn't replace a shower, but it's better than nothing, and it makes me a little less conspicuous. Glut doesn't like the water, but he stays close, and I'm thankful for that. He could've run away like all the other spirits, but he actually seems to like me. After all the pain I involuntarily caused him, I couldn't be more grateful that he's decided to forgive me. The blisters on my hand will turn into a scar and always remind me I need to look out for others as well.

As night falls, the streets seem to swell with people instead of emptying. While most of the tourists have turned in for the night, the locals are coming out in full force. Each guest seems to know the restaurant owners personally and is welcomed with loud and cheery voices and kisses. For some reason, I imagine Wulf, Carina, and her brother Piero settling around one of the candle-lit tables outside. I see Wulf laughing in a carefree way he never really does in Berlin, and my heart tightens. Wulf would've been elated to show me around the city he grew up in. If we'd come here together, I might've even fallen in love with it, when now, despite all its beauty, it appears like a giant trap full of hidden mines.

I miss him. In fact, I miss all of them, especially Aeola. We weren't meant to be separated. Not after everything we've been through together.

"Let's head in for the night," I tell Glut, trying to capture some of the companionship I've gotten used to from my sylph friend. But while I'm grateful for his presence, it's not the same.

We return to the cat colony ruins, which now appear like a square of darkness among the well-lit streets. I have to stroll casually around the perimeter for two rounds before there's enough of a gap in foot traffic that I can climb over the fence and run down the stairs built in for the occasional caretaker access. I scan the area, ignoring the mewling cat pressing itself against my legs. The centre will be too exposed in the morning, so I pick a half-covered ruin in one of the corners to nestle in behind. This low and with all the shadows, I should be near invisible from above.

Naturally, a bunch of cats come strolling by as soon as I rustle with the biscuits I've only nibbled so far. The few scraps I'm willing to share hardly satisfy them, and they politely ignore my attempts to shoo them away. At this rate, I won't get a single minute of sleep. "Please just go," I tell them, too tired to think of a more sensible approach.

"Go!" Glut hisses, his back lighting enough to singe a bit of my hair.

Instantly, the cats scurry away, fleeing from the little salamander. "You're quite the protector, aren't you?" I lift him from my neck to look him in the eyes. "And such a sweet one." Then I settle him in my lap, stroking his back. "Let's sleep, shall we?"

It doesn't take me more than a few minutes to lose all consciousness.

"Che stai facendo lì?"

Shit.

I slept too long. The sun is already shining, though judging by the barely audible traffic, it's still early morning. Above me, a police officer is leaning on the railing, looking down at me expectantly.

"Scusi..." I try, cursing the fact I didn't have enough time to pick up any proper Italian. On my lap, Glut stirs, opening one of his eyes in confusion.

He switches to English immediately. "Get out!"

There's no exit other than the stairs I came in by, so instead of waiting for him to get me himself, I make to follow his order. With luck, this is just another routine job where he gives me a slap on the hand and lectures me about the dangers of sleeping outside and trespassing. But trusting luck is how you get into trouble, and the way things usually go for me, he'll take me back to the station and hand me over to the SSA.

With Glut scuttling back onto my shoulders, I walk up the stairs towards the gate. My intuition is proved right when I see a glint of silver in the sunlight. I climb over the gate a lot more awkwardly than I need to while the policeman mumbles something in Italian, probably complaining about the tourists. Just when he's about to grab my hand, I bolt.

If pursued by foot, always get a street between you. Later in the day, that'd be near impossible with how busy the traffic around here gets. Even this early in the morning, there are enough motorists to honk their horns and hurl insults at me as I duck in between the cars and run along the median strip until I find a gap to cross to the other side.

Unfortunately, the policeman is no stranger to Roman traffic and manages to find an equally fast crossing. His shouts are ringing after me. I know there's a fifty-fifty chance of him calling for reinforcements. I haven't actually done anything wrong, apart from trespassing on some ancient ruins, but now I'm resisting police. Either way, I need to lose him fast. Since the busy street didn't work, I duck into the little alleyways, making sure I change my direction at every opportunity, hoping to lose him in the maze. As much as I try, the footsteps behind me aren't fading. I'm glad for all the circuit training I've done, which helps me push through the exhaustion and continue to seek the most complicated path I can find, but it doesn't keep the police officer off me.

I cut through a courtyard with washing hanging in multiple lines, thinking about whether I could find a quick hiding spot instead, when the linen behind me suddenly catches fire. Within seconds, the entire washing is ablaze, a feat only achievable by spirit intervention. Behind me, the policeman stops and curses. I whisper a quick thanks to Glut and leave the courtyard on the other side.

The good thing is no one will accredit the fire to my mindless flight. The bad thing is this will show up on the spirit seeker's radar.

As soon as I'm a couple of blocks away from the site, I slow down, trying not to look like I'm on the run. More and more people are crowding the streets, going about their normal life, and I'm glad no one spares me a second glance. A fire truck can be heard further down the street, making me feel bad about the little fire I didn't even set.

At last, Glut and I settle at the side of the river, low enough to be out of sight, but not in a way that would seem suspicious. Just a foreign girl enjoying a sunny morning by the water. If only that were true.

I pick Glut off my shoulders, so I can look him in the eye. "Sorry about the rude awakening." If it weren't for me, he would still be sleeping. No random police officer would've seen a little salamander in a cat colony. "And thanks for saving my ass in that courtyard."

"You saved me," Glut says in such a cheerful manner I can't help but smile. That's it. I saved his life; he saved mine. No explanations needed. Spirits can be so wonderfully simple.

"The problem is, if you stick around me, you'll have to do a lot of saving. And unfortunately, I'm not sure I can rescue you again if the SSA finds us." And eventually, they will. "You're not safe with me. You stand a much better chance making your own way. They're after me, not you." I'm sorry to see the little guy go, but I know I can't take on this responsibility. If we get caught, they'll trap him again and who knows what fate awaits him then. "Do you understand what I'm saying?" He's still so young.

Glut sighs, two twin rings of smoke rising from his nostrils. "You want me to be alone."

"I want you to be safe. Honestly, I'd love nothing more than to make it back to Berlin with you, but your chances are much higher without me. I've already failed you once; I don't want to do it again." Tears are stinging in my eyes, half born out of frustration at my own failings and the unfairness of having to do this alone. I'd much rather have a friend with me.

"I understand," Glut says in a low voice, and I sense the sadness pouring out of his body.

Carefully, I press him against my chest, looking for the warm spark of comfort. "I'm gonna miss you."

"I'll miss you, too," he whispers, licking my palm where he burnt me before.

Finally, I set him down on the grass. "Go find yourself a volcano." There should be plenty of them around here.

The pattern on his back lights up once as he turns away. I watch him scuttle away through the grass. Once Glut is gone, I get to my feet. Time to find a way out of this city. And perhaps something to eat.

\#

After a long walk through the city and asking several people, I find my way to Roma Termini, Rome's Central Station. Naturally, there are a couple of police officers casually strolling through the crowd. I can't tell if they're looking for something, or just following routine. I only need to get on one train, preferably an international one that gets me out of here fast. Then again, the national ones might be better suited to hide in, depending on how strict the controllers are. Or I might spend the entire ride in the toilet, hoping the controller passes me by.

As soon as my eyes spot Berlin on the board, my heart skips a beat. Platform 12, leaving in eighteen minutes. All I need to do is to get there safely and hop on board, letting the chips fall where they do. Just the thought of being back in Berlin tomorrow makes my chest ache. I want to go so badly.

And I'd be leaving everything behind, Dante and his academy, Carina and her grief, the friends I've made despite the odds, and most importantly, hundreds and thousands of spirits trapped in the SSA's research lab and education facilities, tortured in countless battles with spirit seeker hopefuls, and dissected and torn into pieces for all their nifty little gadgets, such as staffs made of dryad wood. And then there are the spirits who are being *fixed* by adding other spirit parts, turning them into weapons against misbehaving spirit seeker teams or even states. How can I just ignore that when I'm so close to the source?

Looking at the city I've come to call my home is painful. I watch the board change, listen to them call for the last travellers to board, and see the train leaving the station. I know it's not my only way home. There are plenty of other north-bound trains, but I won't take them. This is no longer about me and my safety. There is no one but me fighting for the spirits. If I don't do something, it'll never stop. No one will ever hold the SSA accountable.

Stroking the blisters on my palm, I turn away and head back into Rome.

# 17

My first order of business is to gather intelligence. Obviously, I can't return to the academy—and not just because I have no clue where it is—so the next best thing is finding some spirits to chat to. I keep walking around until I find a pleasant park on top of a hill, one of the few spots of nature in this city. Even here, the ruins have been left alone. An old-fashioned temple on an island in a lake is the centrepiece, and for a while, I admire the scenery.

Professor Okorie never told us how the ancient Romans approached spirits. Most of them probably saw the wrath of their gods in natural disasters, but what about those who could see the spirits? Nymph is an old word. Was it attributed to the water spirits later or were the spirits revered in ancient times? The idea of humans bringing sacrifices to some spirit deity amuses me more than it should.

It doesn't take long to find a couple of dryads squabbling about whose tree is the most beautiful. "But my leaves! They're so fleshy and green," says a rather knobbly dryad with an impressive mop of leaf hair.

"Leaves? What's so special about leaves?" An oleander dryad dressed in a sea of pink flowers snorts. "Every tree is green. But flowers! Look at my cute little oleander. Isn't it pretty?" She leans forward to a small tree covered in the same type of flowers.

"Fruit. It's all about fruit," a third dryad says. Two bunches of long black bean pods hang from their ears. Carobs. "Mine are not only edible but *sweet*."

Since there's no one else around, I decide to approach them. "Uhm, excuse me." They all turn to me, somewhat aghast, as if they can't fathom how anyone could interrupt them. "Sorry, I couldn't help but overhear. I think you're all beautiful in your own way."

The carob dryad with the legume earrings rolls their eyes. "That's such a human thing to say. You're rather ugly, if I may say so. You don't even grow leaves."

I pick at my blue strands of hair. "Yeah, I know. I would if I could. Beats dyeing my hair."

"The colour is nice," the oleander dryad admits. She steps forward without reservation and arranges a branch of pink blossoms in my hair. "There you go. Now you're not so bad."

The carob dryad still seems to think differently but keeps their mouth shut. Still, I make sure to thank the oleander spirit.

"What are you doing here?" the cork oak dryad with her leafy green hair asks. "You're not one of them, are you?"

I'm wearing their T-shirt, though fortunately it's still inside-out. "Definitely not. In fact, I've just escaped."

Movement goes through the dryads as they bristle in excitement. The oak dryad rustles her leaves, the oleander dryad squeals, and the carob dryad's pods clank against each other.

"Oh, you're her," the oleander dryad says, her eyes turning a dark shade of pink.

I'm so confused I almost take a step back. "I'm her?"

"The one who freed all those spirits," the leafy one explains.

Damn, spirit news travels fast. "You heard about that?"

"Of course we did." Suddenly, my human ugliness is forgiven, and the carob dryad comes closer, eager for gossip. "It's all over the wind. Twelve spirits escaped with the help of a human, a true spirit seeker who actually cares for us." They're so close I can smell the sweet aroma of their fruit.

Who knew recognition would mean so much? Within seconds, I'm tearing up.

At the sight of my tears, the carob dryad takes a step back to assess me once more. Their excitement dwindles as they revert to the criticism that comes so naturally to them. "So, that's you."

Yeah, I'm aware I don't look like much. Especially not after a night spent outside and a day running around the city. I probably smell, too. Nevertheless, I make a mock-curtsy. "That's me."

The oleander dryad flops down into the grass, sending up a cloud of pink blossoms. "You've got to tell us everything. Did you infiltrate the castle? Are you a spy?"

Okay, this dryad has definitely listened to too many movie geeks. The other two are closing in as well, their gaze just as eager. What do I tell them? I doubt they're interested in my whole sorry life story. I decide to do the shortened version, starting with my kidnapping and ignoring the entire time I was stuck in a cell. They're interested in the spirits, not me. So I tell them about the fighting training and my refusal to hurt a spirit, until I get to the part where I led the spirits in a prison break. "And once the wall collapsed, we all made a run for it."

"They've been so brave." Naturally, the dryads focus on the spirits, quickly glossing over my involvement. "Just imagine uniting with sala-manders and gnomes to fight for your freedom. I'd burn a few leaves if it meant escaping from that place."

The oak dryad looks eagerly at me. "Was there a dryad?"

"Were they good-looking?" the oleander dryad asks, eyes sparkling pink.

"Uhm, there was a really handsome tundra spirit named Demyan." I have to admit I'm not an expert in spirit dating questions.

The oleander dryad pulls a face. "I can't stand ice spirits. They always break my flowers."

"Sorry." I'm kind of glad I don't need to tell her how to get to that supermarket for their first date. "Can I ask you a question?" In an instant, they're all sitting attentively again. "The SSA has enslaved many more spirits. I want to free all of them. But I have no idea where they're kept. Perhaps the wind told you about a research lab or something?"

"If we knew where those monsters kept spirits, don't you think we would've freed them?" The oak dryad shakes out her leaves. "We don't need human help to protect ours."

After what I've learnt, I'm not entirely convinced that's true, but I understand the sentiment. The spirits don't need a human saviour. They have their own methods to get back at us. But their methods and our methods are what's led to endless suffering on both sides, and I strongly believe we can only end it if we work together. "Of course not. I'm not asking you to give up any secrets. But maybe..." An idea strikes me suddenly. "Which places do you usually avoid here in Rome?"

"The Castel Sant'Angelo," the oleander dryad and the carob dryad say immediately.

"No one goes near there. They've got patrols around every day," the carob dryad elaborates.

The oleander dryad nods enthusiastically, dropping some petals. "And the headquarters in Aventino, where all the spirit seekers live. Don't go too close to the Colosseum, either," she says, shuddering. "Unless you want to get burnt."

Before I can ask what that's supposed to mean, the cork oak declares, "I wouldn't go near Sapienza." She pulls her leaves in. "They experiment on spirits there," she whispers, her leaves rustling in agreement.

I instantly perk up. "Sapienza? That's the university, isn't it?" Of course! Why didn't I think of that? Henny told me they were involved in a research program over there. I don't know if they keep all the spirits there, but they most definitely keep the ones they're trying to recombine. And if I can set them free—the unmodified ones, not those already altered—I might be able to stop the horrifying project altogether. It would be a start.

The dryads explain how to get there, and they're happy for me to stay the night, probably to see what other bits of gossip they can get out of me. Accidentally, I settle their earlier argument when the carob dryad gives me their fruit to eat. On an empty stomach, they're the best thing I've ever eaten. Saying so out loud leaves one dryad feeling very smug and the others twirling their leaves in annoyance.

When I finally go to sleep, my head is full of exciting and rather frightening new plans. Tomorrow, I'll have a snoop around the university.

\#

The unnatural rustling of leaves wakes me in the dead of night. Deep in the forested area of the park, there's no light other than the moon. But though I can't see them, I hear someone approaching. Someone entirely human.

My heart hammers in my chest. Is it a straggler, just randomly stumbling over my sleeping place? The footsteps seem too light for that. They're almost cautious, as if someone's trying to sneak up on me. Then I see a light hopping over the grass. Someone's searching with the flashlight of a cell phone. Moments later, the beam settles on me, blinding me.

"There you are." I recognise the voice even if I can't see a bit. How often did I dream of this?

My mother has finally found me.

Thankfully, the light lowers, and my vision returns slowly. She looks just as I remember: her hair falling unbound down her back while the wind picks up the lightweight fabric of her summer dress. Her eyes settle on me with all the kindness of the world. "May I sit?"

As dreamlike as her appearance is, I'm aware this isn't a vision. My mother's truly here. "How did you find me?"

She chuckles as she sits with that awkward distance that's too close and yet hardly close enough. "You're not the only one who can listen to the wind."

"So, you decided spirits are worth listening to again?" I can't let myself forget what she said in the castle. She's on Dante's side, not mine.

My mother stares at me wistfully. "Of course they are. Did you really think I could close myself off to the world? Ignore the whispers in the wind, the murmurs in the river, the rattling of gravel under my feet." She turns to gaze into the darkness. "The Castel is my home. Its garden is all I've got, but it's silent, always silent."

I don't dare trust her. I can't let her hurt me again, but my heart yearns to reconnect with her now we share something again. "They kept me prisoner at the castle."

She looks back at me, sadness clouding her gaze now. "I assumed as much. My darling girl wouldn't come here on her own. Not the girl who skipped stones with gnomes, swam with nymphs, and laughed with sylphs. I always knew they'd try to take it all away from you. How did they find you? I remember telling you to stay away from them."

I want to say I did, but that's not true. When Camille offered me a home, I didn't run. Well, I ran a little, but I kept coming back. "It might've helped if you'd told me why." I still remember the loneliness

I'd felt, not being able to share my gift with the world, assuming I was the only one. My team in Berlin has become so much more than a home. They're my family.

"There was no time," my mother recounts sadly. "I should've prepared you better."

I feel myself slipping towards her. It's like an invisible force draws us closer with each breath. I need to confront her or risk getting burnt yet again. "I saw you laughing with Dante. You two seem to get along very well." There was nothing forced in her laughter in the hall.

"Dante," my mother says with a momentous sigh. "He's a complicated man. A lot of responsibility, expectations. When I first met him, he was such a serious boy, never smiled, eager to live up to his family's name. But when I introduced him to the spirits, he changed. Like a butterfly breaking out of its chrysalis. It made him hungry for more. More knowledge, more wonders, more change. He wanted to turn the whole academy upside down. We all did, the entire group of us." Her eyes are suddenly lighting up. "We took over the lectures, making sure they taught real spirit behaviour. We wrote in textbooks, hung flyers, and held speeches. Well, Dante did. I was never one for the podium."

My mother told me so many stories in my childhood. She told me of her childhood in Hungary, of her travels and past relationships, of spirits and ideas. But she never told me about her stint at the SSA or her friendship with Dante. I recognise so much of myself in her words it hurts that she never decided to share with me. "What happened?"

"Oh, the old families got wind of it. We had a glorious few months, but then the board came down hard on us. They threatened to expel all of us, and they were looking for the ringleaders. We got punished—Dante, most of all. But I couldn't go back to what they'd taught us. A fire had been ignited in me that I just couldn't keep contained. So, Dante helped me escape, and I left Rome. But he paid for it. His parents made sure he wouldn't step out of line again, forcing him to repeat the entire year so he'd be at school longer."

I remember Dante's words now. How he told me that he, too, once had grand ideas of peace. How long has this cycle of abuse been going on? Did they keep Dante in a cell like mine? His parents? Their grandparents? The victim became the perpetrator. "He's not a good man."

"Perhaps not," my mother admits. "But who is?" It sounds so deflated I want to take her in my arms and hug her.

Instead, I tell her my truth. "A bunch of people." I remind myself of my team back home, of Wulf who's willing to have his world challenged again and again, of Leon who opened his mind wide to the world around him, and of Rory stepping up to bring peace to the Irish and their spirits. "I would even say most people. Like the spirits aren't all mindless monsters hell-bent on destruction, humans aren't either. So much of what drives us is built on fear, mainly fear of the unknown." If there's one thing I've learnt in Professor Okorie's lessons, it's that fear of the unknown can have disastrous effects. "The spirit seekers fight this fear by hunting spirits, but fear can only be conquered by understanding. We need to learn to listen to each other, to learn from each other. We need to stop the vicious cycle we've let ourselves get caught up in." Just as the cycle of abuse at the academy needs to be stopped. Unconsciously, I've shifted onto my knees, kneeling next to my mother, imploring her to believe me.

She raises a hand and lays it softly against my cheek, a wistful smile on her lips. "Look at you, all grown up."

My heart aches thinking of how she missed me growing up, and how fast I had to do it living on the streets. "Things can still change." With my mother at my side, I feel like I can do anything. "We could convince the world to change its ways. People are willing to listen.

They're aware the SSA's approach isn't working. Things are getting worse, not better. Maybe the academy is the wrong place to attempt this, but there are others. You've heard of Wulf Bachmann?" When she gives me the slightest indication of a nod, I launch right back in. "He's pretty much the SSA's poster boy, and he believes me. He believes in me. If I can convince someone like him, we can convince anyone."

"You like this guy," my mother notes, chuckling quietly.

Blood rushes to my cheeks, heating them up. "That's not the point." If only I hadn't let him get away that night.

My mother lowers her hand and sighs deeply. "You need to go back."

Confusion hits me as her demeanour reverts to the apologetic sadness that carried her here. "Back? You mean back to Berlin?"

"No." She looks at her hands, then up to me. "Back to him."

I still don't get what she means. Wulf is in Berlin, so if I'm not supposed to go there, then...

My thoughts are interrupted by the sound of someone else approaching. A man steps into the small circle of light, his shoes shined, his pants pressed.

Dante gives us both a charming smile. "Good evening, ladies."

# 18

I can't believe my eyes. This has to be a dream, or rather, a nightmare. My mother can't... she couldn't... "What's he doing here?" I hate how brittle my voice sounds.

Dante snorts softly, as if this is all highly amusing to him. "I'm here to pick you up. Léna was happy to lend me her services."

He might as well have plunged a dagger into my heart and twisted it. "You tracked me for him?" Angry tears sting in my eyes.

I should've taken that train to Berlin. Staying here has accomplished nothing. I could've been back with Wulf, and we would've worked something out together. Instead, I'm right back where I started, in the clutches of the SSA.

"I had no choice." My mother looks sorry, but all I want to do is spit into her face. Dante would've never found me without her help. She used the spirits to find me, used my yearning to keep me in place. All her words were just sweet little lies, and I gobbled them up like the Christmas feast in a soup kitchen. I'm so angry, I don't know if I want to scream, rage, or run.

*Run.* Surely, I can escape them just like I escaped the police officer this morning. The dryads might even help me. Their trees are nearby. But the trees are still, not a leaf in motion.

*They're afraid. They recognise this man.*

He was Rome's spirit seeker commander, after all, if I remember correctly.

Well, I'm not afraid. I get up on my feet, glowering at Dante, and turn away from him. A quick dash into the darkness might lead to a broken ankle, but I'll happily break both my feet if it keeps me out of Dante's clutches. Unfortunately, Dante hasn't come alone. Gian is standing behind me, arms crossed in front of his chest.

I've half a mind to try it, anyway. What's there to lose?

Gian must've seen the decision in my eyes. The moment I will my feet to break into a cold run, he moves forward and swiftly grabs my arm, yanking me backwards. My back slams into his chest, and his second arm wraps around my waist. I kick wildly, going for his shins, but he may as well be made of stone for all the effect I have on him.

"Are you done?" he asks when my activity finally slows, sounding terribly bored.

My gaze finds my mother's face. She's got to her feet. Her eyes are wide, but her hand rests on Dante's arm. Gian could slit my throat in front of her, and she wouldn't step in. As I realise this, all the energy drains out of me. My feet settle on the ground as I jerk my head sideways. I don't want her to see my tears.

Dante's soft voice breaks the silence that creeps in on us. "Now this matter's been taken care of, let's go home. We could all use some sleep after the excitement we've had." He offers his arm to my mother, and she takes it, following his lead like the trained puppy she is.

I, on the other hand, have to be half dragged, half carried by Gian. I may stand no chance against the power of the SSA, but I won't go along willingly.

\#

My cell is waiting for me, as cold and dark as before. Gian drops me on the floor and leaves me alone. As the door falls shut, it feels like it's slammed into me. I shudder in a weird mix of rage and despair. My own mother betrayed me. How do I move on from that?

It makes it impossible to breathe, impossible to exist. I look around and see the same impenetrable walls around me closing in. I never wanted to return to this place, and now I've tasted freedom, it's even worse. All the progress I've made convincing Dante he could trust me is destroyed. I'll be in here for weeks, months, even. I'll never see the light of day again.

Faster and faster, the dark thoughts circle, swooping down like crows to snatch pieces of my mind. *I can't do this again. I can't do this again. I can't do this again.*

A sudden click makes me catch my breath and whirl around. Dante has re-entered the room, looking down at me gravely. I search his face in vain for the false kindness he's always displayed. I don't want his smooth lies, the way he twists my words and turns my world upside down. But now I'm not going to get them, I feel trepidation settle in. When the gentle approach fails, what comes next?

"Do you have any idea the damage you've caused?" His voice is heavy. Like a weighted blanket, it presses down on my shoulders. I know what he's referring to. I've freed a dozen spirits and, in the process, destroyed the specialised training court and part of a probably ancient wall.

But that pales in front of the destruction the altered spirits have caused in the name of the SSA. "What about the damage you've caused?"

Dante frowns. "Me? Whatever could you mean by that?"

I hate him. I hate him so much, his smooth demeanour, his spotless suit, everything. I want to tear him down, rip his clothes, and wipe that gentle smile off his face. He's not a good man, and I don't care if he's had a complicated past. Whatever trauma he had to go through—and that's just based on what my lying, Dante-worshipping mother has said—doesn't excuse the fact he's a criminal. He had me kidnapped, he's kept me captive, and he's tried to brainwash me. The worst part is it almost worked. Some of the things he said sowed seeds of doubt in me that have sprouted into the most tenacious weeds.

But I can't allow him to do this to me again. Instead, I get to my feet. I harbour the rage and I claw at the facts. "I know all about the alteration project, or whatever you call it. You create polluted spirits and re-release them into the world so your pretty agency can cash in. People can't possibly be allowed to think spirits might not be as dangerous as you've told them. So, whenever it looks like a country might drop out, you send your tainted spirits to heat the conflict again." I snort. "I've caused damage? What about the College Green in Ireland or the damage you did to Grafton Street. The dryads were marching for the Spire. If that had fallen, people would've died. And Budapest. You complain about a wall but are happy to destroy three historical bridges?"

"You were in Budapest, too?" Dante says with a frown. Apparently, that's the most important part of my speech. "You're definitely getting around, aren't you? Well, I guess that might be expected from a Traveller." The sudden spite in his voice makes me shiver. He truly has let go of all his masks. "Was that where you ran into Wulf?"

Defiantly, I shake my head. "Wulf ran into me. He was on your stupid volcano mission when I joined his team in Berlin. He only came back after we defeated the Erlking." I remember his sombre expression back then. The cold determination when he ran into a sylph in his citadel.

Dante grabs my hands and looks at my arms as if he seeing them for the first time. His gaze trails the dendritic scars I carry from that fight. I try to pull my hands away, but his fingers dig into my wrists, holding them still. Then his gaze searches out mine. "You're the one that caught him."

"What?" I know I've already said too much. I've called out Dublin and Budapest, and now my friends in Berlin as well. Surely, the SSA can't touch them, not with Wulf protecting them.

"The report didn't match up. There were too many details missing. Mr Krassnitz's report was missing altogether, and he was the highest-ranking seeker back then, knocked out early in the battle." A feverish expression has taken hold of him, his eyes still fixed on my scars. "A battle like that should've been broken down, so we could learn from it, teach it, but the report was barely more than 'with a concerted effort, the teams caught the A-class spirit threatening the city'." Finally, he looks up at me. "I chalked it off to Mrs Bouchard's inexperience, but she was hiding you. You caught the Erlking!"

I answer his intense stare with my own, but to be honest, he's scaring me. I feel like the life I've built myself in the last few months is unravelling as I speak. And there's nothing I can do to stop it anymore. "So what if I did?" I yank my hands back, and this time, he lets go.

For a moment, Dante looks confused, overwhelmed perhaps, and certainly more human than ever before. "I don't understand. You're pro-spirit. Why would you trap one?"

"Because they're all individuals. The Erlking was corroded by hate and vengeance over hundreds of years. It's not like I didn't try to reason with him, but he left me no choice. It was either him or me."

Something's changed. Dante looks taken aback, shocked even. It's almost like... he's actually considering what I'm saying.

Eagerly, I press forward. Maybe what my mother told me was the truth. Maybe underneath all that duty and responsibility he's carrying, his questioning mind is still alive. "You know that. You know they're not mindless monsters. That some of them are angry, hateful even, but they're not the majority. And it could be much less if we—"

Without warning, the door opens behind him, and another man enters. He's about ten years older than Dante and vaguely familiar, though I'm a hundred per cent sure I've never seen him before. The moment he enters, Dante snaps back from wherever his mind has wandered. His back straightens, and he gives the man a sharp nod. "Thanks for coming. I know it's the middle of the night."

The man doesn't look like he's just been woken up. Quite the opposite. He could've walked straight into a corporate meeting and never missed a step. "Some matters can't wait." He settles his attention on me, and I finally understand who he is. The scrutinising, slightly disgusted expression is the same I've seen each day in battle training. This must be Carina's father, Wulf's foster father.

"So, you're the little troublemaker?" His voice is as slick as oil. "I've spent the last forty-eight hours cleaning up your mess."

Looks like I'm going to like him even less than his daughter. "My mess?"

"An explosion at the SSA Academy? A multi-spirit attack? From the outside, of course, not the inside," he clarifies, telling me how he spun the story for the press. "One of your classmates was hurt. You were lucky the commander of the Roman spirit seekers was present."

Oh no. Not this again. I won't fall for this a second time. "I'm not a troublemaker. You don't get to blame this on me."

"Who else should I blame it on?" He cocks his head as if he's hard of hearing. "Were you not the one who released all the spirits and blew a hole through the wall?"

"No. In fact, I wasn't. Your daughter released the spirits in a temper tantrum, and the spirits made the hole." That's it. Facts over whatever twisted version they want to serve me. "You don't get to paint me as the villain here." The way Dante has completely removed himself from the confrontation tells me who's really in charge of the SSA. "What did you think I'd do? When you kidnap me, drag me halfway across Europe, and force me into your academy! Of course, I'd seize the opportunity to run." I spread my arms and snort. "I'm in a fucking prison cell!"

Let's just say criticism doesn't go well with Signore Vallesco. Angry red blotches appear on his cheeks and a murderous look enters his eyes. He might as well be frothing. "You're a danger to the world. The nonsense you spout, combined with your reckless behaviour, could undo everything the SSA has worked for."

Somehow, that doesn't really bother me. Let the SSA burn, for all I care. "Good! Let it be undone! Perhaps we can form something better from the rubble left behind. Something sustainable."

"You have no idea what you're talking about, miss." His voice is like a whip cracked mid-air.

I'm done with being afraid of these people, though. They're scared of me! They're afraid that one little Traveller girl could show the world what frauds they are. How they're warmongering fanatics who build their legacy on fear. "Oh, I know a lot more than you think. And I won't be silenced. I won't let you brainwash me like you do everyone else, including your own... Is it brother-in-law?" I check with Dante for confirmation, but he looks tired rather than rebellious. "I'll prove to the world that there are other ways—peaceful ways."

"You're not particularly in a position to make such threats," Signore Vallesco snarls.

He's got a point there. After everything I've said, they'll probably let me rot in this cell. Nevertheless, I decide to grab the bull by the horns. "What? You're gonna stoop to murder now?" I can feel myself shaking. With fear or rage, I don't know. It's all become one.

All of a sudden, Signore Vallesco smiles. It's even worse than his scowl. "Now, that would be barbaric. I think you might've mistaken us for the Mafia." In my opinion, they're pretty much the same thing.

He turns away and faces Dante. "Tomorrow, Rika will return to her lessons."

"I won't do that." What does he think will happen? That I'll sit down quietly and keep my mouth shut? "I'm certainly not becoming a spirit seeker."

Nobody cares about my protest. Dante is frowning, likely thinking the same. Perhaps they'll have Gian sit next to me at all times. I wonder how they'll explain that to the others.

Signore Vallesco has his back to me as he elaborates. "I think it's time for some private lessons in the Colosseum."

The way Dante pales scares me more than the ominous words. Even private lessons with Carina wouldn't elicit such a strong reaction. "She's not ready for that. She's hardly a beginner."

"She's got an NAV of over 500. I'm expecting great things from her." At last, Mr Vallesco turns back to me, baring his teeth as he smiles. "Show us what you can do, little girl, won't you?"

I'm left speechless. Mr Vallesco doesn't wait for a reply. He nods to Dante and leaves the room, probably to return to bed or to chair a SSA business meeting.

When the door has closed, Dante lets out a monumental sigh. His eyes are full of sadness as he turns to me. "All you had to do was listen to me." And with that reassuring food for thought, Dante leaves as well.

I remain alone in the small room, locked behind steel. Something terrible is going to happen tomorrow, and I have no idea what it might be.

# 19

I can't sleep. I don't want to, either. All I want is to get out of here. Preferably before morning comes. I've banged against the doors until my hands bled, and screamed and shouted until my voice broke. Now, I'm sitting in my spot against the wall, knees huddled to my chest. If anybody in this school has heard me, they've ignored me.

I'm tired, and I guess sleeping would be beneficial for whatever it is I'll have to face tomorrow. The problem is, knowing that something *will* happen tomorrow makes it impossible to fall asleep. Signore Vallesco said my training would continue, but why would that make Dante regretful? What's this new training I'm going to face? In the Colosseum, of all places. I have to admit I know little about the ancient monument. Obviously, even I've seen pictures of the round walls and multitude of empty windows. It's a ruin now, but during Rome's Golden Age, it was an entertainment hub; a vast arena where gladiators fought to the death. Oh, yeah, that definitely doesn't help with sleeping.

Nevertheless, my eyes are growing heavy, and I find my chin dropping, when the door opens. Talk about timing.

I'm wide awake in an instant, looking at Gian, who's come to pick me up. Even he seems out of sorts today, missing his carefree arrogance. It's all business this morning as he gives me a sharp nod. "Let's go."

Instead of upstairs, we go down to the garage. Dante's already waiting by the car, dressed sharp as always. "You ready, Rika?"

"For what?" This would all be a lot less unnerving if they bothered with information.

"To continue your training," is all Dante explains before he takes a seat in the car.

Gian forces me into the backseat, and I find myself locked off from the outside world and the two men in the front by tinted windows and a pulled-up wall between the seats. I hear the motor starting and sense the car rolling. Gingerly, I test the doors. Locked, of course.

It's not a long drive, not really worth all the effort, but I guess dragging me down the street wouldn't go too well with Signore Vallesco's smoothing-the-feathers campaign. We stop, and when the door finally opens, I get my first proper look at the day.

It's earlier than I thought it would be. In the cell, it seemed like hours passed, but the sky is still dark, though a faint band of grey is visible in the East. Right in front of me is the Colosseum. It's huge! There's something awe-inspiring about standing in front of a structure you know so well from pictures. We're so close to the back I can hardly capture it all in a single gaze. Dark walls are broken by rounded window holes in four rows—or two on the side where the upper half has toppled down.

I'm so in awe I barely notice Gian grabbing my upper arm and dragging me inside. Dante has the keys to what seems to be a back entrance opposite the tourist's one. I don't know when the Colosseum opens, but the reason we're here so early is probably so we can be done by then. Despite all the window holes, it's dark in the hallway Dante leads us through. At last, we arrive at a small set of stairs leading down to a gate.

"This is where the gladiators were held before it was their time in the arena," Dante explains. His voice echoes slightly from the ancient walls. "Now it's part of our training facilities, though they haven't been used since March."

What happened in March that made the SSA close their doors to this facility? And why are they happy to reopen them for me?

Dante hands me a battle staff, making it clear I'm expected to fight spirits. "Try to... Just give it a try."

Wow. So, there's not even a tip before I'm sent into the unknown. Dante opens the gate, and Gian pushes me forward until the only step I can take will take me inside the Colosseum. "Go."

I find myself shivering with anticipation. There'll be a spirit down here or more. So what? I faced trapped spirits in the castle and managed to convince them. Surely this will be no different. I guess if breaking even more of the Colosseum is my only way out of here, then that's what I'll have to do.

Finding my determination, I step through the gate and down the hallway. The gate closes behind me, but I refuse to look back. The only way out lies forward.

The Romans left behind a maze of half-broken walls and grass-covered floors. I assume it was once all covered by what would be the arena floor, but that's been gone for a long time.

As I go through the empty hallways, I feel... warm. Not that it was freezing before, but it's definitely comfortable now. Perhaps even a bit more than that, considering it's still technically night and in open territory. It's about then I realise something huge is in the arena, so huge I didn't notice until I walked right through it. Or is it over it?

I stop and test the ground gingerly. It's firm, and yet I can't help expecting it to crack and swallow me at any moment. What if there's a second layer of catacombs? One filled with spirits?

Subconsciously, my hand's been gripping the smooth black wood tighter. What am I doing? I don't want to fight any spirits, and certainly not with the chopped-off body part of an unfortunate dryad. I drop the staff on the ground and walk away from it.

My fingers brush over the stones on either side, noting they aren't cold to the touch as they should be. Then the remnant of the hallway I'm following opens into what would've been a room or a cell like mine. I've barely set foot into it when the ground underneath rumbles.

*Earthquake!* I step away from the walls into the middle, not wanting to be crushed by toppling ruins. Nothing falls, though, and the ground settles. Until it doesn't.

With no warning, the ground beneath my feet bulges, and the heat rises instantly. I slip and fall to my knees as the ground cracks. I waste no time getting to my feet and scramble away until I hit one of the surrounding walls. Pressed against the stone, I see the cracks glowing red. I only grasp what I'm seeing when the red flows out of the ground. Lava. The heat wave hits me when the top of the floor explodes and what looks like a miniature volcano forms.

This isn't natural. Or not in any way nature should behave. Volcanoes don't suddenly pop up in ancient ruins, emitting lava as well as hate. I'm strongly reminded of the Erlking and the words he once inscribed into my flesh. This spirit hates me as much as he did, and I haven't even met them yet.

From the crater, a creature is clawing its way out of the earth. Two arms as thick as power poles shift away the rock to pull themselves up from the lava. A head takes shape, culminating in ember-like eyes and a deep, dark hollow that I assume is his mouth. Every centimetre of his skin is flowing lava. The heat shimmers around him. He isn't a salamander like the ones I'm used to. He's not even a lava crawler, which

I've only heard of. He's his own beast. An emperor among spirits, risen like the ghosts from the past.

Perhaps I shouldn't have given up the battle staff Dante so kindly provided me with, but then it wouldn't make that much of a difference. The dryads told me they keep their distance from the Colosseum, so I don't think their wood could withstand the heat of a volcano.

His eyes settle on me. He takes in my sorry figure with contempt. The heat rises as the hatred grows. It's now singeing the hairs on my skin. It isn't until a mighty roar shakes the earth under my feet that I finally manage to take my eyes off him and move.

I scramble back to the hallway, or maybe it's a different one, leading me into another room instead of back to the gate. I don't care. I just run.

The volcano spirit comes after me, not running or anything like that, but moving through the earth. Lava erupts in front of me, blowing up a wall. I turn around and scramble to find another way. The next earthquake sends me flying on my face. Rocks topple above me, barely missing my head as they tumble to the ground.

"I'm here to talk!" I scream, covering my head with my arms and trying to make myself as small as possible.

Beneath me, the ground grows warmer and warmer until it's unbearably hot, and I jump up again, stumbling backwards, away from the spot before it erupts into lava again.

I don't want to fight him. I *can't* fight him. So, how do I stop him from killing me?

The answer is 'not at all'. I can run, but I can't hide. This is his territory, his realm, and I'm the intruder, the most hated person in his world. Or so it appears.

The approaching lava flow makes me spin on my feet and bolt. In every corner, the spirit awaits me, toppling stone walls and melting the ground. Earthquakes slam me into the rock. I twist my ankles and abrade every joint in my body. Smoke has filled the Colosseum, making it hard to breathe.

I've lost all sense of orientation. I just run where he lets me pass, knowing I can never escape him. At one point, I cross the battle staff I dropped earlier, but before I can even think about picking it up, the spirit has seized it and snapped it in half. The sound of the wood bursting sends a shudder through my bones, as if they were on the receiving end of his force. Then the wood is set aflame. It chars and burns up within seconds.

My face is wet with tears and I'm whimpering. "It wasn't mine," I say, as if this spirit cares one bit. He knows I can see him, knows that I'm a spirit seeker.

He roars again, and my feet fly over the grassy hallways, not because I think I could ever outrun him, but because my body only knows this primal reaction. This is what people warned me of. This is what parents tell their children, so they behave. The spirits have no mercy. They'll tear down everything in their way.

Suddenly, I'm in front of the gate, or another gate. I push against the bars with all my might, but these are modern bars, not ones that have rusted away, and it's locked. Despair hits me, and I lean my head against it

Behind me, the heat rises, and I know even as I turn that this time, there's no escape. There's nowhere to run to.

The bars are pressing against my back. In front of me, the spirit takes on his humanoid shape once more, walking now. Each step sends tremors through the ground, as if I wasn't shaking enough already.

"I'm sorry," I whimper.

It's exactly the wrong thing to say. Hate hits me even harder than the heat. He must restrain the latter, or I would've burnt to a crisp already.

"Sorry? *You* are sorry?" His voice is a deep rumble that vibrates in my stomach like a heavy bass.

I understand now that no apology would ever suffice for whatever's been done to him. They've trapped him here. In this human structure, far from the lava conduits of his home. He doesn't belong in Rome. But he's strong. He can melt this entire city down, so why doesn't he? "What have they done to you?"

"What...?" He halts just a metre in front of me. The heat from his body melts through the rocky skin encasing him, yet it doesn't reach me. The hate abates, leaving behind a waft of suspicion. "Who are *they*?"

I wet my lips, hoping I won't pass out from fear. Though that might be the preferable option. "The other spirit seekers. The SSA. They forced me to be here, too." Should I really try to commiserate with this ancient spirit? Surely, my life doesn't matter to anything like him. Nevertheless, I find myself saying, "They want you to kill me." It doesn't even surprise me, now that I think about it. I'm a troublemaker and obviously beyond any manipulation that could've saved my ass. That's why Dante was so full of regret when he'd left last night. He'd failed to convert me, and now I'll pay the price.

The spirit comes closer, so close I can barely breathe without burning my lungs. "You're the one that northern salamander talked about."

"You talked to Glut?"

"You know his name?" The hate has dissipated, replaced by confusion.

I realise I know his name, too. "You're Vesuvius." The spirit they caught in March; that Wulf caught in March. I'm about to pass out.

"I am." He stands tall, and for a moment, rage pours out of him.

I get it now. He's been a prisoner of the SSA's ever since Wulf completed the mission that pulled him away from Berlin in winter. I was in awe of Wulf then, impressed by how anyone could willingly fight a volcanic eruption and come out on top. But so many things have happened since then, and I no longer believe stopping the eruption was necessary. Not like this, at least. "What did he do to you?" My voice almost falters, not wanting to know about Wulf's heroic yet damning deed.

Vesuvius lowers his head until he's almost at my eye-level. His hands wrap around the bars next to my head. This time, his voice is the hiss of gas escaping a vent. "He stole my eggs."

A sizzling sound next to my ears makes me jump forward. I'm now standing right in front of Vesuvius, but though he's hot, he's no longer out to burn me. Instead, I pick up the sound of something dripping behind me. I take a couple of seconds to build up the courage to check what's happening. When I finally do, Vesuvius has already melted down half of the bars.

"You're letting me go?" I ask, not daring to hope.

"Help me find my eggs." It's not a bargain, but a demand.

I almost wet myself with gratitude. "I will." I mean, I have no idea where to start, but as long as I'm alive, I can always figure that part out.

The rest of the gate gives way. A blob of molten metal is all that's left. "Hide. Quickly."

I hear steps behind me. Tourists. Or did Dante stay? Either way, I hasten out the hole in the wall, run up the short flight of stairs, and duck under the tarp hanging from a scaffolding set up to stabilise the Colosseum.

I'm hidden from sight not a minute too early. Through the slit between tarp and floor, I see Dante and Gian return. Dante's holding one of the ancient staffs; I assume the only one left in the SSA. He holds it in front of him, jaw set.

"Back with you!" he shouts at Vesuvius, who growls with anger. "Return to the centre, or else!"

The unspoken threat makes my blood boil. Yes, a volcanic eruption is a terrible thing to behold, and I can understand trying to stop it, but using children as a bargaining chip? That's vile. I'm sure, to the SSA, these eggs aren't the children of a spirit, just something bearing potential for future destruction, yet they use them for blackmail just the same.

Once more, the earth shakes, then I sense Vesuvius retreat from the exit.

"Is it safe?" Gian asks, not sounding so sure now.

Dante takes a while to answer. He's looking down, though I don't know what could've caught his eye. "He'll stay."

Another long moment of silence passes. Once again, it's Gian who breaks it. "So, she's dead?"

I almost snort. He doesn't need to sound so regretful. It's not like he didn't know what he was condemning me to.

"I'm afraid so." Now, Dante's playing the sorrowful one. I almost bring up some bile. "We'll tell the others she tried to free Vesuvius as well and... paid the price."

I'm shaking with anger. So, after all that, they're going to spin my murder into some kind of cautionary tale for future spirit seekers? It's just as well their steps are receding, because I want to burst out of this hiding spot and strangle them. Exploiting my death! How dare they!

But then another thought penetrates my fury. Dante and Gian believe I'm dead. And so will everyone else at the SSA. I'm free. No one will search for me, no one will put me back in my cell, or force me to hurt spirits. I'm finally free to do whatever I want.

At least for a little bit.

<h1 style="text-align:center">20</h1>

Vesuvius and I have settled in what was once a chamber but is now nothing but charred grass and tumbled walls. The sun has finally conquered the sky, turning it into another spotless day. It's still too early for tourists. I reckon it's a couple of hours still, if they open at ten as usual.

Now that Vesuvius doesn't want to kill me anymore, it's like sitting next to an open oven door. A little too hot for comfort, but comparatively safe. Before long, a couple of smaller salamanders have joined us, among them Glut, who crawls into my lap straight away.

"Did you find yourself a nice volcano?" I joke unsteadily. Though Dante and Gian are far away, I'm still shaking from what they've put me through. A lot of shit has happened to me over the last eight years, but no one's tried to murder me in cold blood. Or hot fire.

Glut puffs out a little smoke cloud. "Very nice. And warm."

I stroke his back, mainly to calm myself.

Meanwhile, Vesuvius observes me. "You came back."

I could've fled after Dante and Gian left, but I wouldn't dare. Vesuvius spared my life, and I owe him. "You asked me to help you find your eggs." I still don't know what to make of the fact that Wulf kidnapped what are essentially babies in order to capture a spirit as powerful as a volcano.

"And you actually care," he says, sounding more confused than surprised. "Are you that frightened?"

I'm frightened enough to break into a thousand pieces, but that's not really the point. "I... I don't think what Wulf did was right." I remember that Wulf probably didn't introduce himself to Vesuvius when he took his eggs. "The spirit seeker who took your eggs. He... he must've had a reason." I can't bring myself to say "good reason", because there isn't any. You wouldn't take someone's babies hostage, so why would you do that to spirits?

"If he hadn't taken them, I would've swallowed him whole," Vesuvius growls. Though his words might suggest otherwise, he's not sympathetic or understanding. "He and the others came into my home. They were the intruders."

His anger makes the air shimmer, and I find myself breathing more shallowly. In terms of power, it's like I'm talking to an unsecured grenade. "I get it," I admit, though my distaste for Wulf's action fades a little. He only did it to save his life. "They entered your sanctuary and pushed forward. It's just... you were erupting. Why?" I wet my lips, preparing myself for spontaneous combustion. "Why do you make the volcano erupt so violently?" After all, the spirit seekers were only responding to an emergency.

"Why does the sun burn? Or the rain fall? It's the way things are. You can't expect an ocean to stop its waves or the wind to stop howling. So why would you stop me from erupting?"

He makes some interesting points. Not all volcanoes erupt, though. Some sleep for millions of years. "There are people living nearby. If the lava had got to them, they would've died."

"And why would I care about people?" he asks in the same voice someone might ask about ants. "They're settling on what is mine. Do you not kill the rodent that infests your house?"

Another good point. Humans are literally everywhere. It reminds me of the conversation I had with Dante about how overpopulation was certainly a problem, but human life would always come first. It's only natural the spirits think the same way. Are we truly doomed to always be at war? Is this world too small for both of our species?

"Well, I don't have a house. Never owned one." I shrug. "Rodents don't bother me. They're annoying, especially when they steal your food, but I wouldn't go out of my way to kill them."

"I didn't go out of my way. They're simply in the way. They've built as close as they could, and because that wasn't enough, they send people up my summit every day." Vesuvius snorts, emitting two clouds of smoke. "There are just too many."

"I get it." If he weren't several hundred degrees hot, I'd pat his arm. "I just fear it can't be changed."

Obviously, that was a challenge since, once again, he rumbles loudly. "It can. They're a pest to be burnt off Earth. Starting with those who call themselves spirit seekers. What are they seeking us for if not for battle and ruin?"

I wonder if the spirit seekers ever examined their name. "A dryad told me there used to be true spirit seekers." A terrible thought comes to me. The true spirit seekers existed, but the SSA took their name for themselves to twist and pervert it. A common strategy. I shake my head and continue. "True spirit seekers are people who sought spirits for advice and protection. They struck bargains and worked together to carve out a life for each other." How easy would it have been for the spirits to wipe us all off the Earth when we were only a few? I guess they never thought we would grow to be so many.

"Will you hold up your end of the bargain?" Vesuvius asks, a smidgeon of anxiety in his voice.

This one is a simple answer. "Of course I will. I keep my word. I... I just don't know where to start, and... Well, the SSA is a powerful organisation. I'll do my best, but they might kill me before I get to them." Quickly, I swallow, as if that could take the words back. I don't want to die, but I owe Vesuvius, and I also can't bear the thought that the SSA might win. That they can keep a powerful spirit like Vesuvius captive in their city while probably experimenting on his eggs. That they can murder me and get away with it. "Actually, I have an idea of where they keep them."

"Where?" he asks greedily, his eyes glowing.

"In their university. I don't know for sure, but I believe it's where they keep all the spirits they trap. I was planning to free them before Dante caught me." Or rather, my mother caught me. Did she realise finding me might get me murdered? Would she care? It bothers me more than anything that I no longer know the answer to that.

Tears are stinging in my eyes when Vesuvius suddenly raises a wall of lava behind me. As it cools, black rock appears, hiding us from sight. It's only after that I hear someone calling out. It's far away as first, but then the words become audible.

"Vesuvius! Is it true? Did you kill her?"

My heart skips several beats as I recognise the voice. Before I can fully process it, I'm on my feet, running around the newly erected wall, and throw myself around Wulf's neck. "You're here!"

Not expecting me or my sudden onslaught, Wulf stumbles backward, barely getting his staff out of his way. He drops it to press one of his arms against my back and the other hand against my head, breathing shakily into my hair. "You're alive. Oh, gosh, you're alive."

Almost instantly, a soft breeze breathes through my hair, and I can no longer hold back my tears. Aeola came as well. "We were so worried about you."

"I was, too." My voice cracks, and still Wulf holds onto me for dear life. "I'm okay," I manage to say, though my breath comes short and quick. "Vesuvius didn't kill me. We were just talking."

A laugh breaks free of Wulf's lips, shaky and unsure, but full of relief. "Of course you'd make friends with a volcano."

Just then, the ground beneath us vibrates. A wave of heat rolls over my back, and I sense the hate Vesuvius swallowed for me flare up again.

In an instant, Wulf pushes me behind him and picks up his battle staff. Aeola wraps herself around me, protecting me from the blast of hot air. I look around just in time to see Vesuvius lunge forward.

"Don't!" I push past Wulf and jump in between the two. Aeola flees to the air to avoid becoming super-heated. "He's changed. He's not the same anymore." Panicked, I look at Wulf, who's set for a fight.

Reluctantly, he drops his gaze to meet mine, and I see he's wary as well as determined. "I..." All the tension seems to flood out of him. He drops his shoulders and bends down to lay his staff on the ground. When he rises again, he turns both hands outward. "I'm not looking for a fight."

"I am," Vesuvius declares, but he's stopped as well. "So, it's her I need to kill to get my vengeance." A chill runs down my back that feels even colder under all that sweat from earlier. "Or should I keep her under the earth, out of your reach, suffocating in a dark hole, until you give back what's mine?"

Forget the chill. This is like being doused in ice-water, thrown into a barrel of burning coals, and plunged back into the sea again. I don't doubt Vesuvius would do that to get what he wants. I'd hoped we had an understanding, but I'm just a human to him, after all. And I admitted that I probably wasn't the help he was looking for. But the thought of being stuck under the earth for who-knows-how-long is catching my breath in my throat and slowly squeezing all the rest of the air out of my lungs.

"You struck a bargain with her," a tiny voice says from underneath Vesuvius' feet. My little baby salamander is challenging a volcano for me.

"Vesuvius," Wulf says, pleading with all his heart. "Rika has done no wrong. She doesn't deserve to be punished or hurt. What happened is between the two of us. Take my life if you must, but let Rika go."

"No!" I don't want Wulf to die. What he did with Vesuvius' eggs was wrong, but I don't want him dead for it. "Please, Wulf will help me. He knows them. He... he can actually get them back."

Though I'm hardly coherent, Wulf pieces together the bargain I struck with Vesuvius. "You want your eggs. I'll get them," he promises, without even hesitating.

"You will?" Vesuvius asks, and for the first time since the two saw each other, the heat lowers.

"When I took them, I was desperate to stay alive. Desperate to fulfil my mission, but the mission was wrong, and I should've never agreed to take it on." Something has changed in Wulf. There's a new kind of pain I'm unfamiliar with. The Wulf I know was reluctant to work with spirits and conflicted about the SSA, but he wouldn't have stood against them. "I needed the eggs to get out alive, but I should've given them back once I did. So, I'll do that now. Just let her live. Please."

Vesuvius takes a long while to consider his words. I sense how tempted he is to swallow us both and be done with it, but at last, his gaze settles on me. "It seems like you're right. He truly has changed." Then he glowers at Wulf. "If you betray my trust, I will swallow this city and everyone within. I will have my eggs, one way or the other."

I have to give it to Wulf when he doesn't even flinch. "I'll set things right. I promise."

# 21

Wulf brings me to a small house near the Via Appia Antica, one of the oldest roads of Rome. For a moment, I'm afraid he's brought me back to the Vallescos, but this little abode probably doesn't even qualify as a bachelor pad to them. It's a small house, tucked away in between two larger ones and inconspicuous, but the view is amazing. I stand by the window in the small living room, my back to Wulf, and admire the long, solitary cypresses that appear like a painting.

"Whose house is this?" I ask at last. It's the first proper words I've spoken since we left the Colosseum. I still can't quite believe he's really here.

"It's a long story."

Reluctantly, I tear my gaze away from the peaceful view outside and face him. I can still feel his hot breath against my hair and the fervour with which he pressed my body against his, but the distance between us now couldn't be any wider. Wulf stands behind a table, watching me carefully, as if I might sprout wings and fly away at any moment. It's a gaze that wants so much and dares so little. I can't bear to see him like that.

Running a finger along my side of the table, I take in the rest of the house. There's an open-plan kitchen next to the living room. The light-blue paint on the cupboard is chipped, giving it an antique appearance. The wood has dulled by lack of use; the tapestry is a plain beige. A bowl of fresh fruit is an unexpected splash of colour against the washed-out tapestry. It's like somebody tried to mask the fact nobody truly lives here. It's a dead place for dead people.

I grasp the spokes of a wooden chair and hold on tight as a shudder runs through my body. The reality of what happened today is only now sinking in.

"Do you want something to drink?" Wulf asks, concern etched into his face.

I want to say yes, but my mouth has a different idea. "Why now?" Puzzlement passes over Wulf's face. "Why did you only come now?" How many weeks have passed since our return from Ireland? How many weeks have I spent locked up in a dark cell with nothing but my own fears to accompany me?

Wulf sighs. He gets out two glasses and fills them with water despite my lack of reply. As he sets them down on the table, he says, "I told you, it's a long story. Do you want to sit?"

"No." I feel as if I'll burst into tears as soon as I allow myself to relax. *Don't be silly, Rika. You've survived so much. Surely, you can sit down and have a drink with someone who isn't out to get you.* But is he really? My own mother sold me out.

Just then, a soft breeze brushes my cheek. "You're safe now," Aeola whispers, wrapping me in her air.

Having her by my side makes it easier to let go of the chair and sit down. My fingers wrap around the glass of water and hold it as tight as I did the chair. Unable to return Wulf's worried glance, I stare into the water.

"I had no idea where you were," Wulf starts softly. He sits down at the opposite side of the table, still keeping the furniture between us.

"Aeola came to me, said some evil woman had taken you prisoner, but by the time I ran outside, you were gone."

The water shakes as my grip tightens. I haven't forgotten the feel of the gun's nuzzle against my back. "Her name was Agnes."

If he knows her, he doesn't show it. "I tried finding you at first. Aeola flew through the entire city, but there was no trace of you. So, the next thing I did was call Dante."

Waves of water lap against the glass. My shoulders are drawn back, pressing my elbows against my ribs. How could someone as compassionate as Wulf be friends with someone as murderous and manipulative as Dante? How can he call a guy like that family?

"Aeola said it was a spirit seeker who took you, so I checked with him first." A quick glimpse tells me that Wulf is still watching me closely. "He said he hadn't heard of you, but that he'd keep an eye out."

"He's a liar!" And so much more.

Wulf sighs heavily. "That's what I was afraid of. He suggested you were taken by rogue spirit seekers. Apparently, the SSA had traced a couple of them back to Berlin. Dante gave me all the investigative data on them, convincing me they might've been interested in you."

"And you believed him?" I ask incredulously, finally looking up. Even without knowing what happened to me since, Wulf must've known that Dante can't be trusted. Yet, he was still first on Wulf's list to call.

"I didn't," Wulf replies, looking strained. "I wanted to, but I couldn't. Not after everything Brigid and Rory told us in Dublin. If any of it was true, I realised he'd lie to me. Still, I'd hoped he wouldn't actually go that far. After all, I'm his... I guess I'm nothing to him." Now it's he who looks down.

I try to tell myself how hard it must be for Wulf to learn everything he's believed was built on a lie, but right now, I'd take pretty lies over being abducted, tortured, and almost murdered.

Wulf shakes off his personal disappointment and faces me again. "I couldn't leave that stone unturned in case he'd been telling the truth, so I followed up on it and found the rogue seekers. This is one of their safe houses."

"You went rogue?" Now *that's* surprising.

"Well, I didn't really feel like giving them up to the SSA once we'd sat down and had a chat. I don't like being used... anymore." I pick up from his voice that a lot's happened since I last saw him. When we left Dublin, a huge part of him was still hanging onto the SSA. But they manipulated him just like everybody else, brainwashing him since he was a little boy.

He shrugs dejectedly and continues, "Meanwhile, I contacted Rory for help. He told me he had a contact at the academy and could find out in a way that wouldn't alert Dante and my..." *Family.* The word remains unspoken. After all, what do you call a loved one who'll murder people to get their way?

"Eoghan." Slowly, I'm putting the pieces together. "He's one of the elite students."

Wulf frowns slightly. "I've heard of him. Dante tells... used to tell me all about the promising prospects who came through the academy. So, Eoghan's one of them, then. Another rogue seeker."

"You don't need to sound so disappointed," I hear myself saying. Instantly, I take a shaky breath. It's not Wulf's fault his family's a bunch of psychopaths. "I'm sorry. It's... I don't know what it is." So many weeks I've waited for him, and now he's finally here, I can't bear his presence. Everything we've built together has been washed away. Every chasm we've bridged has widened again. Too much about him reminds me of those who hurt me. "It's just that I'm one of them, as well."

"I'm aware of that." Wulf swallows. "Me, too. I guess." He takes a deep breath after this extraordinary admission. The Wulf I know believes full-heartedly in his mission. "A lot's happened, and each day I'm less sure of what to think, of what to believe. Honestly, I'm drowning. Or I would be, if it weren't for you." His voice becomes more urgent as he stretches a hand out to me. "I'm on your side. That is the one thing I'm a hundred per cent sure of. You're the only thing that still makes sense in this world, and I can't tell you how glad I am to find you alive."

Alive, but not well. Still, I remember his tight embrace once more. Wulf believes in me. He came for me. He's still willing to accept the challenges I present, perhaps even more so now than before. With that in mind, I manage to let go of the glass and put my hand into his. As he grabs my fingers tight and smiles, I feel a knot loosen in my chest. "You never gave up on me." Not like my mother.

"Never," he says, more decisively than anything he's said today. "As soon as Rory told me that Eoghan had met you and Dante had indeed lied to me, I came to Italy. But when I arrived, you'd already left the academy. Something about a spirit prison break?"

So close. We missed each other by mere hours. "I may have freed some of the training spirits."

Wulf chuckles softly, but then a shadow passes over his face. "I never told you. I'm sorry."

I let go of his hand, staring to the side. That's right. Wulf never told me the elite spirit seekers train with live spirits. "I guess there's much I don't know about the SSA." And to think that just a month or two ago Wulf would've sent me to the academy. I shiver.

"Rika…"

"He's learning," Aeola says softly, wrapping me a little tighter in her embrace.

A moment later, I hear his chair sliding across the floor. When I look up in surprise, Wulf is already halfway around the table and goes down on one knee beside me, looking up. "I know there's no excuse. I was blind, still am blind, but I'm trying. You were right about all of it, and it hurt. Never in a million years would I have believed the SSA would abduct people at gunpoint. And I feel... I feel stupid. I grew up with the Vallescos. Dante was my mentor, and yet I failed to notice any of this. And I'm like... when would I have learnt of it?"

He shakes his head and runs his hands over his face, looking as tired as I am. "They want me on the board once I retire from active service. I've known about it for years. I hadn't yet figured out how to feel about it and whether it was something I wanted, but now I'm horrified. I'm horrified I would've said yes and become a person who'd order these crimes for the sake of protecting the agency." He scoffs, his face full of pain. "That's why I'm here, in this place. In my home city, but not at home. I hadn't even told Carina I was coming. I didn't want her to lie to me as well."

Carina. There's another one of Wulf's foster family who didn't quite make a good impression on me. "I met her. I don't think she likes me very much."

Wulf snorts. "I wouldn't have expected her to. She's not exactly an easy person."

I wince. "Try spiteful, instead."

A shadow passes over his face. "Do you want to tell me what happened?" He looks so helpless, broken in a way I've never seen him before. Or maybe it's my own brokenness that's reflected in his face.

My mind forms several words; about Carina's murderous training circuit, my failed escape in Austria, Dante's gaslighting attempts, my cell, or my mother. But instead of sentences, only a sob comes out of my mouth, and then another. In an instant, I'm wrapped up in Wulf's arms again. He holds me as close as he held me in the Colosseum. For a few minutes, I try to explain all that's happened to me, but all I've got for him are tears. Gosh, I'm tired.

Wulf holds me with all the patience in the world. I don't think he's ever seen me cry, and certainly not this much. I used to be so strong, with a skin as tough as concrete built around me. Now here I am, bared to the naked flesh, for all the world to hurt me. And comfort me. That's another new thing.

"I haven't slept since yesterday," I finally admit. All this crying has only exhausted me more. "Or bathed since..." After Vesuvius' ashfall, I must look even worse than usual.

Wulf leans back his head to take my sight in, smiling as he does. "Well, in that case, I'll show you the shower. I'm sorry I didn't think of it. There's a bed upstairs. No garden, unfortunately."

For the first time in a long while, a bed sounds more promising. At least in there, nobody can jump on me. "A bed is enough."

"Alright." Flustered, he stands, pointing to a small corridor. "The shower is over there. There should be a towel. If not, shout out. Do you want some food before you go to sleep? I could make some quick toast or something."

I love how little he pushes me, concentrating on mundane things, such as nutrition and hygiene. It helps me dry my tears and pull myself together. One day, I'll tell him all of it, but for now, food, shower, and a safe space to sleep are top of my list.

#

When I open my eyes again, night has fallen, which means I must've slept twelve hours or more. The room Wulf led me to is not much bigger than the cell at the academy, but it has a broad window that

I've left open all day long. Now the wind's blowing the curtains inside, white billows that mirror Aeola, who's floating next to my bed in the darkness.

"Do you need something? Should I get Wulf?" she asks as soon as I stir.

I shake my head. "Give me a minute to adjust." I rub my eyes, which are awfully dry after all the tears I've shed. Someone has left a set of clean clothes by the door. A shirt and some leggings, nothing fancy. I hope they've burnt that SSA training shirt. I try to shake off the unhelpful thoughts and turn my attention to the sylph. "How have you been?"

"I was worried," Aeola says promptly. "There was nothing I could do. I could only watch and let you go."

"You felt helpless," I suggest, getting all warm and fuzzy. Spirits experience the world different to us. When I met Aeola, she didn't know worry. Now she does. I should be sad about it, but knowing she cares heals something in me. "It sucks. Feeling helpless, I mean. There are so many things we can't change. I used to walk away from them. Now I want to try and face them instead."

I haven't told Wulf yet, but I haven't given up on my original plan. As I focus on that, it becomes easier to push all other emotions away. "I think I figured out where they're keeping Vesuvius' eggs and all the spirits they've trapped. I want to free them. All of them"

"That could be dangerous," Aeola says. "What if they attack you?"

With a shrug, I answer, "Then they'd still be free."

"I don't want anyone to hurt you!" Aeola is surprisingly passionate, blowing into my face as she says so.

"But everyone does it anyway." Maybe she's right. All she can do is watch me get hurt. Gosh! What's wrong with me? Why am I blaming the two people who truly care for me for things they have no control over? Tears are back to annoy me, and I realise what's shaken me so much. "I found my mum," I admit, almost quaking with emotion.

Aeola swoops over excitedly. "You did? Is she... is she okay?"

"I guess so." I blink heavily, trying my best not to be swept away by emotion again. It sucks being so vulnerable. "She hates me. Or... I don't know. She works for them! She's a professor, teaching spirit seekers all the secrets of your kind, so they can fight them better. She heeds Dante's every call, and she..." I pant. "She tracked me down to deliver me to him. If it weren't for her, I would've been safe. Dante would never have tried to murder me." Well, I wouldn't have been safe, but she definitely contributed to my trauma. "What kind of mother does that? I spent eight years looking for her and she... she... she isn't even real!" The mother I longed for certainly wasn't.

Aeola looks at me with wide eyes, full of sorrow. "My father never cared what happened to me."

Her father, the Erlking. "But he never did. I'm sorry. It's just that the woman who lives in the academy is not my mum. It's not the person I knew and loved so much. Who loved me." I lose my battle against the tears. I pull up my knees and wrap my arms around them, letting Aeola brush her wind over my hair like the comforting touch I've craved so much from my mother.

"You don't need her," Aeola says softly. "I know you miss her, but you've managed on your own for so long. You're strong and compassionate, full of hope for both humans and spirits. If she's not on board with that, then that's her loss. You don't need her to guide the way." As I raise my head, frowning, Aeola smiles. "You're the guide. You're the one who shows us the future that can be. At least, you show me. And Wulf." She giggles suddenly. "And Lukas and the others. Did you know Lukas took up meditating? Each day, he sits a little closer to Grune. When we left, he was just barely under his branches."

I can see Lukas edging closer to the danger zone each day. The image is so vivid in my mind I have to laugh. "I can't believe he stuck to his promise." He wanted me to teach him, but I never had a chance. "Does it help?"

"He's become more at ease, I'd say. Just a bit," Aeola admits. "He's still blind as a bat."

Once again, a laugh bursts from my lips. "He must be terribly frustrated." Lukas is used to succeeding on every course he sets himself. His breakdown in Dublin was when he couldn't do that anymore.

"He's all right. Leon keeps his feathers smoothed. Speaking of Leon, he's got a girlfriend." Aeola is so excited the room charges, and my hair is rising.

"He does?"

"Well, I think so. He likes Inga. She's one of the rogue spirit seekers who came with us. She's probably downstairs. Her and Bijan came back earlier," Aeola explains.

"Bijan?" How much time has truly passed? It's like the world's kept turning while I've been stuck here. And there are strangers in this house. Wulf might work with them, but I don't know these rogue spirit seekers. They're not outspoken spirit activists. As far as I'm aware, they've just left the agency that taught them.

Aeola blows away the tears on my cheeks, leaving me a little wind-swept. "He's a software engineer, whatever that is. Wulf tried explaining it to me, but all I understand is that he sits in front of a computer for most of the day." It's amazing how comfortable Wulf and she have become with each other while I've been out of the picture. It makes me a bit jealous. "Anyway, he... hacks holes into the SSA and pulls out data."

I giggle. "He hacks into the SSA's database. There are no holes." The rogue spirit seekers are considered criminals, defectors who betrayed the

SSA for different reasons. "He's probably the one who hides their traces. Alright." I take a deep breath and clap the bed. "I think I'm ready to meet them. And talk to Wulf. We've got a promise to keep, after all."

"I'm glad you're better." Aeola flies up and seeps through the gaps in the door.

I throw off the blanket and get dressed quickly. Then I open the door and listen carefully. Downstairs, I can hear muffled voices. If it weren't for Aeola waiting on the stairs, I probably would've hidden in the room a little longer. Then my stomach rumbles, and that settles it.

"Hey," I say shyly as I enter the room.

Wulf and two strangers are sitting around the table, open pizza boxes and drinks between them. A Middle Eastern guy has his laptop up, while the tall woman with a strawberry-blonde ponytail is spreading out a previously rolled-up plan. The woman and Wulf glance up at me in surprise. Then Wulf's face stretches in a smile. "You're up. Do you want some pizza? We've still got heaps left."

Grateful for his offer, which allows me to be occupied, I sit down at his side. Wulf pulls a pizza carton closer and opens it, exposing a world full of cheese. "It smells delicious."

"Do you want a Coke, or a glass of wine?" the woman, who I assume is Inga, asks me. When I opt for the Coke, she turns around immediately to get it for me.

As I wait, I glimpse the building plan she's left behind. "What's that?"

"The SSA research lab at Sapienza," Wulf explains. "That's where they keep Vesuvius' eggs. I haven't exactly figured out where, though."

"Here you go," Inga says, handing me a can and sitting down again. "We're trying to find a way inside."

"So, you're all on board?" I ask innocently while picking the cheese off a slice and tasting it. The food in this country has been nothing but excellent, and this pizza is no exception. I don't think I can ever go back to a German replica after this.

"I've explained why we have to do it," Wulf says. "This whole experimenting on spirits is..."

"Disgusting?" Inga offers. Then she looks at me. "Decades of advocating for animal rights and we're doing the same thing to spirits. Or even worse. But it's okay because nobody can see them or hear their cries." She puffs out some air and shakes her head, deeply frustrated.

I think I like her. "Can you see them?"

Inga shakes her head. "My NAV is only around 200, but I know they're there. I mean, if you can fight and trap something, then it's obviously alive."

"So, you left the SSA because you didn't agree with how they dealt with trapped spirits?" I ask carefully.

"That's pretty much it. Whenever I asked why we were trying to catch all spirits, even if they didn't attack us, I was blown off." She seems pretty annoyed about it, though judging by her apparent age, it must be at least five years since she graduated from the academy. "It was all, 'but they could become a problem'. We don't go out and shoot all wolves or tigers because they *could* eventually become a problem. I mean, it's bad enough we do that once they attacked someone, but pre-emptively? Gosh, I could never get behind it." Slowly, she calms down and smiles. "I've tried the whole spirit seeker thing, but seeing all those traps lined up did something to me. So, one night, I took the current catch and ran away."

That settles it. I like her, and I strongly approve of whatever kind of relationship she might have with Leon. "And you?" I ask Bijan, who has been so focused on his screen he hasn't even looked at me yet.

Now that he does, I see he's quite good-looking. Heavy black brows, warm brown eyes, and gorgeous cheekbones. "How I went rogue?"

I nod, and he takes a moment, as if to remember correctly. "Well, I had a pretty shitty commander, didn't like her at all. So I tried to transfer myself and stumbled over some interesting details in my file. Apparently, I was yellow-coded, which stands for 'seems okay, but wouldn't trust with intel'. Well," he grins, showing slightly crooked but white teeth, "I love me some good intel. I think I should be trusted with all the intel." His grin fades as a shadow passes over his face. "Only, then I found the red-coded ones. A friend from the academy who never called. I did a little digging and found out he'd had a traffic accident. That's what happens to them. Heavy observation, unfortunate accidents, placements to the farthest or most dangerous corners of the world. And I don't mean spirit dangerous."

An icy chill runs down my back. "I guess I'm red-coded, then."

"You don't even have a file," Bijan exclaims. "For all intents and purposes, you don't exist." Then he nods at Wulf. "But he went down from a lovely shade of green to orange. Under active observation. Haven't found out who's observing him, though."

Wulf looks rather displeased, though it's obviously not news to him. "Apparently, the change happened a few weeks ago."

Heat burns in my cheeks. "I think that's my fault. I tried asking Carina to contact you, and then Dante came. He wasn't pleased to learn you'd had me tested and kept quiet about me."

"Or he figured when I asked about you and chose to lie to me." Wulf shrugs. "Anyway, right now, he doesn't know I'm here, and apparently thinks you're dead."

"Because I never existed in the first place." It's true. I don't even have an ID. Just then, something strikes me. "Do you have access to Magdaléna Csorba's file? C-S-O-R-B-A."

"A moment."

While Bijan returns to his laptop, Wulf raises an eyebrow at me. "Isn't that one of the new lecturers they hired a few years back?"

"You..." No, he had no idea. I never told him my mother's name. I scoff. He could've told me the whole the time. So could've Lukas. He probably learnt from her. But no, I kept my promise and never told anyone.

"Oh, heavily red-coded," Bijan says. "They let someone like that teach their youngsters? It says here she staged a coup at the academy when she was still a student. Protested for spirit rights, caused quite a movement. What the hell?"

I don't know if I should sigh in relief or disappointment. Knowing they haven't upgraded her should make me feel better about it, shouldn't it? I carefully test the words. "She's under heavy observation. I have no idea why they didn't have her killed, but perhaps it's because she knows so much about spirits. She's useful. They... they brainwashed her. When did she start teaching?"

"Five years ago."

So, it took them three years to get her there. Three years spent in a cell like mine, probably. With only Dante as a point of contact. Kind, charming Dante. No wonder she's so into him. I shake my head. "It doesn't matter. She's unreliable. Don't contact her."

Suddenly, Wulf's fingers are on mine, holding them gently. He frowns. "Who is she?"

I can't look at him, so I focus on the pizza instead. "My mother."

# 22

Bijan wants nothing more than to hack his way into the research lab, but when that fails, I come up with another idea. Now Wulf and I are back at the academy in the wee hours of morning. Turns out, they don't actually have tight security but are more like a university in that regard. Not that I've ever had the chance to find out before, since this is the first time I'm entering the Castel Sant'Angelo via the main entrance.

Inga has hidden my tell-tale blue hair under a blonde wig, which scratches horribly. I'm also wearing ridiculous sunglasses, but it doesn't really matter, since we don't encounter anyone, and if we did, Wulf would be the more interesting person by far. I wonder how he feels seeing his own face in so many displays. He leads me up a set of stairs to the normal bedrooms. I've never been up here. The cold stone has been covered with long carpets. The bedrooms are behind wooden doors, not soundproof metal ones. They're probably comfy, as well.

Thanks to Bijan, we know which room we're going for, and Wulf knows his way around these corridors blindly. He's still tense as hell, though. Last night, I told him all about my mother and the little I'd learnt about Dante. Not in front of the others, but up in my room. He listened, then he held me again, and we slept like that until Inga knocked on the door. If anything, he seems more determined than ever, but I'm afraid he's hurting.

"This is it," he says in front of a door like any other. "Room 232. You sure about this?"

Am I? I nod, anyway. What's the worst that could happen? I get caught again? In front of Wulf? "Let's do this." I knock on the door.

It takes a while, but I hear movement behind the door. Joana opens the door. "What's—" Her eyes fall on Wulf. "Are you for real?"

"I guess so," Wulf says. "Can we come in for a moment?" He doesn't want to be out here any longer than I do.

Joana opens the door wider. "Sure. Come on in." She's sharing the room with Henny, who sits upright in their bed, looking confused.

"How can we help? You're really him, aren't you?" I've never seen Joana this flustered. I guess it's not every day a living legend decides to walk into your bedroom. "What's going on?"

I take off my sunglasses and rub my nose, unsure how to proceed.

"Rika!" Henny jumps out of their bed and flings their arms around my neck, gasping. "What... I don't understand. They... they told us you were killed by a spirit. That you tried to free Vesuvius and got—"

"Fried? Roasted? Burnt to a crisp?" The sharp tone of my voice helps get Henny off my neck. They scrunch their nose in confusion.

Joana stares at me, her eyes even wider than before. "How is that possible?"

"I didn't try to free Vesuvius. I had no idea he was even there. But I will now." The time for keeping my intentions close to my heart is over.

"You can't do that," Henny protests, predictably. "He's an S-class spirit. If he's freed, he'll exact vengeance." They look up at Wulf. "Tell her."

"Vesuvius is my responsibility," he says, determined. "I was the one who tricked and captured him." Apparently, he's no longer holding back either. "I did it because I was fed the same crap you are, because

I believed it was necessary. That we had to control Vesuvius or people would die. There was doubt during the mission. Some said it was nothing but a vanity project. That the SSA wanted the fame of capturing a spirit as powerful as this. And they were willing to risk the lives of ten good spirit seekers on it, some fresh from the academy." As he speaks, his voice gets colder and colder. This is deeply personal to Wulf. "Two men died, one woman lost her eye, three teams were heavily sanctioned, and thus weakened. I lost my brother. And for what? So the SSA could parade their spirit around the Colosseum and use it as an executioner."

Henny's eyes widen even more. "An executioner?" Their gaze flickers back to me.

"Signore Vallesco called it 'special training'," I mumble. "Dante gave me a staff and pushed me through the door."

"But why? I don't understand. You were one of us. You're talented." Joana looks back and forth between us, unable to make sense of the situation.

I guess that means they never realised what was going on. "I didn't come here of my own free will. Dante called it 're-education'. The first week, or more, I was kept in a cell in the basement. I could only study once I pretended to forsake everything I believe. I'm sorry I lied. Gian was always hovering. And if I misstepped, it was back to the cell again." Talking about it makes my throat constrict. Despite all its comfort, their room is still made of stone.

"You weren't really sick," Henny finally surmises. "When you had that fight with Carina and refused to fight spirits..." They're so pale now it looks like they're gonna collapse.

Wulf steps forward. "It's a lot. This whole organisation is built on lies. I... I believed all of them until I met Rika."

"You've met before?" It's as if Joana only now realises we came here together.

The heat rises in my cheeks. "I may have lied about where I got my experience from... I *was* in Ireland. But Wulf and the rest of us travelled there together from Berlin."

"Yeah, she usurped my team while I was busy playing fetch for the board," Wulf jokes bitterly. "She's right, though. Fighting spirits isn't the only way to prevent deaths." He smirks. "I mean, I found her and Vesuvius making plans."

"So, you can talk to spirits!" Joana crosses her arms, looking smug.

I remember how it amazed her more than frightened her, and give a little shrug. "Yeah. It's really not that hard."

Wulf chuckles. "True. It's still awe-inspiring to watch her do it. Anyway..."

I blink quickly, as if that could keep the blush away from my cheeks. Joana laughs. "You need to teach me."

"So, if they did all these horrible things to you, why are you back?" Henny asks, recovering slowly from the surprise.

Straightening my back, I reply, "We need your help. Do you have an access key to the Sapienza research lab?"

"I do, but why—You want to free the spirits there." They take a deep breath, and I realise there isn't enough time to convince them. It took me weeks to get through to Wulf.

Joana, on the contrary, looks ready to start a rebellion. "Like you did in the courtyard?"

"You remember the project you're working on?" I ask Henny, who nods in response. Of course they do. "It's not just theoretical. Spirits have been combined, and it's the most terrifying thing I've ever experienced. It turns them vicious and unpredictable. It turns them into exactly the kind of monsters the SSA wants everyone to believe in."

"Only, they're ten times as strong and mess up all our trapping procedures," Wulf adds.

"We first encountered them in Budapest," I continue. "It took the entire team there and some brave dryads to defeat those spirits. That was a test run. And it worked so well the SSA employed them in Dublin. Henny, that project endangers people's lives. The SSA uses these spirits to punish their own people and countries that aren't willing to fund them any longer; that think they don't need the SSA."

"I didn't want to believe it, either," Wulf says quietly, "but the evidence is staggering. We know for a fact the SSA ordered these spirits to be released in Dublin. Dante gave the order."

Henny looks shaken, and I don't blame them. It's a lot to take in. It's even worse, seeing how they were a part of this. "I had no idea. I thought it was all just theory, just—You need to stop this."

"Totally." Joana looks equally horrified. For her, it's all out of the blue.

"We will," Wulf promises. "So, will you give us the key?"

"I'll come with you," Henny says, suddenly determined. "I know my way around the lab. At least the front part. There are other doors, and people know me." There's another reason, one I can emphasise with. They can't bear being in this environment any longer. "Besides, I need to see it for myself."

\#

Henny and Joana take remarkably little time to get dressed. One quick brush through Henny's short brown hair and it curls around their ears. "You're lucky it's my research day. Nobody will wonder where I am."

"I'll go and see if it's clear," Joana announces, tying her hair in a quick knot.

She slips outside and shortly after waves to us to follow her. "There'll be a couple of early morning runners, so we need to be quick," she explains as we walk swiftly back down the halls. I can't wait to be out of the academy. Hopefully, I'll never have to set foot in it again.

Just then, a door opens between us, fortunately obscuring me, Henny, and Wulf from sight. The startled voice is one I recognise. Marit. "Jo... since when are you up so early?"

Joana's eyes flicker to us and back. Her shoulders sag a little but she puts on a big fake smile. "I was actually looking for you. It's about the history test coming. I was wondering if we could go over our notes. Well, your notes, mainly."

"Oh." Marit seems surprised. I don't think Joana's ever showed her much kindness. "Sure. I... Never mind. Come in."

With one last glance at us, Joana follows her, and the door closes again. All three of us let out a breath of relief, and Wulf takes the lead. "Okay, let's hope we don't run into anyone else."

Luck is on our side for once, and the rest of the academy is still sleeping soundly or at least staying in their rooms when we reach the exit, and just like that, we're on the bridge outside. Out here, Rome is waking up, early commuters making their way through the city. Aeola joins us once we're on the other side of the Tiber, giving Henny a fright.

"Don't worry," I tell them, "she's with me. Henny, this is Aeola. Aeola, this is Henny. They're gonna help us enter the university."

Shyly, Henny waves at her. "Hi. I think."

Aeola is much more friendly. "Hello," she whistles, before telling me, "Can you smell the fresh bread? Should we get some?"

"Not now." I'd love nothing more than to share some bread with Aeola, but at the moment all I want is to be done with the whole affair. "We'll bake some bread once we're back in Berlin. I promise." Not that I have any idea how to do more than heat up frozen bread rolls.

I notice Henny staring. "What?"

"I can hear her," they say with awe in their voice. "I had no idea sylphs ate bread."

"They're smell junkies. Buy her some perfume, and she'll love you forever." Aeola messes up my wig for that dig.

"Wulf?" a familiar voice calls out.

Instantly, my heart hammers in my chest, and I accelerate my steps, dragging Henny with me. Behind us, Carina climbs off her moped and starts talking to Wulf in Italian. It's not until I reach the corner ahead of us and find cover behind the trellis of a restaurant that I dare look back at them.

"She was so mad at you," Henny whispers, thankfully accepting my need for hiding. "Never seen her like that. You're lucky you ran away."

"Was she aware I died?" I can't help it. I don't like Carina, and I like her even less when I see her embracing Wulf and kissing his cheeks. She holds onto him far too long for my liking.

Henny sighs. "Yes. Dante told us at the training session. Her face stiffened, and then she said it served you right."

Oh, yes, the cautionary tale. I have no idea what Wulf and Carina are talking about, but Carina's body language is so full of movement. It could be anything: a rant about my misbehaviour or a passionate love declaration. Or maybe they're just talking about where to go for breakfast. As the minutes pass, I notice Wulf gesticulating more emphatically. It's as if he's slipping back into an old but familiar suit. His true suit? I have to admit the language sounds beautiful from his lips. I wish I understood more than the occasional word.

They talk for ages, and I'm getting nervous. Can't they catch up another time? Preferably when I'm not at risk of discovery. It only gets worse when they finally do wrap up because Wulf is bringing her to us. I freeze, staring incredulously at him through the trellis. He can't be serious, can he?

"See," he says to Carina, "she's alive. Now why would he lie about that?"

Awesome. He's decided to trust Carina. Now she can call her daddy, and we can go for murder attempt number two.

Carina stares at me, probably judging me for the wig and ridiculous sunglasses. I take them off. It's not like they serve for more than a quick glance, anyway.

"My uncle is not a murderer," she declares. "He must've seen you walk into the Colosseum and assumed you died."

I give Wulf a pointed stare. "I must've dreamed the whole late-night kidnapping, then. Oh wait, you're probably going to say that was an arrest. But if so, how did I escape again? I had no idea you kept a volcano spirit in the city!"

"Cari," Wulf starts, and I suddenly wish I had a nickname, "I know how it sounds. But the evidence is staggering."

"You only have her word." Carina crosses her arms and glares at him. "She's dangerous, Wulf. She doesn't understand the severity of her actions; she just spouts nonsense and digs her heels in."

"So, she's as stubborn as you?" he asks. Carina looks like she's going to slap him. Gentler, he says, "When I first met her, I had the same reaction. I thought I knew better, because clearly, I had all this education and experience."

"You do know better!" Carina points out. "She's what? Twenty? Why should a little girl know more about spirits than us? Than the entire SSA?"

"Because I don't close my eyes to the world around me!" This entire conversation has dragged on long enough. I search Wulf's gaze and hold him down. "Is she with us, or is she going to get me killed for real this time?"

An uncomfortable look passes between them, and I realise they've already been through this. Carina just doesn't want to accept it. She purses her lips and glares at Wulf. "I'll check out these experiments and decide for myself." Then, for the first time, her voice softens. "And I would never try to get you killed, Rika. It must have been a misunderstanding; an accident." It sounds almost desperate.

I hold my tongue. Maybe Wulf was right about her. Even if she's mean, we may be able to trust her. Or at least he can. They're practically siblings, after all. *And ex-lovers,* says an annoying voice in my head. Before I can think too deeply about how weird it is that two quasi-siblings should fall in love, I get going, leading the way with Henny, so I don't have to see the two together.

"There's a sylph hovering above us," I hear Carina mutter.

"That's Aeola," Wulf replies. "Don't worry about her."

"Don't worry about a sylph?" Carina sounds incredulous.

"She's a friend of Rika's," Wulf says. Then he adds, "And mine."

The audible gasp makes me grin wildly. *Take that, Carina. This little girl managed to teach Wulf how to see past his trauma and befriend a sylph. I can teach you, too.*

# 23

Half an hour later, we meet Bijan and Inga at the university. Unsurprisingly, they're both wary about Carina's presence. "What is she doing here?" Bijan asks.

Annoyed, Carina pushes past the two rogue spirit seekers. "Come on, Henny, let's show them there's nothing sinister going on in this lab. Unless we start calling all research on spirits sinister now," she says, glaring at us over her shoulder.

Inga looks as if she has something to say about that, but after taking a deep breath, she follows Carina and Henny inside. I wait for Bijan to do the same before I ask Wulf, "Why did you bring her?"

"Because I believe that when she sees what's really going on, she'll be on our side. She's not a bad person, Rika," he pleads, as if he needs my permission. Well, it's too late for that.

"We'll see about that," I say. The best I can do is accept I've only seen one side of Carina. The one that tells me how she treats those she thinks beneath her. It's not a good look.

Nevertheless, I keep my mouth shut and decide to trust Wulf with this. One step at a time.

Henny's access card gets us into the university and the large sector dedicated to Spirit Studies. At the end of a long corridor of offices, the SSA lab awaits us. A note on the door tells us every visitor needs to contact the lab manager and complete safety induction. Unauthorised access is not allowed. Henny ignores all that and opens the door with their card.

"Here we are," they announce. "I practically never go here except to find my supervisor. This is the main experiment area, but there are more labs further in."

The lab's huge! It's like the size of an airport hangar. Some of it is sectioned off, usually around chemical equipment or quiet spaces such as the microscope area, but the majority is filled with huge machinery I can't make any sense of. "What is all that?"

Carina shrugs. "Research stuff." She has no idea either—or doesn't care.

"Spirit processing machines," Henny explains, much more helpful. "I don't know how each of them works. But this one, for example, is a universal material testing machine that tests the tensile and compressive strengths of gnome rock. Over there is a centrifuge, which is used to separate liquid spirit components. That machine over there—"

"Stop!" I beg, already sick to the stomach. "They're machines to torture spirits, I get it."

"Don't be so dramatic," Carina says. "It's called research. Nobody's torturing anyone."

Inga coughs, but instead of speaking up, she quietly takes out her phone and starts filming. I realise she and Bijan didn't just come to help us get Vesuvius' eggs. They've got their own agenda. Those images will probably be used to expose the SSA. Which suits me fine. The more people learn about this, the easier it'll be to shut the whole thing down.

Henny keeps quiet, deep in thought, and leads us past a row of empty aquariums and a giant furnace. Their card lets us through another door, and we find ourselves in a stairwell. "As far as I know, the storage facilities are down there. I've never been here, though."

We go down the stairs to find another lab. A similar note to the one in the other lab hangs at the door. Carina puts her hand on it, uncharacteristically gentle. Then I hear her whisper a name. "Piero." It's not until she lifts her fingers from the paper that I notice what they've touched. '*All enquiries: contact Piero Vallesco.*'

"This is his lab," Wulf says in a raw voice, stepping up next to her. An intimate look passes between them, a gentle touch, and I realise they share something that will forever connect them.

"We need another key," Henny announces softly, after trying to find the card mechanism. "This is as far as we can go."

Well, that's not very far. Bijan looks at the door and tries the handle, but before he can give it a jerk, Carina hisses, "It's secured! Do you want to set off the alarm?"

"Then how do we get in, princess?" he asks, shooting Wulf a dark look.

Carina huffs, her face showing her inner struggle. I assume part of her wants to report our sorry asses, but she surprises me by letting go of all that haughtiness and pull out a key ring instead. "I've got Piero's keys."

I'm almost sorry for her when she gives up her dead brother's keys to unlock the door. "They must still be looking for a replacement," she says, sounding a little like she's suddenly contracted a cold. "It'll take ages, of course."

"Of course," Wulf says, his voice gentle. "Piero could never be re-placed."

It eases the tension in Carina's shoulders, and she nods. Then she pushes the door open and lets us into the next room. It's rather unimpressive, more office than lab. A door on the other side leads to the storage facility.

Instead of going for the door, Wulf and Carina head for the last desk, strewn with paper. "What is it with researchers and their lack of order?" Carina says.

"Piero's room was the same; always a mess," Wulf jokes, and once again, I envy them these shared memories. It makes me feel as if I'm intruding on something.

The others are similarly restless. Inga takes pictures of some research papers, while Bijan saunters over to the computer on Piero's desk. "I could probably hack into that."

"And why would you do that?" Carina asks, the acid back in her voice. She turns around to Wulf, who's looking at an old notebook of his dead brother. "What are we doing here, Wulf? You think Piero committed acts of terror? This is ridiculous. You knew him. He couldn't hurt a fly."

He obviously could hurt a spirit, but I hold my tongue. Besides, Wulf's face has turned ashen. "Cari..."

"What?" Carina asks. "What is it?"

I see Wulf's hand shaking. He's wetting his lips, searching Carina's eyes first, then mine. When I hold his gaze, he releases a breath and calms. Looking straight at me, he explains, "It was Piero who came up with the spirit recombination project."

Carina snorts and tries to snatch the notebook from Wulf's hands, but he holds it out of her reach. "Give me that!"

"Carina, listen." This time, the gentleness of his voice has gone. "We both know how brilliant Piero was. It says here," he opens the book again, "'What if we pit spirits against spirits?' Then a whole lot of plans for how they could alter spirits and control them."

"By recombining different parts," Henny says. Their face shows a pale green tint now. "Oh dear, I did the grunt work for the recombinations."

"So?" Carina asks, crossing her arms. "He came up with a brilliant idea, using spirits to fight other spirits. That's ingenious. We all know how little effect our staffs have. Only spirits can hurt other spirits, so pitting them against each other sounds great to me."

"You also into animals tearing each other apart?" Inga asks, finally snapping.

"I'm into humans surviving! Lives saved!" Carina shouts. Then she turns around to each of us until finally her eyes settle on Wulf. "This is what we're fighting for. The sacrifices that need to be made. You're one of us." Desperation clings to her voice, and I almost feel sorry for her.

That is until Bijan pipes up from behind the other computer in the room. "Holy shit. You were right about this whole thing." When everyone stares at him, he clears his throat awkwardly. "First test balloon: Budapest."

"'Test balloon'?" Wulf asks, his voice shaking. I wish I could hold his hand and tell him it's all just a dream.

Bijan hunches his shoulders. "They had to deploy them somewhere. There's a shitload of test data from the Battle of Budapest. Energy readings, effectiveness…"

A chill takes hold of me. When the polluted spirits appeared in Dublin, we figured it was to counteract the political movement. Dublin wanted to get rid of the SSA, stop their payments, and bring back the old treaties with spirits. But Budapest hadn't done that. Budapest was loyal, invested in finding a better way to fight spirits and further the SSA's development. Yet they used them as a test balloon. They risked the lives of countless people and their own spirit seekers to test their new weapons. And then they punished them.

And for what? The spirit seekers in Budapest were doing the exact same thing as the SSA, trying to develop a weapon, using trapped spirits for more research. "Hypocrites. They're such hypocrites." I think I'm actually going to be sick.

Wulf goes over to check out the file Bijan has brought up. He glares at Carina. "There's your evidence. Powerful spirits, much more powerful than they should be, have been released in a highly populated area. For testing reasons. I almost died there."

"What were you doing in Budapest?" Carina asks. Her voice is shaking when she fumbles for an explanation. "I guess they had to be tested somewhere. They might have tested them in a city because they knew spirit seekers would be there to keep them under control."

"Why are you defending this?" I just don't get her. Yes, it's a lot to take in, but she just accepts what they did and finds reasons to justify it. "I thought you cared about human lives. But just particular human lives, right? Your people, your country. Who cares about Budapest?" Maybe it's not fair. Maybe I'm projecting, but I'm sure the SSA would've never picked a West European city for mere testing reasons. Punishment, yes, but Dublin was justified—at least in their eyes.

Carina stares at me for a moment, then she snaps, "What do you care about Budapest?"

Before it can get really ugly, Wulf speaks up, "It's not just Budapest. One of those spirits was released in Berlin. You don't care about that, either? Oh right, I know you don't." There's a bitterness in his voice that's as old as the comfort between them. I've never asked what drove them apart, but Berlin seems to be part of it. "You know what, I'm actually beginning to think Yllka had it right. Vesuvius was a vanity project. Got the SSA some nice publicity and a strong spi—" His eyes meet mine.

I understand at the same time. "They're gonna turn Vesuvius into a weapon." Of course he'll be more than a tourist attraction; more than a handy executioner. "We need to get the eggs."

"Agreed." He straightens his back and marches to the back of the office, where another door leads to the storage area.

"Eggs?" Carina asks, her face horror-stricken. "Wulf, what are you planning?" She strides after him. "What are you—" The words get stuck in her throat as Wulf throws the door open.

I gasp. There are shelves upon shelves alongside a long, dark corridor. "Traps." The morning light through the tall windows makes the tubes shine silver. Hundreds, no, thousands of traps are lined up in shelves, each of them containing an unfortunate spirit. My mind tries to make sense of it—of course, dozens of teams throughout Europe would catch hundreds of spirits each year. I knew that. I just never realised how many that would add up to. "So many spirits."

"Yes," Carina barks back sharply. "So many spirits who tried to hurt people."

"But I thought most of them were released into the wild," Henny says, their face mirroring my surprise. So, that lie is part of the curriculum.

Carina shrugs. "We can't. There's just too many of them. A few very weak ones, yes, but all of them? That would be asking for payback."

Oh, yes, can't have spirits taking revenge for being abducted from their homes and thrown into tiny little cells away from fresh air and the elements they love so much. "We have to free them."

"Are you mad?" Carina's eyes widen. "Wasn't it enough for you to damage the academy and cause mayhem in the city?"

If there was any mayhem, it sure didn't travel far, but I don't care about Carina's opinion. If spirits suffer only a fraction of what I've suffered at the hand of the SSA, they need to be released. And I'm sure it's not a fraction. Being cut off from the natural world would be a lot worse for them than it is for me. I push past Carina through the door and grab the first tube—a storm sprite. I'm just about to open it when a hand closes around my wrist.

Wulf looks at me with pained eyes. "We can't set them free, Rika. Not here. Not all of them."

I jerk my hand free, and he lets me go. "They're suffering."

He stares down at the tube, his lips moving nervously. "I believe you, but it's too dangerous. With time and patience, I'm sure you could set all of them free, talk to them, and calm them. But there are thousands of them, and we don't have the time. If you open the traps now, they'll blow up the lab, and us with it."

"This lab deserves it," I reply stubbornly, but I know he's right. Carina released fourteen spirits at the same time, and while they were weakened, they were strong and angry enough to break through an ancient stone wall. I can't even imagine the storm that would form if we let all of them go in this confined space.

"Perhaps it does," Wulf admits. "But that would only serve the SSA's narrative. Especially if they find out about us. If Dante used your 'accidental' death as a cautionary tale, how do you think he'll spin this one?"

My throat tightens as I imagine the scenario. I'll be painted as a terrorist, a madwoman. And if those spirits hurt anyone, I'd deserve it, too. It sucks. Am I truly willing to endanger people for the sake of spirits? But how can I walk away? How can I leave, not knowing if I'll ever find my way here again?

Wulf offers me his hand, waiting for me to make up my mind. He's not comfortable setting free the spirits he and others have caught, but he's willing to step back and let me take the reins. I've never felt so conscious about the consequences of my actions. "Let's move on." I put the trap away and take Wulf's hand instead, trying not to be hurt by his subtle sigh of relief.

The only thing that makes this a little better is Inga stepping up to photograph it all. Perhaps there's another way to get these spirits freed: with caution instead of brash action.

"This lab proves nothing," Carina says, stepping up on Wulf's other side, ignoring our clasped hands. She's breathing surprisingly hard. "If we checked those reports in detail, I'm sure there'd be an explanation. The board would never endanger Berlin."

I'm not so sure about that, considering Wulf's downgrading. Then again, the dryad was released long before he got put under observation, and far away from humans. There's the possibility they used it just as Piero intended—against other spirits. Spirits, such as Grune, who've never shown aggression, but spirits, nonetheless. Not that it makes it any better, and I'm glad Wulf snorts at the suggestion.

"I can't believe you're still playing that fiddle," he says. "Even if none of this were true, how is that fair? Why do I get first dibs? Why help Berlin and condemn Budapest? This is exactly the kind of bullshit they always pull. This playing of favourites, this nepotism. It has to stop."

"You're a favourite because you're capable!" Carina protests. "As am I. Should we step back from our duties just because we're Vallescos?"

"*You're* a Vallesco, not me."

Something momentous is happening and I grasp Wulf's fingers tighter. The tension in his jaw tells me how much he wishes he could take those words back. He's practically told Carina she isn't his family anymore.

For once, Carina doesn't fly into a rage. She huffs, but it's a dejected little puff, full of disbelief and... hurt. At last, she manages a reply. "I see."

Fortunately, we're saved from the awkwardness by reaching a second door, yet another lab, this one small and dark. Instead of unlocking the door, Carina hands Wulf the keys, obviously unwilling to be part of this any longer. "Do what you must." She turns around and stalks back down the long corridor.

"Carina!" Wulf calls out, but she ignores him.

"I'm sorry," I say. I only know too well how it hurts to see a family member turn away from you.

Wulf sighs, and we let go of each other's hands so he can open the door. There isn't a lot of machinery in the room, but there's a soft red glow coming from what looks like an industrial oven. I sense the life stuck inside of it. Vesuvius' eggs. They're really here.

"How are we gonna transport them?" Inga asks. "Aren't they incredibly hot?"

"Not really," Wulf says. "Like a hot potato, basically. They're just babies after all," he adds, more quietly, and I realise he really does feel sorry about using them for his escape.

"Here." Henny hands me a pair of thick gloves. They look as anxious as I feel. "I never knew spirits could have babies."

"They're living beings," I whisper. How these spirit seekers can go through the world with eyes closed, I will never understand.

I put on the gloves and grab the huge handle with both hands. Turning it is incredibly tough. I'm glad I've had strength training during the last few weeks, or this would've turned out embarrassing. But at last, the handle turns, and the oven door opens. A flash of heat envelops my skin, and I step back quickly.

I don't know what I expected these eggs to look like, but it isn't what's in front of us. Three eggs the size of ostrich eggs are lying separately from each other on different levels. The glowing-red outsides are flowing, but there are black flakes in them, moving around sluggishly like debris caught in a river of honey. The top parts are attached to a tube and several heat-resistant measuring tools. On that side, the eggs are solid, and I pick up immediately that this is not how they're supposed to be.

The eggs feel wrong, terribly wrong.

"They're using them for their next stage of recombination," I whisper. Vesuvius believes they've kept his eggs captive. That they're the SSA's insurance for his pliability, but that's not what's happening here. They couldn't resist researching, couldn't resist the opportunity to hatch their own spirits.

"This is awful," Wulf says.

Neither of us moves. The SSA is corrupting innocent babies. You can't tell me that's for the best.

"Let's get them out of there," Henny says with sudden urgency. They take what looks like a giant prong from the wall and approach the oven. "This is not what I signed up for," they mutter as they carefully pick up the top egg and pull it away from the tube that's injecting whatever vile concoction they're using for these experiments.

Wulf grabs a towel and opens his arms, allowing Henny to drop the egg there. He doesn't even wince at the heat.

"Who's taking the next?" Henny asks before turning around to the oven again.

"They belong together," Wulf says in a coarse voice. "They should never have been separated."

The moment he says it, I realise he's right. Yet another failure to attribute to the SSA. They separated what should not be separated, causing the eggs to solidify before their time.

Henny drops the second egg in Wulf's arms, and immediately, the two eggs flow into each other. Somehow, they still retain their individual shapes, yet the magma flows from one egg to the other. When the third egg rejoins the others, the small specks of rock start melting.

I wasn't aware of the tension in my shoulders until I sigh in relief. "They're recovering." I imagine returning damaged eggs to Vesuvius and shudder. The eternal city would've faced its end. "Let's leave."

Though she can't see the spirits, Inga helps Wulf wrap the eggs and put them into a backpack. It's amazing how they can burn Wulf's skin and yet don't affect the material of the backpack.

We walk back through the rows of traps while Wulf takes care to lock up after himself. I can't help myself and snatch three random traps to take outside. Saving three spirits is better than none. One step at a time.

"Are you done?" Bijan asks, still sitting behind the computer. "I've transferred some files and installed some spyware so we can get the rest later. Got everything about those test missions and the Dublin attacks."

Wulf only nods at him, seeming as tired as if he's had to walk through the volcano again. We close up the lab and make our way up the stairs and through the main lab. Nobody's here yet, but judging by the noise outside, the university is about to resume business.

"You okay?" I ask Wulf, to which he scoffs.

"Are you?"

I don't think I can ever be okay after what I've just witnessed. I can still see the broken rock blocking the life flow of the eggs. Hopefully, they'll fully recover. Not for our sake, but for theirs.

"We'll start a media campaign," Inga says. "I've got a few journalist contacts. They'll rip these accounts out of our hands. This time, we've got them."

"Yeah, I don't think so."

We come to a sudden halt in front of a group of spirit seekers, all dressed in combat gear, staffs at the ready. In front of them stands Carina, her arms crossed and her face hard. "I'm afraid you're going nowhere."

# 24

My stomach lurches at the sight of the spirit seekers while my mind jumps several loops ahead of itself. They've caught me again. They'll throw me into a cell for three years. They'll kill me right now. Then Wulf's hand lands on my shoulder and squeezes gently, and I calm a little. I'm not alone this time. Wulf is here. Wulf, who still holds some sway over these people, no matter his security rating.

As he steps forward, I take a quick look at Carina's team. Most of them seem to be Italian, which is not unusual, but there's one ginger standing out. Eoghan has followed Carina's call. He stares at me wide-eyed, and I know exactly what he's thinking: *Why is she alive? Is she going to get me into trouble?* I wish I could tell him I won't blow his cover. I couldn't do what he does, but I'm not judging him for the choices he's made to keep himself safe.

"What are you doing, Carina?" Wulf asks, as if the rest of them don't exist. "You called your team?"

"I'm stopping you from ruining your life," Carina says. "When Dante told me you weren't coping very well, I felt sorry for you. I knew Piero's death wasn't easy on you. It wasn't easy on any of us, but what you're doing is dangerous. It's madness. You're destroying everything." Her voice is on the edge of breaking.

So, Dante didn't even spare his niece—or his mentee. He's used his soft-spoken manipulations to twist Wulf's intentions, to make him seem like a victim of his circumstances, deeply troubled by PTSD or something similar, instead of a man who's had an honest change of heart. It was a trap set long before Wulf reached out to Carina, or perhaps a safeguard to make sure he wouldn't lose her as well.

"You're wrong about that. Of course, I grieve for Piero, but I didn't lose my mind because of it. I'm coping. What I'm not able to process is how corrupt the whole organisation is." Wulf shakes his head, anger pouring out of him. Squaring his shoulders, he forces himself to calm down. "We can talk about this calmly, in quiet. Rika can introduce you to some friendly spirits, and you can see for yourself that there's more to them than what we've been taught."

Carina laughs it off. "Friendly spirits? Like the one that killed my brother?" Her face darkens, and she steps closer to Wulf, shoving a finger into his face. "I know what you're planning. You're gonna return Vesuvius' eggs to him and set him free. And you're telling me you haven't lost your mind? He killed Piero!" She screams the last words at him, and I see the spittle hitting Wulf's face.

I want to show compassion for Piero Vallesco, but if what we've found is true, it was their brother who came up with the abominations concocted in the lab downstairs. Without his ingenuity, there never would've been an attack on Budapest or a strike of vengeance against Dublin. Good intentions or not, he created monsters—spirit and human ones alike.

"Cari—" Wulf starts.

She slaps him hard. "Don't you 'Cari' me. You've turned on Piero. On the family who raised you, the organisation that supported you." At last, her death stare finds me. "And all for a girl who still believes in fairy tales."

"They're not fairy tales," Wulf protests. "I've seen the truth. I've heard it, and I felt it." When she tries to slap him again, he catches her hand in the air. "Don't. Just because you've always accepted everything that's been handed to you doesn't mean it's right."

She glares at him before jerking her hand free. Wulf lets go of it with a shake of his head. They seem to have had this conversation before, if with fewer stakes. Carina huffs. With a last contemptuous look, she turns around and walks away. But then her hand reaches back in a flash, and before I can really grasp what's happening, she's whirled around, staff in hand, and hit Wulf's shins.

Wulf staggers forward, grunting in pain, and I run to his side, only to be faced with the end of Carina's staff. "This is all your fault!" She's never resembled her father more.

From the corner of my eye, I see the rest of her team moving in. None of us have brought a weapon. They would've been too visible. On top of that, I've never fought another human above a quick shove and run, which doesn't really work if there's, like, three people for each of us and a wall at our backs.

"You corrupted him! You..." As in the training yard, a flash of anger comes over Carina. She raises her staff, ready to hit me over the head, if it weren't for Wulf grabbing the other end.

"Carina!" He tries to tear the staff out of her hands, but she's got the better angle and brings it back around, barely missing me in the process.

The rest of the team is spreading out, staffs ready to make contact. Henny has raised their hands, mortified at the sudden aggression. A guy slams his staff into Wulf's shoulder from behind, almost hitting the backpack with the eggs. In a minute, it'll be over. There are just too many of them and they're out for blood, thanks to Carina.

I need to do something. But what? Another spirit seeker moves into the gap between Carina and me, forcing me to stumble backward. I hit the wall with a metallic clank. The traps!

Hastily, I pick the first one I can reach and open it, barely registering that it's calibrated to a gnome. "Please," I say, "we need your help. This would be an awesome time for an earthquake."

The gnome isn't too damaged, though he's a bit wobbly on one side. At the sight of the spirit seekers, he dives into the Earth, likely never to be seen again. I, on the other hand, have to duck under the staff and jump to the side. Next to me, I see Bijan being slammed into the wall by two spirit seekers, one of them pressing his staff against the hacker's throat.

I barely escape another staff, only to be faced by two more spirit seekers. A third moves in behind me, staff raised. This is it. If I don't surrender, they'll beat me, maybe even kill me—*accidentally.*

In that moment, an earthquake hits, causing the ground to lurch under our feet. I fall to my knees, hitting the concrete hard, but so do the others.

"Spirit attack!" the one in front of me shouts, looking for Carina.

*Ha!* They have no idea where the gnome is. A second wave follows, but this time, I know where it's coming from and shift my balance accordingly. While the others fall back down after scrambling to their feet, I dash through to where Wulf wrestles a staff from one of Carina's followers and whirls it around to stop another attack. His eyes meet mine for a split second. "Run!"

He's expecting me to leave him here surrounded by these thugs? Small chance, Wulf. I reach for the other two traps, stick them under my left arm and open them quickly, freeing a patchy fog maiden and another scrappy gnome, cracks all over her stony face. "I need you to help get us out of here. I need a fog."

Another earthquake hits, and I stagger into a spirit seeker. Eoghan. Instantly, he grabs my upper arm, causing the traps to clatter to the ground. "Hold it!" His fingers dig painfully into my skin.

The temperature sinks as droplets of water descend. Sudden fog spreads out rapidly. Eoghan howls in pain as the second gnome bashes her head into his thigh, but his grip is relentless, and the gnome finds another target.

"Let me go!" I shout as he drags me away from the fog, past Carina, who's trying to get the situation under control.

"Paolo, next to you! Everyone, don't let spirits or these rogues escape." She catches sight of Eoghan and me and nods. "Well done, Eoghan. Keep an eye on her!"

"Will do." He continues to drag me away from the fight.

I throw myself against his grip, calling out for Wulf, then turning around to hit Eoghan's chest. "I don't care that you're playing it safe. I'm not. I'll never be safe!"

"Don't you think I know that?" he hisses, then glances over his shoulder as if to check if anyone's following us. "They tried to kill you once. They'll do it again if they catch you here."

Stunned, I stop my assault. When did his we become they?

Eoghan uses the moment to press a little object into my palm. A key. He glances back once more, before explaining quickly, "There's a moped, first one on the left. Take it and get out of here. I'll hold them back or lead them astray."

"But your cover..."

"Screw my cover," he blurts out. "Do you think I can sit by and watch people being murdered for their beliefs? Now, go. Go!" He pushes me away, down the corridor.

I get about two steps before two others catch up to us: Wulf, followed by another spirit seeker in hot pursuit. "Take your hands off her!" Wulf barks at Eoghan.

The Irish boy raises his free hand and steps aside. "Fine with me."

"Hey, kid," the other spirit seeker shouts, probably as confused as Wulf.

Wulf recovers quicker, though. He strides past Eoghan and takes my waiting hand as Eoghan intercepts the other man's path. "For Dublin!" he cries and attacks the guy furiously.

I don't want to leave Eoghan with them. It feels like exchanging my life for his, but I have no choice. Wulf is dragging me down the corridor now, out the doors. Sirens are closing in.

With the fresh air, Aeola arrives, swooping around me. "Are you okay? I saw them go in, but I couldn't figure out how to warn you."

"All good," I say, completely out of breath.

"We have to get away fast," Wulf pulls me down a small set of stairs.

I still have Eoghan's key in my hand. "There's a moped." Actually, there's an entire line of mopeds. Looks like the Italian spirit seekers aren't big fans of public transport. "But I don't know how to drive one."

"Which one?" Wulf asks, throwing his borrowed staff into the bushes.

"The one on the left."

"Let's go!" He takes the key from my hands and hurries over to them.

A minute later, I'm holding on tight to his backpack, my hair fluttering in the wind as we race down the tight streets behind the university.

# 25

By the time we arrive at the Colosseum, the attraction has already opened to the public. Wulf and I stand in line for what seems like half an hour, disguised as just another couple of tourists. My heart is hammering in my chest so loud I'm surprised nobody turns around in wonder. Only Wulf's fingers in mine and his deep, gentle voice, occasionally pointing out the sight, keep me from running and hiding. At any point, I expect the police or another group of spirit seekers to turn up and pull us out of the queue, but we enter the Colosseum as planned.

The arena itself isn't accessible to the public, so instead, we follow the crowd sweeping around the circular ranks outside, looking down at the ruins occupied by Vesuvius. Our flight and pursuit yesterday have left surprisingly little effect. There's no lava field, and if any of the crumpled ruins have been left in this shape by us, it's impossible to distinguish them from the ones damaged by time. There's no sign of Vesuvius, only his powerful presence against my mind, like a ticking bomb under the surface.

Strolling around the ancient floors of the Colosseum puts me in a weird mood that is half anxiety and half lull. Not knowing how Vesuvius will react once the eggs are returned to him forces us to wait until it's closing time before we can find a way down. That means we have the entire day in front of us with nothing to occupy ourselves but worrisome thoughts.

After two rounds, one of them on the inside circuit, we stop at the far side of the arena. Wulf leans his forearms on the balustrade, staring into the distance. A little lizard, almost invisible against the stone, skitters away. The sun is shining down on us, not a cloud in the blue sky.

"Show me a miracle," Wulf says, so softly I almost don't hear it at all.

"A miracle?" Last time I checked, I wasn't a miracle worker.

His shoulders heave, and I hear the sigh. "How did we get here?"

I know he doesn't mean the Colosseum. That was thanks to Eoghan's moped.

We fought spirit seekers. Other humans. His sister. "All I ever wanted to do was live in peace with the world around me," I admit. And now my life is full of terror and lies. We left Henny, Eoghan, Inga, and Bijan behind. I don't want to imagine what that means for them. Hopefully, they've managed to escape. If not, their fate is in the SSA's hands, and I don't like that outlook one bit.

"And what do you want now?" Wulf asks, still not looking at me.

"Honestly? To be tucked away in a dryad tree, safe and sound."

My answer makes him turn his head slightly to me, lips curled into a smile. Then Wulf takes my hand and pulls it closer, resting his lips on them. My heart suddenly skips a beat as my breath hitches.

"There's no dryad here, but I'll keep you safe," he says.

It didn't work the last time he said it, and I know it won't work this time. He might be the greatest spirit seeker of all time, but it's not spirits I'm afraid of. Still, hearing him say it makes me glow from inside. How different would it be if we were here on a trip? Just Wulf showing me the city he grew up in? We could enjoy the sunshine, try out all the different food, and marvel at the sights, and instead of looking over my shoulder, I'd be gazing into his eyes.

But that doesn't really work when the SSA is on a manhunt for you. "Things need to change," I say quietly, pulling away. "The world needs to see things differently, see spirits for what they are. I don't want to be safe if that means others will suffer. And by others, I also mean spirits."

"Also, or mostly?" Wulf asks, sounding a little tired.

I know he's struggling with all the changes in his life. Would it be easier for him to run back to the SSA and admit he was wrong? With his connections, he'd probably get away with a slap on the hand. Then he could go back to fighting spirits, not thinking about right or wrong.

"Does it matter? I want there to be an alternative. I want more than just one option. More than just fight or die. Spirits can be argued with. They can be negotiated with. If humans can make peace with one another, then why can't we do that with spirits?" He winces, but I hold his gaze, putting more urgency into my voice. "I've run away and hidden who I am my entire life. I no longer want to do that. The person I am is nothing to be ashamed of. Believing in a peaceful co-existence is nothing to be persecuted. Once we get home, I want to speak out. I want to make the world see that there's more to spirits than what we know. What the SSA dictated. People with a high natural attunement need to be able to be more than just soldiers."

Wulf looks away as if hurt, studying the ruins under us. "Carina turned on me."

It surprises me much less than him, but I don't say that. "She made her choice." She saw everything we did in the lab, learnt of the same atrocities, and yet chose ignorance for the comfort of knowing her place.

"So did I," Wulf says. He looks up again, his face hardening when he returns my gaze. "So did I," he repeats, a lot firmer. "I chose you. I chose the truth."

Such an enormous weight slips from my shoulders that I gasp in relief. Giddiness fills my head, and I realise how much his support means to me. Not having to make a stand alone is everything. "Thank you."

Wulf turns around to me, pushing away from the balustrade. He lifts one hand to brush the blonde streaks of the wig to the side, his fingertips brushing my temple. Once again, my breath hitches, my entire body going rigid in anticipation. "Thank *you*," Wulf stresses, "for opening my eyes."

The touch of his hand becomes firmer as he presses it against the side of my face. He leans forward, and I suppress the sudden urge to wet my lips, holding my breath instead.

A wind rushes through us, pushing us apart, and waking me from my trance.

"Aeola!" I protest, hoping she has a really good reason to interrupt now. Wulf has already stepped back, looking as if he'd been caught fraternising with a spirit.

"They're here!" Aeola hisses. "Spirit seekers."

All thoughts of kisses never kissed vanish in the panic. I rush to the balustrade, looking down into the ruins, until Aeola sweeps my head around to where a woman with a blond pixie cut is making her way through the crowd.

"That's her," I tell Wulf, clutching his arm. My heart is beating furiously while my mind replays images from the night she pointed a gun at me. "Agnes. She's the one who kidnapped me."

Wulf takes some time to spot her in the crowd. "They know we'd come here, then."

"What do we do?" We can't climb down into the arena with so many people watching, and we can't leave without running into Agnes and who-knows-who-else on the lookout for us.

"You think we could talk to her?" Wulf asks, and I almost kick his shin.

"Talk? To the woman who held a gun to my face? Why don't I just climb onto the balustrade and jump into the pit?" With luck, I'll break my neck on a wall before I even reach the ground.

Wulf sighs. "Look. We're in a crowd. She can't do anything."

Aeola floats back and forth, thinking deeply. "She needs to breathe, right?" Her shimmering form is darkening a little, a sign of sheer determination.

"Thank you, Aeola!" At least someone understands how dire the situation is.

"She needs to breathe?" Wulf asks, his face alarmed. "What are you suggesting?"

I know I should be more aghast, but I'm not entirely thinking straight. Agnes is coming closer and closer. Her gaze sweeps the crowd. Any moment, it'll land on us. There. Agnes looks straight at me, and my entire body turns to ice despite the warm sunshine. Her hand reaches to her side. My mind reels with the consequences. "Aeola, quick!"

"No!" Wulf shouts, but the spirit is my friend first and his second. We've been through too much together for her to leave me high and dry.

She speeds towards Agnes, who's raising a small black object. Is she going to shoot me right here? No, it's not a gun but a walkie-talkie.

Agnes opens her mouth, but instead of speaking, she gasps. Or she would've if she had any air to draw from.

Aeola has wrapped herself around Agnes' face, cutting off the airflow. Agnes' eyes widen in sudden panic. To her, it must seem as if her lungs have stopped working for no apparent reason. The walkie-talkie falls from her hand as she staggers on the spot. Her hands clutch the stone wall, fingers clawing at the surface. Someone next to her realises her struggle, moving closer in concern.

Wulf's shoulder knocks into mine as he strides towards Agnes. It makes me realise what I'm doing here, or rather, what Aeola is doing for me. I don't want her to become a murderer. Not for me, not for anyone.

Quickly, I follow Wulf. A small crowd has formed around Agnes, who's on her knees, clawing at her own throat. Someone is calling emergency services. Just then, Agnes passes out, and the guy next to her checks her vitals in a panic.

"Aeola, stop!" I shout. No one pays me any attention, but ahead I see the sylph rise into the air and search for me in the crowd. Wulf stops, having almost broken through the last line of people to assist Agnes.

Someone shouts, "She's breathing again!", and a collective sigh of relief goes through the crowd.

As Agnes slowly comes back to herself, Wulf turns around. He glares until he reaches me, whereupon he grabs my arm and drags me to the nearest gap in the ranks that connects the outside circuit with the inside of the Colosseum. There are far fewer people milling around here, nearly all of them just passing by. A siren howls in the distance.

"Have you lost your mind?" Wulf asks, letting go of my arm.

Aeola swoops down on my shoulder, looking askance at Wulf. "What's wrong?"

"You could've killed her!" He jerks an arm towards the crowd outside. Then he runs his hands over his face. "I can't believe you let Aeola do that."

"She's an evil woman, Wulf," Aeola explains, in all her naïvety. "She hurt Rika. She'll do it again."

I see the muscles in Wulf's face straining. To save him from inner combustion, I turn to Aeola. "What Wulf is trying to say is we can't lower ourselves to the same level. Killing people is wrong, and if we want a chance to change the world, we need to play by the rules," I explain, for Wulf's benefit. Then it's my turn to glare at him. "Even if the other side clearly doesn't."

Wulf crosses his arms stubbornly. "That's right."

He steps back as an employee leads ambulance staff up the stairs. We watch in silence as the crowd parts and the emergency services attend to Agnes, who's clearly annoyed with the whole fuss. Fortunately, though, stopping to breathe in such a dramatic fashion warrants a trip to the hospital, and Agnes can be convinced to accompany them. We quickly move down the steps and hide behind the corner while Agnes walks past us, shielded by the emergency services.

"I'd call that a success," I mutter, knowing fully well Wulf doesn't agree with me.

"Just don't do it again," he says, only for his eyes to widen.

I want to turn around, but Wulf grabs my shoulders instead and shoves me behind him. The man walking down the stairs, eyes scanning the crowd, is no stranger to me. "That's Dante's security man," I gasp. Seeing Gian again in this place is almost worse than Agnes. Wherever I ran, he was always there to stop me.

"I know." Wulf hushes me and pushes me back into the darkness. This corridor of the inner circumference is a dead-end, containing nothing but a set of modern toilets. No one else is around. Unfortunately, that means we can't find cover quick enough before Gian spots us. "Wulf."

"Gian," Wulf says, his shoulders tense. So, these two know each other as well.

Gian sees me peeking at him from behind Wulf's back, and a lazy smile curls his lip. "And there's our runaway queen." Gosh, how much I hate him! "Not so much this time."

"If you want Rika, you'll have to go through me," Wulf declares, and I could kiss him right here.

The smile on Gian's face falters, replaced by something that could almost pass for regret. "I wish you wouldn't make me, but since you insist." He raises a similar walkie-talkie to Agnes'. "They're here at the back, near the toilets."

"Aeola could—" I say, but Wulf stops me.

"Not again!"

It's too late, anyway. He's already informed the others. How many spirit seekers are there?

"Now we'll wait for the others, and then it's home for you two," Gian quips, but his grimace appears strained.

"I'm not going back with you," I say, desperately looking for a way out. Perhaps I could lock myself in a toilet.

Just then, Wulf steps forward and makes a grab for Gian. With the element of surprise, he manages to get a hold of his arms. "Rika, go!" he yells at me.

Before I can get my feet to move, Gian has thrust his elbow into Wulf's side and freed himself. With practised movements, he turns around and rams his knee into Wulf's stomach. Wulf grunts, looking as if he's going to keel over.

I will not watch Gian beat up Wulf in front of me—and accidentally destroy Vesuvius' eggs in the process. With a feral cry, I jump onto Gian's back, wrapping my arm around his neck. The sudden weight makes him topple backwards, and we both land on the ground with a thud. I'm seeing stars while Gian rolls around, frees himself from my arm, and turns the tables, pressing his arm into my neck.

His weight is only on top of me for a second before a powerful breeze knocks him off-balance. As Gian staggers to the side, Wulf grabs his shoulder and punches him straight in the temple. Gian topples like a sack of potatoes, knocked out cold. Before he can come back to his senses, Wulf helps me up. "We need to leave," he says, his hand almost crushing mine.

We ignore Gian's groans and the stares of some tourists who have noticed our scuffle, and plunge back into the crowd leading to the exit. We get about a quarter around the Colosseum when I see two other men pushing through the crowd with determined looks. Wulf sees them, too, and jerks me to the side. Another connecting passage is not too far behind us. But before we get any farther, a sudden lurch of the ground sends me stumbling into Wulf. Dust trickles from the ceiling as the Colosseum shakes. In an instant, people are screaming and running for cover.

Wulf pulls me to the side and forces me to huddle down with him. "Cover your head!" he instructs, as a second earthquake hits the Colosseum.

When I felt the volcanic tremors in the arena, it was frightening. Now, covered by rock on all sides in a structure that has already partially collapsed on one side, it's a nightmare. Screams fill my ears. Somewhere, rocks are tumbling down, smashing into walls. I cower on the floor, hands held so tight over my head it hurts. Everything is shaking. *I'm shaking.*

"Rika!" Wulf grabs me by my shoulders, repeating my name over and over again. "It's Vesuvius, Rika. We have to go to him. We have to go to him now." Then he pulls me into a hug, patting my back. "Rika, it's okay. I've got you. You're safe."

Slowly, I unclasp my hands, only to realise the only thing shaking is me. The crowd from outside is pushing past us, sweeping the spirit seekers away in their panic. I wish my feet would carry me to safety, if there were any to be found.

"That's it," Wulf says when I manage to get to my feet. He puts his hands on both sides of my face. "Vesuvius is losing his patience. I need you to calm him down. There are too many people here. Do you think you can do that for me?"

"How…" I'm still shivering. Wetting my lips, I try speaking for a second time. "How do we get down there?"

"We might be able to talk to him from up here. Come!" Wulf offers me his hand.

As he pulls me up, I notice my wig is gone. It must have fallen off when I rolled on the floor with Gian. Aeola brushes my face, and the fresh breath of air eases my breathing. By the time Wulf has led me back to the inner circumference, I almost feel like myself again. Only very few people are still outside, most of them cowering on the floor like I had.

Wulf leads me back to the far side where we're directly above the gate the spirit seekers used. Everyone has already left this area. Clutching the balustrade, I look down into the arena.

To the normal eye, it would probably look the same, but I see the volcano spirit roaming the empty maze of catacombs. He roars, and in the next moment, a third earthquake shakes the Colosseum's walls. Rocks fall on the opposite side, and muffled screams rise all around.

"Vesuvius!" Wulf bellows, but from up here, he might as well have shouted in the wind.

Wind. "Aeola. Tell Vesuvius we're here. We've got his eggs."

"Got it." The sylph flies down in a rush, and soon, I can't see her anymore.

A few tense seconds later, the ground rumbles under us. Then red-glowing lava appears between the ruins, slowly spreading.

"Oh, no!" Wulf turns to leave, but I grab his arm.

"Wait!"

Vesuvius has turned around, looking in our direction now. The lava keeps moving. It flows in strange ways that ignore all gravity because it rises from the ground and arcs towards us. Closer and closer, the molten rock comes, until the heat sears the hairs on my arms. Still, we hold out, and just before it melts down the stone balustrade, the lava flow stops, cooling quickly.

"You don't want to walk down on that, do you? It's too hot to... it probably doesn't even exist," Wulf says, looking awfully pale in the sunlight.

"It exists for us," I tell him, somehow calmer than I've been all day. I grasp Wulf's hand. "Trust me." I trust the spirit.

Wulf waits for my cue. I don't actually know how hot the newly formed bridge is—perhaps it'll melt off my shoes on the first step—but it appears safe. After all, I trust my intuition above everything.

We take the first step together and then another. The stone beneath us is warm, but more like a heated blanket and less like all-consuming lava. Wulf follows my lead, bravely setting one foot in front of the other until we reach the ground. There, Vesuvius and Aeola await us.

"You have my eggs?" The volcano asks when we set foot on the miraculously untouched grass.

Wulf slowly takes off his backpack. "I do."

"Give them to me," Vesuvius says. Though he's growling, I sense the fear beneath his churning skin. This is a spirit concerned for his children.

I watch as Wulf opens the backpack and plunges his hands in to retrieve the wrapped-up eggs.

"Don't you dare!" a voice calls from behind us. Dante and Carina, both with their staffs ready, come running down the corridor leading to the molten gate. For the first time, Dante isn't in a suit, but the same black combat gear Carina wears. It makes him look ten years younger and much more dangerous. They must've been ready to engage Vesuvius in battle.

"Do not hand over those eggs!" Dante repeats, looking past me straight at Wulf, who has frozen mid-action. "Please, my boy."

# 26

There are a lot of places I would like to be right now. Caught between fanatic spirit seekers and an angry volcano is not one of them.

I wish it were me who was carrying the eggs. I would've taken them straight to Vesuvius and handed them over. I'd take my chances with the potential gratefulness of a spirit over people who were happy to leave me for dead. But the eggs aren't in my hands. They're in Wulf's, and to him, the people he's facing aren't ruthless murderers but his family. Will they manage to get through to him and pull him back from the edge or will he stand by his choice?

"Please, Wulf. You promised," I remind him.

But Wulf takes his hands out of the backpack without the wrapped-up eggs, and shoulders it. Then he takes a few steps back. Towards Vesuvius, not the people he knows. "Hold it, Dante," he growls.

Immediately, Dante stops, stretching out his arm to stop Carina's advance as well. They're only two meters away from me. Carina glowers at me. Dante, however, ignores me completely, not letting a little thing like me surviving his murder attempt slow him down. He runs his gaze up and down over Wulf before settling on his face. "So, it's true? You've gone rogue?"

Wulf snorts. "Is rogue just another word for not following blindly?"

I'm so proud of him. He's not caving at all but meant what he said half an hour ago. Behind him, I see Aeola whispering to Vesuvius. For now, the volcano spirit holds back, letting the ground settle.

"This isn't you, my boy." Dante takes a tentative step forward, shaking his head. "Have you forgotten everything I've taught you? I'm not the bogeyman Rika's told you about. I'm your family. You're like a son to me."

"A murderous family," I mutter. Dante is close enough for me to strangle him, but he doesn't even flinch.

Wulf shakes his head. "Everything you ever taught me was built on a lie!"

"You think my feelings for you are a lie?" Dante gasps. He does offended very well.

"It's not your feelings I doubt, but your cause," Wulf says harshly.

Dante frowns. He crosses his arms and plants his feet firmly on the ground. "You mean the cause where we risk our lives to protect all of humanity from spirit attacks?"

Behind Wulf, Vesuvius growls, and a low tremor goes through the earth. Carina looks nervous, but the two men ignore the spirit.

"You call letting loose polluted spirits in our cities protecting humanity?" Wulf scoffs. "Don't tell me you didn't know about Piero's project. That it was all going on behind your back."

For a moment, it looks like Dante will do exactly that, but instead, he shakes his head. "I knew about it."

Behind us, Carina gasps. "Tio!"

"But I didn't sanction it," Dante explains. "Yes, Piero came up with the idea. You know we've always struggled to build effective weapons against spirits. Only spirits can hurt spirits. So we thought, why not *use* spirits against spirits?"

"That's not what you've been doing," Wulf says, his voice shaking ever so slightly. He raises his hand to stay Vesuvius, who's picking up on his anger and hurt.

"But that was the plan Piero and I hatched. The rest of the board wasn't convinced it would work, so they decided to test it where there would be spirit seekers to step in. They picked Budapest, hoping we could conduct the test in a low-key fashion that wouldn't draw too much attention if it failed."

Once again, I feel Dante's gentle voice lulling me in. He always sounds so reasonable. But it's all a lie. "If that's so, why didn't you tell the Budapest spirit seekers? Why have them be unprepared if they were meant to be a safeguard?" I ask.

Dante's gaze flicks to me before he refocuses on Wulf. He knows there's no way in hell he can convince me after throwing me in here. I'm a lost cause, always have been. "The board didn't want them to temper with it prematurely."

"And Dublin? Was that another test run?" Wulf scoffs. I'm glad to see he doesn't believe a word of this pitiful excuse.

"Dublin was... an outright rebellion," Dante admits in a surprise move of honesty that stuns me. "Again, I was merely the one executing the board's will. But something had to be done. Ireland could not be allowed to turn the public against us. They were talking about abolishing the SSA, thinking they could somehow control spirits by leaving sacrifices to them." He scrunches his nose in disgust. "Give in once, and who else will follow? If the Irish stop their payments, the whole of Europe will cry out. People are now questioning the very things that keep them safe. We're back at square one. 'Oh, I never saw a spirit,'" he says, imitating some hapless member of the public. "'They must be fake, a tale told by the SSA to frighten us.'" His voice normalises again. "Wulf, they had to be dealt with. This way, Ireland was reminded of how dangerous spirits truly are." Finally, he turns his gaze on me. "Or they would've been, if not for your interference."

"Because I showed them there are other ways to deal with the threat spirits pose? Peaceful ways?" Well, Rory did most of that, practically marrying himself to the Liffey. But I'm not going to throw him under the bus. There's still a chance the SSA doesn't know how far things have progressed in Dublin since their failed meddling.

Dante shakes his head. "Peaceful doesn't work. It never has. There are always spirits too powerful to be bargained with, too hateful to be reasoned with."

"Well, we'll see about that," Wulf says. He takes yet another step toward Vesuvius, taking off the backpack to retrieve the eggs. "I'll return the eggs I wrongfully took from Vesuvius."

"And release him over Italy once more?" Carina shouts, distraught. Her voice is breaking. "He killed Piero, Wulf! You'll doom us all!"

Compassion flickers over Wulf's face, but his mind is made up. "I don't believe that, Cari. I believe Rika's future deserves a fighting chance. And this is how it begins."

"Wulf!" Dante shouts, passing me. "You really want to do this? After everything we did for you? We raised you! We gave you a home! We gave you everything we've got!"

"You turned me into a monster!" Wulf shouts back.

"I turned you into a soldier!" Dante bellows.

Wulf stops, then he scoffs. "Like a son, huh? Guess that was just another lie." The anger returns immediately. "I'm not blind anymore, Dante. How dare you turn the grief of a nine-year-old into hate!"

"Sylphs killed your family, not me." Dante shakes his head. "You saw them murder your family! I didn't teach you those images. You're the one who witnessed their deaths."

"You made me believe all spirits were bad," Wulf replies, his voice shaking again.

"Those spirits were!" Dante scoffs, overcome by anger, just like Wulf. "Did you do anything to them? Did you step on their eggs or however sylphs breed? Did you pollute their air pockets by taking a hike? Was your laughter offending them? No! They simply hated humans. They threw your parents off the path, pushed them to their death. Just. For. Fun!"

Wulf's face has turned ashen. There's no doubt he's seeing his parents' death once more, feeling the wind, hearing their screams.

Aeola feels his distress. She floats down and gently brushes his cheek, whispering in the wind. "I'm so sorry, Wulf."

Wulf swallows heavily. "But not all sylphs are like that. And neither are all spirits. There's been hurt on both sides. Sure, we can continue to kill each other or we can stop doing that and start to heal." His eyes lock with mine, and when I nod, his chest shudders in relief.

"But not by letting loose this monster," Dante says, and behind us, Carina sniffles.

Wulf turns his back on Dante. "Well, we'll see about that."

Eagerly, Vesuvius bends forward.

"Don't!" Instead of jumping forward, Dante steps back, and suddenly, his arms are wrapped around me, his battle staff pressed tightly against my throat. "You do it, and she dies."

I want to call out to Wulf, but I can only croak. Pain is shooting down my throat and panic claws at my skin. I kick and try to push the wood away, but Dante's grip only intensifies.

Until now, Wulf hasn't truly believed Dante could do something like that. Now, his eyes widen, and he quickly walks back. "What are you doing?"

I shake my head. Wulf needs to hand over the eggs. It'll never stop, otherwise. Just spirit seekers against spirits, trauma replicated for all of eternity.

"Carina!" Wulf prompts, desperation unravelling his features.

"Just return the eggs to us," Carina says, her own voice thin and meek. "Please, Wulf."

*Please,* I want to say as well, but the pressure against my throat is squeezing my windpipe shut. Little daggers of pain stab my temples. My vision flickers at the edges. Wind blows into my face, but the air can't find a way in.

"Let her go!" Aeola shrieks, pulling and tearing at Dante's clothes and hair.

"Carina, deal with that sylph!" Dante orders.

*No!* My eyes find Wulf again. He's caught in indecision between us and Vesuvius. "Pl..." *You promised.*

"I will kill her, Wulf!" Dante says when it looks as if Wulf is still following through with his plan. "I swear to all that's holy, I'll end her if she costs us your loyalty."

"Dante, don't!" Another voice enters the fray, and I'm pretty sure I'm now beyond saving, because it can't be real.

"Mum," I croak, for momentarily, Dante has loosened his grip ever so slightly.

He whirls me around with him as he faces my mother striding down the corridor, her face horrified. "Not now, Léna!" he barks.

"What is she doing here?" Carina asks.

My mother looks stricken with fear. "Dante, don't... she's my daughter. Rika is my daughter. Our daughter!"

Suddenly, I can breathe again. Dante has pushed me away so forcefully I crumple to the ground. "She's what?" I hear him asking over the rush of blood in my ears.

Then Wulf is there, wrapping his arms around me, while Aeola breathes down on us. Before I can even process what's happened, the ground rumbles. Fire erupts, engulfing us, and then we're falling. Falling into darkness.

# 27

The darkness is hot, suffocatingly hot. I can't breathe. Or I might be breathing too fast. My lungs are burning, screaming in pain, while my mind grasps at the fraying seams of reality, unable to make sense of the pressure and heat, and complete darkness. All I know is Wulf is holding onto me, enclosing me tight in his embrace.

Then we're dumped on the cold stone floor, and I scream. It's still dark, though the faintest shimmer of orange tells me we're completely encased by stone. Stone and darkness, and not enough air to hold.

I scream until my voice is raw, my fingers clawing at the unforgiving surface until blood runs down my knuckles. I can't get enough air. I'll never be able to breathe again.

Someone grabs my wrists, keeping me from getting out of this hell. I kick and twist, grunting and sobbing at the same time.

"Rika, calm down! Rika, please."

How can I calm down when we're going to die in this stony grave? How can I...

Suddenly, there's crushing pressure all around me, squeezing my arms against my chest and my ribs against each other. And somehow, this complete and utter lack of mobility brings me out of it. I blink, gasping, and realise it's Wulf who's holding me, just as he held me when we were moving through the darkness.

It's still dark here and awfully quiet. My laboured breathing is painfully loud in my ears. That's right. I'm breathing. I can breathe.

"Better?" Wulf asks in a small voice.

I don't trust my voice yet, but I try to nod.

"Listen," Wulf says, still holding onto me. "I need you to stay calm. We're going to be alright, okay?" Another nod. "Vesuvius brought us out of the Colosseum, away from Dante and Carina."

And my mum. My mum was there. She said...

"We travelled through the earth. How, I've no idea. But we're now in the catacombs under Rome."

Catacombs. My heart rate accelerates. I'm hyperventilating. Catacombs are for dead people.

"It's alright," Wulf says hastily. "I know the exit."

That doesn't make sense. How would he know the exit? But I hold onto that, cradle the hope in my hands.

"We're going to get out of here soon. You've got nothing to fear. Understand?" He waits until my breath has slowed again. "I'll let go of you now, but I'm here, and if you need me, just squeeze my hand. Can you do that?"

His arms around me loosen. One of his hands slips into mine, giving it a gentle squeeze. I clutch it desperately, pressing myself against his arm, in search of the comfort of constraint. No. I don't need that. I'm alright. Wulf is going to get us out of here.

As my heart rate slows, my vision becomes clearer. I now see we're in a room, but there are two exits. Long, dark tunnels under the earth. Aeola is there, wavering in worry, and so is Vesuvius, his magma covered with a dark crust. Slowly, it's melting. As it does, the room brightens and warms. He must've cooled himself down to transport us safely.

"That's it," Wulf says, a feeble smile on his ghastly white face. "Nothing to fear."

"I want my eggs now," Vesuvius growls, and the ground shakes in response. Oh, please, no earthquake while I'm under tons of stone and soil.

"Can't you give us a minute?" Wulf asks.

"Are you okay, Rika?" Aeola asks, gently brushing tears from my cheek I didn't even realise were there.

I nod at her and try this whole speaking business again. "Give them to him. He's waited long enough."

"That's right," the volcano grumbles.

Unwillingly, Wulf lets go of my hand and takes off his backpack. He unpacks the eggs and offers them to Vesuvius. "I hope they're okay."

Vesuvius bends forward, gently plucking the eggs from Wulf's hands and cradling them in his arm. "So cold," he mutters.

"Will they make it?" I ask. They felt alive earlier, but that was before we took them on a trip around Rome.

I don't get an answer for a long time. Vesuvius strokes the eggs, softly massaging heat into them. At last, he turns to us. "They will sleep a little longer. A few thousand years. But they will hatch eventually." He looks at Wulf. "You did well. For a human."

Wulf scoffs slightly, but I can tell he's relieved. "I'm sorry I took them in the first place."

"You had your reasons, and I forgive you." Then Vesuvius shifts and the heat is mixed with an air of discomfort. "I'm sorry I killed your Piero. And the other one."

"We had no business being in your volcano."

That weird sense of embarrassment intensifies. "Well, maybe you did. I did erupt a bit."

I step forward before these two die from shame. "Perhaps we can all be considerate of innocent beings next time." Talk about a double glare. "Vesuvius, I know you have no reason to take my advice or strike a bargain, but Wulf is right. We have to break this cycle of hate. We have to stop hurting each other. So, please, if you can find it in yourself, don't take vengeance. Let this rift be closed here."

"What about those people?" Vesuvius asks. "The spirit seekers?"

"I believe that far fewer spirit seekers will continue the battle if they learn spirits can be negotiated with." All people can't be ruthless psychopaths that happen to be my... No. I can't even think it. "You have to allow us to deal with ours as we see fit. If you attack them, innocents will die." I think of the tourists visiting the Colosseum. Will the spirit seekers get punished for their reckless endangering or will they get extra funds for excellent fear mongering? "That's the thing. It'll always be those not at fault who take the brunt of our actions. The children who lose their parents." Next to me, Wulf winces. "The parents who lose their children."

Vesuvius cradles his eggs closer, probably deciding he'll never leave them out of his sight again.

"Let's break this cycle of hurt and pain by doing things differently, by forgiving each other and moving forward together." If I can't convince a single volcano, there's no hope for my vision. I take Wulf's hand and squeeze it. "We must let go of what we've been taught and open our eyes, our ears, and our hearts." Aeola nuzzles against my other side. "Talk to each other, listen to each other, and care for each other."

Vesuvius regards his eggs for a long time, so long I'm sure he won't answer, but then he heaves a sigh and turns his glowing eyes on me. "I will hold my fire. But not forever. The pressure is too much to bear for all of eternity." He needs to erupt, and I can't deny him that. That's just how volcanoes work. "But maybe until after my children are born. When humans are long gone."

I gasp. Facing the mortality of your own race is too big a thought to behold. But he's right. One day, humans will be no longer, whereas the magma will still be churning. "You'll go dormant?" I ask.

"For a little," Vesuvius promises. Then he grins in a ghastly fashion. "I might check how you're doing with your future plans. It'll be interesting to see if an understanding can be reached."

It might never happen, but I'm hopeful now. "I'll pledge my life to this cause. For better or worse." There's no going back now. Not after everything the SSA has done to me; to all of us.

"And I'll be with her, supporting her every step of her way," Wulf claims, returning my squeeze now. "We'll show the world what true spirit seekers are."

"I can't speak for all spirits," Aeola pipes up, "but I'll stay with Rika. And I'll do my very best to help her communicate with our kind."

Aww, I wish I could hug all of them.

Vesuvius nods gravely. "In that case, I will need someone to keep me in the loop. And I happen to know just the salamander."

There's the skitter of little feet on the ground and a hiss of flame. Then Glut rushes out from under Vesuvius and towards me. I kneel on the floor to let him climb my hands, nuzzling my nose into the warm scales of his skin. "There you are. I haven't said thanks yet for putting in a good word for me."

"You saved me," Glut protests, but I can tell how much my thanks mean to him. He puffs out a little smoke ringlet in deep contentment.

"Glut will accompany you back home. He will keep tabs on your progress," Vesuvius says. "For now, I must go. My eggs need my attention. Thanks for bringing them back to me. I trust you can find your way out of this place."

Now that he's reminded me, the walls have become that much more oppressive. It's even worse when Vesuvius sinks into the earth, taking his light and warmth with him.

"You know the way?" I whisper, holding tightly to Wulf's hand.

"I do," Aeola replies. "There's an airflow. It's small, but we can follow it."

Wulf squeezes my hand. "We'll be back outside in no time."

Glut lights up his back to show us the way, and together we move towards freedom.

Getting out of the catacombs becomes our sole focus. We spend what seems like hours in dark tunnels that all look the same. But eventually, Aeola leads us to an old door, and after a bit of force from Wulf, it opens to a warm afternoon on the Via Appia Antica. From here, it's not far until we reach the tiny safehouse tucked away between big houses on each side.

To our surprise, it's not abandoned. Instead, Inga, Bijan, Eoghan, and Henny are all sitting around the table, making plans. Henny jumps up and squeals as they run toward me. "Oh my gosh, you're alive! Again!"

I can't help but chuckle. Somehow, I made it out of the Colosseum a second time. "You're all here." I look at Eoghan. "How come?"

"Someone called the police," Eoghan explains. "Suddenly Carina's team weren't so keen on being caught on the scene anymore. I'm afraid they're not really interested in me joining their team for missions anymore either." He's quipping, but I'm well aware how much he's given up to help me. His cover's blown, and if he goes back to the academy, they'll start re-educating him.

The same goes for Henny, I assume. "What are you two going to do now?" I ask. "The SSA won't let you get away with this."

"Well, that's why we're here, I guess." Henny shrugs.

"I'll return to Ireland," Eoghan says. "Apparently, my brother's looking for spirit seekers to join his new government program. Gosh, I can't imagine Rory being a politician."

"We all become what we must," I say. I can't really see myself becoming an activist, and yet, that's who I'll have to be: standing up for others, when all my life I've only had to fend for myself.

Eoghan looks at Henny. "You could come with me. With the recent changes, Ireland might be the safest place to be."

"You can't return to the academy," I tell Henny. "It's too dangerous. They'll..." I can't even bring myself to say it. I wish I could say Carina wouldn't let that happen, but she looked away when Dante threatened me; begged Wulf instead of her uncle.

My mind veers dangerously close to the thing I don't want to think about. "Well, you could always come with us," I announce. The cheerfulness of my voice sounds painfully wrong against my ears. "We're going to return to Berlin, right?"

I realise Wulf has been watching me closely. He nods now. "As soon as we can. Bijan?"

"I'll get us some tickets," the hacker announces. "Don't worry, they'll be paid for."

Henny shares a look with Eoghan and says, "Get one for me, too. I've always liked Berlin." The Irish recruit sighs, but he doesn't protest.

I, however, hug them fiercely. During my time at the academy, I was never sure if I could trust them. Now, I'm glad I did. "Thank you."

"No, thank you! Without you, I would've been drafted into their research program, continuing Piero Vallesco's work. And I would've been honoured." They roll their eyes. "Can you imagine that? I'm glad I never went that far." They hold their breath and glance up at me. "What do I do now?"

Considering how it was practically their childhood dream to join the SSA, I feel terribly sorry for them. "You could learn to combat your fear of spirits, rather than the spirits themselves. I'd be happy to teach you."

They hug me again. "Thank you. I want as little ties with the SSA as possible." They shudder in disgust.

Ties. I don't want any ties with the SSA, either. I shouldn't. But now they're everywhere. Like tendrils of weed, they've wrapped themselves around me, pulling me deep into their web of lies and corruption. Dante is...

"Rika?" Henny asks, concerned, waving a hand in front of my face.

I must've spaced out. My tongue feels foreign in my mouth, and my eyes are stinging. What's happening?

"Right," Wulf says, putting a hand on my shoulder. "Before we leave, Rika and I should take a shower and get some rest. It was a long day."

"You're showering together now?" Bijan quips, but I don't get the joke. My mind and body are numb.

Wulf steers me upstairs to the little room where I slept last night. Once he has me sitting on the edge of the bed, he closes the door, letting only Aeola and Glut inside. Then he crouches in front of me, looking up in concern and brushing a blue streak from my forehead. Where his fingers tingled before, I hardly feel them now.

"Hey," he whispers. "How are you?"

When I don't find the words to answer, he takes my hands in his, gently stroking over the dried blood on my knuckles. I've always disliked tight, closed-off spaces without fresh air. I even avoided taking the subway if possible. And then the SSA locked me up in a cell. No air, no light, for days on end. And what was an uncomfortable thing to think about before has grown into an outright phobia. I thought I was dying down in the catacombs. After what I've learnt at the Colosseum, some part of me wished I had.

Teardrops fall onto Wulf's fingers, then mine. We're both holding our breath. Today wasn't easy for him either.

*That's right. Concentrate on Wulf's challenges.* I raise my head to look at him, wishing instantly I hadn't. There's so much fear in them, so much compassion. I swallow hard. "How are you?"

It's clear he doesn't want to talk about it either, but with a shudder, he indulges me. "Pretty terrible, all things considered. I think I've burnt all my bridges here in Italy."

"I'm sorry." No one should have to go against their family to fight for what they believe in.

Wulf shakes his head. "Don't be. They're the ones who should be sorry for what they did... what they allowed to happen to me, to so many people, to all of Europe. When I was training at the academy, I figured that things weren't perfect. I had so much privilege. Miro... He's a friend of mine. Our NAVs are pretty close, but I was hailed the golden boy while he was the troublemaker. The one to watch. We started out as rivals because of that, but as we progressed to friends, I noticed how differently we were being treated, and all because I was a Vallesco-raised seeker and he just a boy from Russia. I struggled with that and all the other little things that became apparent once I knew where to look for them. It made me want to go to Berlin instead of staying in Rome as Dante had planned."

I wince surprisingly hard at the mention of Dante's name. It's like someone's plunged a dagger into my chest and is turning it slowly.

Immediately, Wulf's face is overshadowed with worry. "I wish with all my heart that a bit of nepotism and prejudice were the worst diseases the SSA nurtures. But today... It's just the same all over. Now I know where to look, I see the corruption everywhere. I just hoped it wasn't as bad." He casts his eyes down. "But it is. It's even worse than I could've ever imagined. I'm so sorry for what my family did to you."

"My family," I croak, then quickly press my hands against my mouth. Why did I have to say that? They're not my family. It can't be. It just can't. But it's all rushing at me now. My mother's fear, her claims, Dante's immediate and strong reaction, everything I've learnt about their past. They knew each other during the academy. Dante helped my mother escape twenty-four years ago, my pregnant mother. The laughter in the dining hall, her hand on his arm. My head reels from the onslaught of images.

*Our daughter.*

I gaze at Wulf through a veil of tears. "He's my father, Wulf. Dante is my father."

He says simply, "I know," and pulls me close, stroking my back as I cry my heart out.

Dante is my father. My father tried to kill me. And my mother is lost. What does that make me?

**Nature spirits and humans can co-exist, but proving it might be the death of me.**

I've escaped the death trap in Rome, leaving behind a slew of mortal enemies—and not the spirit kind. At least, Wulf is completely on my side now. Together, we will stand up to the SSA and ring in a new world, where humans and spirits live in peace once more.
At least, that was the plan until we get invited to attend a Spirit Seeker conference in Brussels. Wulf still thinks he can convince everyone with pretty words, but I'm not fooled. This conference is a trap. But to dismantle it, I'll have to step into it and play their game. A game that I can only win if I'm willing to risk it all. The spirits. Wulf. My life.

**Join Rika and the Spirit Seekers in their grand finale as they unearth monstrosities in Brussels. Get your copy now to find out who lives and who dies!**

Continue Reading!

Join Rika, Wulf & Co. in Brussels

**Nature has declared war on us, and we're here to answer that call.**

Wulf might be the greatest spirit seeker the agency who leads the war against nature has to offer. A new mission calls him and other elite spirit seekers to Italy where they face off against an active volcano. Two thousand years ago, Vesuvius obliterated the city of Pompeii. Now the fire spirit has set his eyes on Naples.
Leading the spirit seekers into the volcano, Wulf begins to realise that his biggest challenge might not be the spirits but keeping this group of big egos in check. Tensions rise as the heat is turned up and one false move could spell out their death.

**Join the Spirit Seekers in this prequel to meet the greatest of them all in action!**
**Get this book for free by signing up to my mailing list**
**www.janna-ruth.com/newsletter**

Magic, Demons and High School Drama

Urban Fantasy with French Flair

## About Janna Ruth

Once upon a time, Janna Ruth studied the plate boundaries of this world. Now, she's creating her own worlds. Born in Berlin, Germany, Janna lives in Wellington, New Zealand, writing both English and German books.

Janna's writing career kicked off when she won a writing competition for German publisher Ueberreuter. Her first self-published novel "Im Bann der zertanzten Schuhe" (Melody of Curse, coming in June 2022) went on to win the 2018 SERAPH for "Best Independent Title". She debuted in English with her witchy novella "Witching with Dolphins" in 2020 and has since published urban fantasy, YA sci-fi, and contemporary coming-of-age novels and series.

When Janna isn't writing, she has a plethora of hobbies, such as aerial acrobatics, cake decorating, drawing, reading, and anything crafty you can throw her way.

**Find out more about Janna and her books here:**

Website: www.janna-ruth.com
BookBub: www.bookbub.com/authors/janna-ruth
Facebook: www.facebook.com/authorjannaruth
Reader Group: www.facebook.com/groups/storyseeker
**Goodreads:**
www.goodreads.com/author/show/16513923.Janna_Ruth
BlueSky: https://bsky.app/profile/janna-ruth.bsky.social
Instagram: www.instagram.com/janna_ruth
TikTok: www.tiktok.com/@jannaruthwrites
Pinterest: www.pinterest.com/jannaruthwrites